KILBRIDE HOUSE

KILBRIDE HOUSE

SHEILA FORSEY

POOLBEG

Published 2019
by Poolbeg Press Ltd.
123 Grange Hill, Baldoyle,
Dublin 13, Ireland
Email: poolbeg@poolbeg.com

A catalogue record for this book is available from the British Library.

ISBN 978178199-7734

Printed and bound by CPI Group (UK) Ltd, Croydon, CR0 4YY

www.poolbeg.com

ABOUT THE AUTHOR

Sheila Forsey's childhood was filled with the legends, folklore and mysticism of Ireland's intricate past. This instilled a deep connection to those who had gone before her and was the stepping stone for her into the world of writing. Ireland's windswept coastline, rugged mountains, valleys and ever-changing sky inspire her writing. She is an honours graduate from Maynooth in Creative Writing. She is the recipient of a literature bursary award from Wexford County Council and Artlinks. A deep love of drama led her to receive an all-Ireland best actress award from the Drama League of Ireland. She facilitates creative writing workshops throughout the country.

She lives with her husband and three children, close to the tapestry of the Wexford Coast.

This is her debut into historical fiction.

ACKNOWLEDGEMENTS

I feel haunted by the ghosts of the past. They compel me to write. During the writing of this book, I stepped back in time, into the fifties, into an Ireland that has changed so immensely that other than its mystical landscape, it is a different land. Ireland's intricate past is full of different shades, and sometimes the brightest light was covered in darkness.

My childhood was filled with stories of the past. Stories of people with cardboard boxes standing at train stations, stories of the Ganger, the Kilburn Road, boats to New York and of those who came back and those for whom the road back simply vanished. This rich tapestry of storytelling had an immense effect on me. I grew up in a house filled with buckets of tea, tons of relatives and tales of the past. I was the youngest of a very large generation and we soaked up hours and hours of recitations and songs from a cornucopia of colourful characters that will forever remain in my memory.

I am indebted to the wonderful Paula Campbell, Caroline and all the team at the incredible Poolbeg Press. This book stole a piece of my heart during its writing and the researching of it. I am forever grateful to Poolbeg Press for turning my words into what it is today. I must mention the gorgeous cover that was designed for it. You captured every emotion in it, thank you so much.

To my editor Gaye for your wonderful work and honesty in making this book a reality. Thank you for your commitment and dedication. You are truly amazing. I feel so blessed to have you in my corner.

Sincere thanks to Wexford County Council and Artlinks for awarding me with a literature bursary recently. Your belief in my writing means a great deal to my life as a writer.

To Maynooth Campus and the wonderful facilitators and friends that I have met along the way.

To the Presentation Centre, Wexford Libraries and Gorey Adult Education for giving me the opportunity to facilitate creative writing workshops. To my friends at The Underground Writers Society. Also, to my friends at Wexford Literary Festival that I had the pleasure to meet during my time as PRO at this wonderful festival.

Thank you to my late father Tommy whose poems and recitations inspire my words. Growing up as a seventies child, my mother and father brought us to numerous plays in our village of Kilmuckridge, a village that was and still is steeped in drama and theatre. This instilled in me a great love of drama and the power of words.

I am lucky to have some very true friends who have stood beside me through thick and thin. I would be so lost without you.

I feel blessed to have made such great comrades in the writing world in Ireland. Friends that have shared so much of this path into publishing with me.

To my lovely kind agent Tracy Brennan from the Trace Literary Agency in America. Thank you for encouraging me to write the book I felt passionate about. It has made all the difference.

To my mother, father, brother, sister and extended family for being the best storytellers and greatest supporters and a special mention to my mother Kathleen who has the most vivid and descriptive memory when recalling Ireland's past. Thanks to my brother Richard who constantly enquires how the writing is going.

My sister Jane brought me to an auction of antiques and, as we walked around, she showed me how each item carried a story, how the memory of those gone before could be found if I knew how to look. This instilled a huge passion in me for the stories of the past and for all things vintage.

To my three children Ben, Faye and Matthew for simply being who you are. I am so very proud of you and I love you to bits. You are my greatest cheerleaders. I know that my love of words and theatre has found new lights in all of you to shine the way forward.

Finally, to Shane my husband. Your support is immense in so many ways. In a world that I sometimes don't understand, you help me make sense of it. Love you always.

To my family and all those gone before us

*'Come away, O human child! To the waters
and the wild …'*
William Butler Yeats

PROLOGUE

Kilbride Graveyard
1954

An old graveyard. Surrounded by a stone wall, crumbling, in need of repair. Jagged steps lead up to a stile and there is also a rusted iron gate. It creaks on opening. Adjacent is a small Protestant church. In daylight you can see wisteria wrapped around it and in summer a wild rambling rose covers the mottled wall with silken petals and an evocative scent of the past.

Edward Goulding and the local vicar walk silently side by side, dressed in heavy overcoats against the cold. Edward is carrying a small coffin. The vicar lights the way with a torch. They find the spot, big enough to fit, yet small enough to hardly notice. It's close to the stone wall, sheltered by a willow tree. Slightly away from the rest of the cold grey slabs.

This very church is where Edward attended Sunday service every week of his childhood. As children they had run up and down the stile steps, clip-clopping and chasing each other. If he closes his eyes he can almost hear their laughter – Victoria and Edith, dressed in velvet coats and hats, all pink cheeks and rosy lips. Edith holding Victoria's hand, just in case she slipped on the withered frosted leaves. Edith, always looking out for Victoria. Victoria who seemed to have no fear, just a wild curiosity. In winter the stone steps would glisten like crystal, cracking under their warm boots as they jumped and hopped, and Edith held Victoria's hand, just in case.

'This is the spot,' the vicar says, dragging Edward back to the present.

Edward is glad his friend is with him – a brother could not have been more loyal. The charcoal night is lit by a thousand ancient stars, like street lamps in the velvet darkness. The call of a nightingale breaks the silence. Something scurries near them. A flash of the torch reveals a mouse. They can see their breath as they breathe. Edward takes out a cigarette and a matchbox. He strikes the match and the little flame flares. He takes a long puff and the tip of the cigarette glows as he inhales.

He walks back and gets two shovels from the car.

The ground is hard, it takes longer and is a more difficult task than they anticipated. The earth smells of rot. They discard their coats and hats. The dawn is almost upon them. Eventually the task is complete, and they lower the coffin in. They throw the earth back, filling in the grave.

There is so much to say, yet they say so little.

'You did the only thing that you could,' the vicar whispers.

'I am broken inside.'

'Time, Edward, time will help.' The vicar fixes a simple cross to mark the spot.

They bow their heads and pray for a new day.

They put their coats and hats on and gather up their spades, then walk back towards the stile.

Edward takes one last look. The small cross is barely visible. The smell of the night air fills his nostrils and he knows it will always make him remember. Even when his hair is silver, and the years have passed, the scent of this place will haunt him, remembering all that was lost.

CHAPTER 1

Kilbride, Dingle Peninsula, County Kerry
1954

Canice Meagher loved and hated Ireland in equal measure. Born on the mystical Great Blasket Island, the cliffs, the gulls and the hardship of the ancient landscape was in his very being. He had left before, but it was as if the Dingle Peninsula could claw him back, denying him any chance of a different life.

To escape, he had left the peninsula on different occasions, losing himself in the dark pubs of Cricklewood and Kilburn where the Irish sang and drank and talked of Éire with sentiment – a land of love, song and poetry – not like his rugged island. A piece of land in the wild sea that tore at his soul and dragged him back to it. Over the years, everyone who could leave had left, with their battered suitcases and few quid. They would find a squalid place to live and dream of coming back as The Big Man. Some did. But most got married over there, the long nights eating at them. They married their own or met a Londoner and began a new life, away from the Island, the sea and the shifting fog. But some might never make it either way, caught in some no man's land off Kilburn Road, eaten up by memories.

And now, of course, there could be no more returns to the Great Blasket. In 1953 the government had removed its people from their harsh lives and increasingly extreme weather, and housed them on the mainland in Dunquin, leaving only their sheep to reign over the island.

It was almost dusk, and the haunting sound of a curlew broke the stillness. Then came the muffled thuds of a galloping horse. It was then that he saw her move across the bog field on a majestic grey mare whose hooves were digging up the wet earth. The gallop softened to a canter and they headed straight for the ditch.

He thought she was a vision summoned up by the Celtic stories that had filled his head since he had first heard them from the island people. This strange beauty of a woman was confidently negotiating the jump. It looked far too risky. She was oblivious to anyone watching. His mind was racing – it was madness to think of jumping it.

He had seldom seen such a display of fearlessness and to make it even more incredible it was a woman, a woman so striking that he wondered had the longing for porter brought him to imagining her. But she was as real as the dirt on his shovel. He thought of trying to stop her, but he knew it was too late – he would only startle the mare and that might lead to something worse. He blessed himself and watched as they made the jump, her body in harmony with the mare's as if they were one. It had to be six feet wide. The graceful horse jumped like she had been taken up by the wind, landing heavily on the other side as her mistress screamed in pure delight. Canice was caught between fear at what could have happened and admiration for such a daring jump. The horse was now cantering towards him. The woman drew on the reins and slowed the horse down.

They reached him and halted. The girl – she was just a girl – stared down at him.

'Are you trying to kill yourself?' he said.

'Of course not,' she said haughtily.

'It was dangerous,' he pointed out.

'I am more than capable and who are you to question my jumping skills?'

'I never questioned your ability, I just questioned your common sense, to jump such a ditch here in the bog. You could have fallen and broken your neck and the horse's too.'

'I would never put my horse at risk. You must know very little about horses.'

'Granted, I know more about work horses than fine thoroughbreds. And she is a fine one – what is she called?'

'Silver.'

'Suits her. And what, may I ask, is your name?'

'You can tell me who you are first and what you are doing on this land.'

'Canice Meagher.'

'Where are you from? There are no Meaghers around here that I know of.'

'An Blascaod Mór – the Great Blasket Island – up to a few years ago.'

'Ah, I see.'

He wondered what exactly she 'saw'. He grinned at her and wiped the sweat from his brow.

'I'm putting up a bit of fencing for the Gouldings.'

He knew who she was, by her clothes, the quality of

the leather saddle and bridle, the way she spoke and the horse that she rode. She had to be a daughter of the Gouldings. But he wasn't going to say that. He had met another daughter briefly, up at the Big House when he was working on a roof. Edith Goulding, striking too but very prim, maybe slightly older. Looking at this girl, he figured she couldn't be more than seventeen or eighteen.

'So, are you working on the farm too or are you just trespassing to use their ditches to jump?' he teased.

'I most certainly am not trespassing! I am Victoria Goulding – we own the land,' she replied with an air of authority.

Canice grinned. 'So, you are one of the Gouldings. I had no idea any of them were like you.'

'What is that supposed to mean?'

'I would expect you to be at piano lessons or doing needlework, not out here trying to kill yourself on a wild horse.'

'I have no interest in needlework or piano.'

He knew straight away she was out of his league and not only his league but his religion. He was a Catholic born and bred and Victoria Goulding was a wealthy Protestant. But in that bog field, for now, religion could be forgotten.

His mother would warn him not to have anything to do with a Goulding. They were gentry, he was an islander. But what harm could there be in a little flirtation?

'Where do you live now?' she asked then.

'Ventry.'

'Ah, I see,' she said again.

'We built a cottage there after we left the island.'

'You have a family?'

'Just my mother.'

Neither of them noticed the hare jump from the ditch. The mare startled and reared, but the girl kept her seat.

The mare whinnied loudly as Canice caught the reins. He whispered to her until the fear had left her while the girl also soothed and patted her.

He put his hand on the girl's in reassurance.

'Are you okay?' he asked softly.

'Fine.'

His hand remained on hers, his eyes didn't leave hers. Then something happened that almost knocked the use from his legs: she leaned down from her horse and kissed him, full on the lips. It only lasted a second, but he knew he would remember it for a lifetime.

With that, she laughed and rode off, galloping away from him, leaving him wondering if the fairies had taken his brain and tricked him into imagining the whole incident.

It was in Kilbride village that he saw her again, her dark curly hair pinned back under a hat. She stopped to chat to another girl and he pretended to tie his boots, then he walked on and followed her.

'Hello there, Miss Goulding. How is that fine mare of yours?' he said as he drew level with her.

'Silver is fine,' she replied, not breaking her step.

'I am heading out to do a bit of fishing later this evening. You are welcome to join me,' he heard himself saying. It was out before he thought about it. She might tell her brother Edward or that mother of hers who would scare the life out of you that he had propositioned her. He would never get work again on the estate. He was about to say that he was only joking when she spoke.

'What time? I'd better see if I can get out of my needlework class.'

He could hardly believe it.

'About four. Down past the lake, at the bog entrance.'

'Look forward to it,' she replied.

'Bring something warm, it gets cold on the boat.'

'See you then.'

She walked off and again he wondered if he had dreamt the whole conversation.

If anyone knew, they would surely stop it. He knew himself it was not right, but he also knew that the wilds of the sea in all their power could not stop him from seeing her again.

CHAPTER 2

New York
2018

In her grandmother's dressing table was a drawer that contained her jewellery. Lainey opened it and from a small velvet-lined wooden box took out a gold hair slide decorated with tiny ruby-red roses. She knew how precious it was to her grandmother. Edith had brought it over from Kilbride when she arrived in New York sixty-four years ago. It belonged to someone very dear to her. That was all Lainey knew.

When Lainey was a child she had taken it to dress up her doll. It had looked so pretty in the doll's black hair. But then she had lost it and had to tell Edith. They searched the apartment and Edith barely slept for two nights, worrying about it. Eventually Lainey had found it stuck into the pages of one of her storybooks. Edith's eyes had filled with tears when it was found but she had never scolded Lainey for taking it.

At times, Lainey had been curious about their family in Ireland, but Edith always looked so strained if they mentioned them that it was almost a taboo subject. But now, looking at her frail grandmother about to leave her, she wished she had persisted long ago.

Edith was only eighteen when she arrived in New York. The Gouldings had wanted for very little, yet Edith had left her beloved Ireland and chosen to live away from everyone she knew, marrying Claude, a wealthy Canadian, shortly after arriving in America. Catherine, her only child, was born soon after but within a few years Claude died, leaving Edith everything. Edith had bought this beautiful apartment for her daughter and her to live in. She had never remarried.

Whatever the circumstances of her leaving Ireland, Edith's memory of the beauty of it was as clear in her mind as the day she left it. Lainey could remember that often when she was young her grandmother would almost go into a trance as she spoke of Ireland.

'The Dingle Peninsula was where I lived in a grand house called Kilbride House. The Atlantic glistened like silver milk when the moon was shining on it and the rugged beauty of the place would capture your heart and soul all at once. We had a pond with golden fish. A rose garden that scented the air so gently that you would think you were in heaven. My room sat at the top of the grand staircase and I had a view of the Blasket Islands. On a clear night the stars were like diamonds glittering in the velvet darkness and in spring the lambs danced like children in the morning sun.'

Lainey had loved listening to the grandeur and the beauty of it all. But again, there was no mention of the family that lived there. The Goulding family. Her grandmother's family. Lainey knew she had a Great-uncle Edward who still lived there, and he had a daughter, but time had erased any curiosity that she had about them.

Edith's breath was getting slower. Her skin white,

angelic. If only she would open her eyes for one last time! Lainey tried to compose herself. She checked her mobile to see if there was a message from Catherine – her mother and Edith's only daughter. None! She had rung at least an hour earlier to let her know that Edith was dying.

She put on a piece of music that her grandmother loved – a song by John McCormack. The Irish tenor's voice filled the bedroom with the haunting ballad *My Lagan Love*. Her grandmother's eyes were closed but Lainey liked to think she was young again in her dreams. Whatever untold secrets from her past in Ireland there were would now forever be with her grandmother.

She turned again to the jewellery drawer and was smoothing out the layer of scented paper that lined it when she felt something underneath the paper. It was an old photograph. She had never seen it before. It was a photo of her grandmother and a man. It was in black and white and slightly frayed at the edges. Her grandmother looked young and her hair was pinned up. She was smiling. She had a long swing coat on and peep-toe shoes. They were standing outside the door of a thatched cottage which looked very much like it was in Ireland. He was tall and broad with a thick head of hair. He was wearing what looked like a Crombie coat over a wide-legged suit.

Lainey stared at the photo. So many questions. How come she had never seen it before? Who was the man in the photo? What was he to her grandmother? Perhaps he was her brother? It was strange her grandmother had never shown it to her. Was he something to do with why her grandmother left Ireland, never to return?

She put the photo back in its hiding place and closed the drawer.

She had grown up in her grandmother's apartment with her mother Catherine after her parents divorced. But her mother had spent most of her time at the theatre. A nanny had looked after her, but Edith was always around if she needed someone to talk to. Lainey wanted to remember the laughter that had filled her childhood, how Edith could make everything look brighter. Like a falling star, she was disappearing from her. It was strange to watch someone pass away. Lainey wanted to believe she was happy. She caught her hand and held it to her cheek.

Doctor Blake arrived. He was a friend of Edith's. Lainey had watched him play card games, which often went on until the early hours, in Edith's apartment.

'I don't think there is much time left,' the doctor whispered.

Lainey thought she looked younger than her eighty-one years, as if any stresses, like the secrets of the past, were released now. The secret of why Edith had left Ireland, never to return, would die with her.

CHAPTER 3

Catherine checked her make-up. She was meticulous about her appearance both on and off the stage.

Her assistant Lucille brought in a cup of Earl Grey tea served in rose-coloured china cup and saucer. Classical music played in the background.

Catherine went through her notes for her understudy. She was playing a Russian Empress in a new play written especially for her by one of Broadway's most respected playwrights, John Henderson. The play, *Vilma*, had received critical acclaim and was deemed to be a classic. Having trained as a Shakespearian actor, Catherine adored classical roles. The roles were fewer for an actress of her age but her reviews were tremendous. Her performance would possibly gain her another Tony award. She already had one for her performance in Tennessee Williams' *A Streetcar Named Desire*. She had played Blanche Dubois sublimely. One review had said: '**Catherine Lee Miller, the American stage actress, is a rival to the late Vivien Leigh and she is just as beautiful if not more so.**' She had always taken extreme care with her looks. She ate a strict diet and took every vitamin

14

supplement that she could. She had constant facials and spent a fortune on creams and potions. She went to a health spa in Switzerland twice a year for a complete detox and came back feeling and looking years younger. It all paid off. She looked at least twenty years younger than her real age. Her auburn hair shone with health. She never arrived at the theatre or anywhere unless she was immaculately presented and that included her hair, make-up, high heels and gloves.

The theatre was where she could leave everything else outside and that included her family. She knew she appeared cold to them, but it was only at the theatre that she felt truly at home. As soon as she walked in the backstage door, it hit her. *Home.* This was what she was born to do. She believed that theatre was on a different level of acting to anything else. The connection was almost spiritual. The audience came to be entranced and she was their goddess.

Normally her head space would be totally focused on the performance ahead, but she had arrived in to check on her understudy who for tonight would play her part. Edith, her mother, was dying so she knew it would be inappropriate to be on stage tonight.

There was a knock at the door. It was Lucille with the latest reviews.

'Excellent reviews again in the papers,' Lucille said. 'Is there anything I can get you?'

Catherine eyed her from head to toe. There was not a hair out of place with Lucille. Catherine hated when people made no effort. It came with the territory if you worked for her. You certainly did not arrive in with messy hair or unkempt clothes if you planned on keeping your job with Catherine Lee Miller.

'Have a car ready shortly, please. I need to go to my mother's apartment.'

'Certainly.' Lucille left, closing the door softly.

Catherine had put off going to the apartment for as long as she could. Her mother might be dying but the last place she wanted to be was beside her. They were close once, but time had almost erased the memory.

Yet there was a time when she did love being with her mother. She remembered Edith brushing her hair and telling her how much she loved her. She remembered lighting the Christmas candle and decorating the tree with the most beautiful decorations that could be bought in New York. It was a childhood of glamour, theatre and laughter.

Even though Claude had died young, he had left them wanting for nothing financially. Edith had bought Catherine beautiful clothes, often shipped from Paris. Velvet coats and hats, silks and chiffons. Designers were commissioned to make dresses for every occasion. Crystals, gems and pearls adorned her clothes. Vintage lace edged her dresses.

Every weekend Edith took her to the theatre and then the magic began for Catherine as she immersed herself in the performances on Broadway. A whole new world opened for her. She knew that one day she would wow the crowd with her own debut.

For Catherine's eighteenth birthday Edith organised an extravagant party and commissioned one of New York's finest designers to make Catherine's dress. They chose a delicate pink with pearls and crystals handstitched all over the fragile bodice, and layers of chiffon billowing from the waist. She was a vision and

16

the toast of New York society. Edith had so many plans for her beautiful daughter. With no family, she obsessed about her. There was nothing she felt she could deny her.

But Catherine felt differently. There was one thing she wanted that Edith could not seem to give her. It was freedom. Freedom to live her life as she wanted, without the watchful eye of her overprotective mother. She felt strangled by her.

Catherine insisted on leaving to go to London to train at the prestigious Royal Academy of Dramatic Art. When Edith refused, she applied for a scholarship and won it. Edith had no option but to give in. She begged her daughter to allow her to go too and live in London while she was studying. But Catherine refused. It broke Edith's heart when she left and the guilt that Catherine carried built a wedge that destroyed their relationship. It was not until Catherine got married and had Lainey that Edith seemed to again have purpose in life. Catherine was relieved not to be the centre of her mother's life anymore, but their relationship had become so strained that they never became close again.

She turned on the laptop beside her and for some reason searched for Dingle in County Kerry in Ireland. Images of the vast cliffs and the islands flashed on the screen. She had watched *Ryan's Daughter* when she was younger. She was a huge fan of Robert Mitchum who played the lead role. She knew it was set in Dingle where her mother had lived but she had never dared mention it to her. That was the irritating thing. She was never allowed ask any questions about her family there and there was no question of visiting them. Being immersed in the theatre, her interest in Irish writers was immense.

She was mesmerised by Beckett and Joyce. There was something about the writings of the Irish that she connected with. She had studied George Bernard Shaw. An Irishman, an emigrant, just like her mother. She had thought of auditioning for a part at the prestigious Gate theatre in Dublin. But her mother had forbidden it and even threatened to cut off her allowance which was hugely generous. She had never crossed the water to see Ireland which seemed ridiculous now.

She put on a cream cashmere coat and cream leather gloves and picked up her Prada bag. She closed the door behind her.

She got into the car that was waiting for her and sat back as the driver took her to the apartment from where, two hours earlier, Lainey had phoned to say that Edith was dying.

CHAPTER 4

Kilbride
1954

Victoria walked away as confidently as she could, with her head held high. Edith had taught her how to walk properly. It came naturally to Edith, she was born like that – she always walked with great elegance and poise. But, right now, Victoria felt like running with excitement, but she knew that would just look childish. She knew he was watching her, but she didn't dare turn around. So, she held her head up straight and walked away, just like Edith had shown her.

Her heart was beating so fast she thought that surely the people on the street could hear it. What had she just done? Agreeing to meet a man she knew nothing about and to meet him in one of the remotest parts of Kilbride? On her own, no chaperone. Her mother would lose her mind if she knew. There was no way she could tell Edith either. How would she get away with it? Edith watched her like a hawk, always ready to tell Mother what she was up to. And Edward would not like her meeting a man on her own like that – at twenty, four years older than her, he always felt responsible for her. He might even want to come along to vet Canice! She could tell

19

Sarah Quinn her best friend, but Sarah would want to know every detail and Victoria wanted to keep him a secret for now.

If Edith knew she would tell her that it was ludicrous to even suggest it. For so many reasons it would be forbidden. He was a Catholic, which was of course an issue. He was a labourer and from the Blasket Islands so probably penniless. Edith was forever trying to do the right thing and not upset Mother. She had accompanied her to social events since their father died – although these outings were very few except for church service, the odd church meeting and tray-bake events. Edith had become her mother's companion. She herself, on the other hand, could do little right in her mother's eyes – she watched her like a hawk, terrified she would go astray.

Victoria had adored her father. It was he who had first lifted her up on a horse. The smell of the leather, the horses, even the air around Kilbride reminded her of her father. When he died, she had run and saddled up her beautiful grey mare Silver and had ridden for hours on the beach, crying, until she had almost got caught with the tide coming in, only escaping in the nick of time.

Her mother had decreed they should wear black for a year and, even though the year had passed, she was still insisting on it and had not allowed her out to any party or dance. She had thought she would never laugh again. It was only taking Silver out that had kept her going. She felt closer to her father when she was out riding, as if his spirit was with her as she lashed across the beaches of Dingle. What would he have thought of what she had just done? Arranging to meet with a labourer who used to live on the Island. A Catholic. Her father would not have approved, Edith would not approve, and her mother would literally forbid it.

Gertrude Goulding encouraged her children to mix only with their own circle, that being the small community of Protestants who lived on the peninsula and beyond. The family was Church of Ireland and part of a small community in Kilbride, together with a few Presbyterians on the outskirts.

She knew from an early age what was expected from her. She needed to marry well. They kept company with lots of Protestant families and she had attended the small Protestant school in the village of Kilbride and then a Protestant boarding school. She had hated every second of being away, counting the days and hours until she could be back on her beloved cliffs and in her own bedroom overlooking the bay.

'Stay with your own,' Bessie the housekeeper at Kilbride House had warned Victoria. Bessie had looked after the Gouldings since Victoria was a baby. Born and raised in the village of Kilbride, as she said herself she knew how it worked. 'There is always unease when Protestants and Catholics cross the line. Neither side will ever want it. Stick to your own. Too much has happened between them.'

'*Stick to your own.*' Easier said than done.

Most of the boys that Victoria met were nice, but she had never met anyone that she wanted to step out with. She was only allowed to go to certain dances – those held in the local Protestant hall or school. Tea and cakes were served and everyone there was Protestant. She longed to go to the local dances in the village that were held in the hall there – she often saw the young people going o their bicycles, with bright-red lipstick and rainbow-coloured dresses. They were always laughing and chatting, and it looked like incredible fun. Mother said they were rowdy and there were often fights. Victoria thought that this sounded like bliss. A fistfight at a dance! How splendid! But her mother would not hear of it. They were not, according to her mother; 'their sort'.

Edward had met a girl called Ingrid at one of the church dances held in a hall in Kenmare and he seemed to have fallen for her. She was a sweet girl and adored Edward. Edward was a rogue but a very loveable one. She was glad Edward had met Ingrid – he deserved someone who really cared about him. Edith was so prim, it was hard to imagine who she might eventually fall for. She was very striking with dark hair like Victoria, always adorned with gold slides, high cheekbones, green eyes and alabaster skin. Victoria was like a wilder version of her older sister – her dark-green eyes had flecks of hazel and her hair was wild and curly. Gertrude Goulding had always bought her two daughters beautiful clothes on their trips to Dublin city. Velvet coats, silk blouses, tailored suits and dresses with lace collars and pearl cuffs. She also purchased taffeta, satins and chiffons and had elegant clothes custom-made for herself and her daughters. But as much as Victoria loved the clothes, she adored the jodhpurs and tweed jackets for riding much more. But she did like to dress up when she went to the church dances.

Unlike Edward, she had not met anyone at the dances that had taken her fancy. But that was certainly not something she could say about Canice Meagher whom she had met in the bog field. There was something so

22

different about him. As if he were an extension of his surroundings. His mad red hair and his blue eyes glinting at her, drinking her in. She was tall herself, but his big frame dwarfed her. When she had leaned down and kissed him, she was nearly more shocked than he was at what she had done. Edith would die of shame if she knew. But she couldn't help it. Afterwards she knew it was wiser to ride off – she didn't trust what she was feeling. But she had thought about him ever since, picturing him working on the fields, working on the bog. Climbing the cliffs.

If Mother knew what she was up to she would lock her up for a month and perhaps try to teach her embroidery or crochet to take her mind off him. She would be shocked to the core that one of her daughters had behaved in such a fashion. A hussy!

But Victoria already had a plan. She knew her mother liked her to do some work for the church and at present Gertrude was writing out duties for the annual church fête that was held for the upkeep of the church. So, she thought her plan out well before she put it into action.

Gertrude Goulding was an austere figure as she sat at her desk in her customary black clothes, Victoria noticed how thin and strained she looked, as if any joy or fun had vanished from her life.

'I'm going over to Mrs Warren, Mother – she's going to show me how to dry flowers for the church hall for next Harvest Thanksgiving and then I'm going to call to see Sarah.'

Her mother arched an eyebrow, not looking like she was entirely convinced. Victoria knew she needed to convince her or she might tell Edith to go with her.

'Really I am, Mother. I might stay a while with Sarah – you know how she loves to sew and she is making this beautiful dress made of a cream organza. She wants me to help with stitching the pearls on the neckline. I can keep her company.'

Gertrude Goulding studied her daughter, a look of concern flashing across her face.

'Don't be late for dinner and change your blouse, it looks grubby. And, for goodness' sake, Victoria, put on a skirt – those trousers are so unladylike. I have no idea why you insist on wearing them. It's bad enough that you wear those jodhpurs all the time – put something nice on. You have a wardrobe of beautiful clothes, yet you insist on going around dressed like a boy.'

'I love trousers – they're so comfortable and make me feel free.'

'Victoria, you are impossible. Go clean yourself up. Tell Sarah that I can help her with the beading and to be careful not to drag that organza. Oh yes, tell her she will be helping you with the jumble sale again this year. I want you both on your best behaviour. I will put Edith in charge of it. Last year the two of you were a handful. I need you to start acting more like a lady, Victoria.'

'Why is Edith always in charge of me? She is only one year older than me. I am fed up of her always correcting me.'

'Edith is only trying to help, Victoria.'

Victoria shrugged.

'Right, I'd better get changed.'

Victoria had met Sarah earlier, when she was out riding. Sarah knew exactly what Victoria's mother was like as her mother was much the same, only less serious and very cuddly which could not be said about Gertrude Goulding. They were Presbyterian and Sarah was encouraged to mix with her own circle. God forbid that her mother might meet Mrs Quinn in Kilbride village and find out that Victoria was not with Sarah. But Sarah would cover somehow for her – she could convince her mother of anything. Victoria reckoned she should be an actress, she was so good at pretending to be the perfect daughter. Sarah had agreed earlier to help her, but she had not been happy when Victoria would not tell her where it was that she was going and more importantly who with.

'But where are you going that you can't tell me?' she asked.

'I will tell you later but just cover for me,' Victoria pleaded.

'You know I will, but you better tell me what you are up to and what has happened to make that glint in your eye appear.'

'I will tell you later – I promise.'

'Be careful, you know what your mother is like. My father said last week that she would skin you alive and eat you without salt, she is in such bad form since your father died.'

'He's not far wrong. She never laughs any more, and she's so cross all the time. Edith is driving me crazy, trying to please her all the time. She is a real little Miss Perfect and Mother is on my case and Edward's constantly.' It was true – her mother seemed terrified that her youngest daughter would go down a wrong path now that her father was not here to guide her and Edward had

25

taken to going to the pub every chance he could get, much to her dismay.

Victoria wanted to look good but, if they were going fishing, she thought she had better dress warmly. She wrapped herself up in a heavy coat. She put her shoes on but put some boots in a bag. She pulled a dress out from the back of her wardrobe – she would slip into it and the shoes before she returned home. She took out her bicycle. Luckily her mother didn't see her off or she would have insisted she should change.

As she cycled towards the cliffs, she knew it was madness. Anything could happen to her, she barely knew him but the pull towards him was like a magnet and she had no choice but to go. She hid her bicycle in a ditch and made her way across to the place on the beach where he had said he would be.

She could see him. He had a traditional currach – a skin boat – and he was bending over it. He looked up and his face broke into a wide grin. He grabbed her and hugged her. It was strange, but it felt the most natural thing in the world to her.

'I was afraid that you would bail,' he said in a whisper.

She looked at his face, a face that had faced many storms in his childhood. He had long fair lashes and his blue eyes were brilliant. He was grinning as if he could hardly believe she was there.

'I am not meant to be here,' she said.

'I can imagine your mother might have something to say if she knew you were meeting with me. I'm not exactly what she would pick for her daughter, I suspect!'

'How about you, would your family approve?'

'There is only my mother. She's a quiet woman. Sure, she would warn me that it would be asking for trouble. But I wanted to see you. I had to.'

'I know.'

She knew she was being more honest than she had intended. But it was the truth – something was pulling at her to meet him and she knew he understood completely what she meant.

He pulled her towards him again.

'I did not dare dream that you would actually come here.' He was staring at her as if afraid to blink in case she vanished. 'I know I should stay away but staying away from you would be like trying to stop the sea from lashing against the rocks.'

She had asked Bessie who the Meaghers were. Bessie had confirmed that they were from An Blascaod Mór, The Great Blasket, the largest of the group of islands off the Dingle Peninsula. Bessie had said they were good honest people, but the hardship of the sea had claimed a son and a husband. Leaving only one son called Canice, who was known to be a great singer. He and his mother had left the island and moved to where his aunt was living near Ventry. Of course, the government had since evacuated the remaining families to Dunquin, the nearest mainland village to the islands. Canice Meagher had a built a little cottage, with money he had saved from periods working in England. But, by all accounts his mother was finding it hard to settle. She spoke no English, only the Gaeilge.

Bessie had looked at her astutely. 'But why do you ask?'

'Sarah and I are gathering clothes for the jumble sale

… we wondered if they would need some.'

Bessie had flung her hands up. 'If I know Mrs Meagher, she would rather die than take any handouts. She may be poor, but the woman has her pride. These do-gooders giving castoffs! I know Sarah and you mean no harm, but people have their pride. The people of the island would rather run naked than accept clothes from any Protestants. No insult to yourself, pet, I know you mean well. But the wounds of the past run deep.'

Victoria knew what she meant. She understood that the past ran deep. The land in Kilbride had almost all belonged to the Gouldings at one stage. Her ancestors had come from Norfolk in England and been granted the land centuries before. But in the 1920s, after the War of Independence, most of the land reverted to Irish hands. Bessie was right. The wounds were still there. They might live side by side on this island of Ireland, but the history could not be rewritten.

Canice Meagher might not have much – he was an islander eking out a living – but, when Victoria looked at him, he was everything. His red hair like fire gave him a Celtic look that only the storybooks told of and those eyes melted her heart. She didn't know him but she felt instinctively that there was a raw honesty about him.

He helped her into the boat and then rowed out to sea.

It was then she kissed him again, and this time she didn't run off on any horse. He kissed her back and wrapped her up in his arms. This wild island man was everything she had dreamed of.

They spent hours on the boat until darkness was falling. They laughed and talked, she had even cried when she told him about her father. She knew he understood.

'When will I see you again?' he asked when they were at last back on the beach.

'On Sunday – I'll take off on Silver and I will see you here – but I won't be able to stay long.'

He held her, not wanting her to go. 'I know this sounds crazy – I can hardly sleep thinking of you. But they will never accept it, they will never accept us.'

Victoria knew what he meant, but a determination so strong overcame her that it almost shook her.

'They will have to, I promise you, they will have to,' she said. She could see the fear in his eyes. She kissed him again then touched his lips with her fingers. 'We will find a way, we will.'

He walked back with her to where she had left her bicycle.

'Go quickly before it's dark,' he said, reluctantly relinquishing her.

She cycled away, her heart light at what had just happened. She would probably get in trouble with her mother for being out so late, but she didn't care. Nothing was going to destroy this feeling. She cycled as fast as she could, getting home at the edge of dark.

As she entered the gate of Kilbride House, she jumped off her bicycle and quickly rolled it between the estate wall and some thick bushes. There she quickly changed into the simple black dress she had brought with her and threw her boots and clothes into her bag. She then put on the shoes that she had brought. She was just about to emerge from behind the bushes when she heard someone walking in through the entrance. It was Edith, dressed in a black linen suit, her hair pinned perfectly under a prim black hat.

Edith stopped and stared at the bushes which unfortunately had rustled as Victoria pulled the bike back. Victoria held her breath.

'I can see you, Victoria. You may as well come out.'

Victoria came out. What would she say? She could easily say she had been desperate to pee and so had ducked behind the bushes – but why on earth would she have taken the bicycle with her?

But that, it turned out, was the least of her problems.

'Where have you been, Victoria? Don't say Sarah's because I was just talking to Sarah's mother at a church meeting and she was asking how you were and when you would call round.'

Victoria had no answer. 'Are you going to tell Mother? Please, Edith, don't tell-tale on me!'

'Where were you?'

Victoria tried to think fast. 'I was with the Fort Woman.'

The Fort Woman lived alone in an old cottage up on Slea Head. She had arrived there many years before, from where no one knew. She was known for cures and herbal tinctures. Victoria knew her mother would not approve of her going there.

'The Fort Woman! What did you want from her? You never went there on your own, did you? Anything could happen to you.'

'I asked her to make something for Silver's leg – it tends to get a little lame and she makes a rub to put on it. Father used to get her to make one.'

'Where is this rub?' Edith asked, unconvinced.

'I have to pick it up in a few days' time.'

Edith shook her head. 'I really don't think you should have anything to do with her. Mother thinks she is very strange.'

'Very well – maybe I'll just ask the vet to look at Silver. Look, say nothing to Mother – she'd only get upset – she's so easily upset lately.'

Edith nodded, and Victoria felt her secret was safe for now.

They walked up the drive, Victoria wheeling the bicycle beside her.

'I hope you're telling me the truth?' Edith said, raising an eyebrow.

'Course I am. You worry too much, sis. Honestly.'

CHAPTER 5

Sarah and Victoria always worked on the jumble sale with Edith for every village fête. They gathered clothes for weeks in advance, then washed and ironed them. The money made would go towards buying a new organ for the choir. Mrs Fitzgerald had been playing the organ for over fifty years and the organ had been there longer. Most of the village people would attend. Even though it was run for the Protestant church, it was a day for the whole community. Of course, Protestants would travel from different villages around the area to support it. As Bessie always said, 'Sure they all stick to their own – them Protestants will come for miles to Kilbride Fête!' The fête was held in the small Protestant school – the jumble sale in one room, the teas in another and games like Lucky Dip and Guess the Weight in the playground, weather permitting.

The big day had now arrived, and Edith was busy trying to make sure she displayed something from everyone who had donated. She had some really nice clothes on her counter display – pinafore dresses in candy colours, some good quality short trousers and braces. She also had a couple of Crombie coats and a collection of dresses and skirts.

Sarah and Victoria were meant to be helping but Sarah was having much more fun trying on the hats that were up for sale.

'Vicky, look at me!' Sarah put on a huge orange-and-lemon hat with big flowers and a sickly lime-green scarf tied on top. She wrapped a brown fox fur around her shoulders. Sticking her head in the air, she swaggered across the tiny floor.

'My name is Mrs Olive Hempenstall and I demand excellent service,' she said, putting on a very posh accent, 'as I am the lady of Ballythomas House, the grandest estate in the whole of Kerry. I will not tolerate anything less than the best for my big head.'

Edith almost dropped the box of clothes that she was carrying.

'Sarah, take that off at once! You are a disgrace!'

Victoria almost fell into a pile of boots as she tried to stop laughing.

Sarah giggled and took the hat off, just before the real Mrs Hempenstall walked in.

'Good afternoon, Mrs Hempenstall, how are you?' Edith said, her face puce. 'You know Sarah Quinn and of course my sister Victoria?'

'Good afternoon, ladies, lovely to see such an orderly display, Edith – you are such a treasure! How is your poor mother? We don't see her very much at all. I really must arrange for her to come for afternoon tea soon – it would do her good to get out.'

Edith smiled, relieved that Mrs Hempenstall had not overheard Sarah mimicking her. 'I am sure she would love that. It would do her good.' Mrs Hempenstall looked at Sarah. 'Sarah Quinn, I believe you are stepping out with Richard Wilkinson. A very fine young man and his father is a Wilkinson from Rothe House in Kenmare.'

'I am indeed,' said Sarah. 'Sure, we are only seeing each other a wet week but I'll see how it goes. Here's a lovely hat – it would suit you, Mrs Hempenstall. I can't think of anyone that it would suit more – didn't I just say that, Victoria? I said, there's a hat for an elegant lady like Mrs Hempenstall who knows style.'

Victoria pretended to cough as she hid a giggle. Sarah held up the hideous hat. Mrs Hempenstall shook her head.

'I have no intention of buying anything. I will, of course, donate a sizeable sum as I always do – and, speaking of donations, I do have some of my clothes. The quality is excellent, so only show mine to someone who may appreciate quality.' She landed a bag of clothes on the small table.

'Of course, Mrs Hempenstall – thank you – I'm sure they are lovely,' Edith said.

'I get all my clothes custom-made by an excellent dressmaker in Dublin. They are very slim-fitting so only someone very trim and in proportion will fit into them. Unfortunately, I don't have any to fit the likes of Mrs Walsh – goodness, she has become very stout lately! I must recommend my dressmaker to her.'

Sarah leaned over to Victoria, whispering in her ear. 'She gets them custom-made because her chest is too big to fit into anything.'

Edith glared at them. 'Thank you, Mrs Hempenstall – it's very generous of you.'

'It's a pleasure. And now I must go to the tea tent where I shall donate one of my secret-recipe fruit cakes.'

With that, she left them.

'Well, the secret of her cake is not brandy because Daddy says she drinks every drop herself,' Sarah remarked.

'Your father has a lot to say, Sarah,' said Edith as she opened the bag of clothes. 'You are unbelievable. Go and help with the teas for a while. Victoria, you can help me sort Mrs Hempenstall's donation.'

Sarah winked at Victoria. 'Ah, Edith Goulding, you are no fun. That dried-up old prune is trying to fob off her old smelly mothball clothes here. Look at them! I know what we'll do with them – my father could use them on the scarecrow – we call her Mrs Hempenstall already. Although the birds only shite on her – they are not afraid of her.'

'Sarah, keep your voice down!' Edith was beside herself.

'Ah, don't get your knickers in a twist, Edith – she is only an auld bag, thinks she is better than everyone and her auld gobshite of a husband groping anyone that he can! I gave him a good wallop for himself last Christmas. "Give me a squeeze, Sarah Quinn," he says, putting his arms out to grab me. I gave him such a kick on the shin that I would say he was black for a week.'

Edith crossed her arms in vexation. But Sarah was on a roll.

'Daddy reckons Mr Hempenstall – Smelly Hempy, I call him – he reckons he doesn't get a bit of you-know-what at home. Daddy says –'

'*Sarah! Go!*' said Edith.

35

Sarah grinned and picked up her cardigan. 'I'd better put on my best voice and serve some teas. I'll bring you in some scones and tea in a minute – that is, if Olive Binchy hasn't got in there and scoffed them all. My father says she will burst at some stage and a heifer will come out of her. The size of her, she must eat a sack of spuds every dinnertime. My father reckons they must kill a bullock every Saturday to feed her. He says her rear end is the size of Munster.'

'*Sarah!*'

'Hold your knickers on, I'm going!' Sarah skipped out before Edith could say any more.

Victoria was in a fit of giggling. Sarah always made her laugh. She was clever too, and well able to talk right and proper when she had to.

'Seriously, Mrs Quinn has her hands full with her. I have never heard anyone so rude. I hope she's not leading you down the wrong path, Victoria.' Edith shook out a dress that did look like it could only look good on a scarecrow.

'You sound like Mother – give it a rest, Edith. Anyone would think you were forty not merely a year older than me. She's only having a bit of a laugh. Anyway, I have a mother – I don't need two. One is enough to be dealing with, watching my every move.' She began to pull old shoes out of a box and sort them into rows. She normally enjoyed the fête, but today she had so much more on her mind than sorting out old smelly clothes.

'Where were you last night? I know you were out.'

Victoria was caught unprepared.

'How do you mean?' She bent over the box of shoes, hoping Edith could not see how red her face had just gone.

'I heard you come in – it was almost midnight. Mother thought you were in bed hours before. You had said you wanted to read and went to bed early.'

'And I did!'

'Victoria, this has been going on for months, don't think I haven't noticed.'

Victoria had been having a feeling that Edith was on to her, forever watching her with her big green eyes. She had been so careful that she was exhausted trying to cover her tracks.

'You're right,' she said. 'It was a mild night and I thought I would just sit outside for a while.'

She had sneaked off to meet Canice. There were very few that she and Canice could trust but Finbarr and Tomás Ó Faoláin from the Blaskets were trustworthy. Like Canice they liked to sing, and she had spent the evening listening to them sing songs from the Great Blasket and play the melodeon. It had been so nice to just sit and hold Canice's hand and not be afraid of being seen. Every now and then he would look at her and she knew there was nowhere in the world she would rather be.

'I'm not a fool, Victoria. Mother has enough on her plate without you acting up. Are you going to tell me where you were? I'm worried about you. You're not yourself and you're not eating – even this morning, you only pretended to eat.' Edith grabbed another bunch of clothes and began folding them.

'I told you – and I don't really care whether you believe me or not. Just drop it – you are driving me mad. I can't stand it. There is nothing wrong with me. I wasn't hungry, that's all, but I can't say that or mother would get in a fuss. I don't need you getting in one too.'

37

Sarah arrived in the nick of time with scones, cream, homemade jam and tea.

'That Mrs Hempenstall is some piece of stuff! She's after telling poor Mrs Walsh that she should stay at the wash-up, instead of serving the teas. But Agnes Bolton put Mrs Hempenstall in her place and told Mrs Walsh to stay where she was.'

She deposited the tray on a table and the others gathered round to help themselves.

Victoria drank the tea gratefully but when she tried to nibble on a scone she almost retched – she hadn't eaten anything that morning. She knew that Edith was watching her to see if she would eat. She really was on to her.

She had been with Canice every chance that she could since that first meeting months before. She had been so careful, always pretending to be out on Silver or meeting with Sarah. Sarah had covered for her lots of times. She had to tell her, and she knew she could trust her.

'I know him,' Sarah said. 'He's big and broad – I wouldn't call him handsome but there is something about him, kind of in a wild way. He has really blue eyes and that mad shock of red hair. I heard him sing – my father said he sings like someone gifted. Your mother will kill you, Vicky. Canice Meagher won't be good enough for her precious daughter, not by a long shot. He's a Catholic too – not a hope. An islander. It's doomed, Vicky. She will do everything to pull you apart.'

'I can't let her.'

'Are you truly in love with him, or is it just a passing fancy? I have lots of them. Passing fancies. But I have never really been in love. If it's love, you would jump into quicksand if you thought he was drowning – most of them, I wouldn't get my dress mucky to save them.'

Victoria laughed but said nothing.

'Well, which is it?' Sarah pressed.

How could Victoria describe how she felt about Canice Meagher? How she felt she would surely die if she couldn't be with him?

Sarah searched her face. 'Oh, you have it bad! And is he as bad for you?'

'Every bit as.'

'Well, you can't hide it forever – what will you do?'

Sarah spoke truer than she was aware. She didn't yet know about the pregnancy. Victoria hadn't dared to tell even her. Soon, her stomach would be showing. She was terrified that Edith would notice her being sick.

'I don't know what we'll do, Sarah, to be honest.'

Sarah looked worried. 'Well, don't go running off and leaving me here in Kilbride with all these boring farts. Promise me that. I couldn't bear you to do that.'

Victoria knew that Sarah would miss her – she would miss Sarah too. But Canice was the love of her life. She knew too that she had crossed the line and the sickness that reached her every morning was a result of that. She was going to have a baby and she was terrified. She had told Canice, and he had cried with joy and anger at their situation.

'I love you, Victoria, I will love you until the day I die, and I will love our baby. Whatever we have to do now to stay together we must do.'

Victoria knew what that meant. Falling in love with Canice Meagher had changed her future. She would have to leave Kilbride House, her home, her family and her heritage. She would have to leave and start a new life away from Kilbride. A panic came over her when she thought about it. Kilbride was part of her, her very being. She wondered if she could live anywhere else. If only she could wrap it up and take it with her. The scent of the air, the way the puffins landed on the Blasket Islands, the wild crashing of the waves on Slea Head. How could she leave it? Kilbride House, her childhood, her memories. But she loved Canice and they had to make the right choice for their baby.

A baby. She had never thought about being a mother. But now that it had happened it was all that mattered. Every waking hour was about how to protect her baby.

It was getting hard to hide. It wasn't that her stomach was noticeable, but she was feeling so ill all the time. She was worried was there something wrong. She knew women could feel ill, but did they feel like they were going to die at times? When she awoke in the morning it was hell. She kept some dry bread beside her, hidden in her room. When she awoke, she nibbled on it and it tended to settle it – if not she retched like her insides were turning inside-out. Worse thing was that she could only talk to Canice about it. She longed to confide in Edith. They had always been so close. But she knew she would just run and tell Mother. There was someone she could tell, though, if the sickness didn't pass. There was one woman who was known to keep secrets forever. She had held her own secret from everyone – the secret of how she came to live at the Fort. She might be able to get her to help her.

CHAPTER 6

Victoria wrapped herself up and headed to a special place on the peninsula. In the morning mist, the steep cliffs of Slea Head looked almost ghostlike. It was like the edge of the world, this place that had seen tribes come and go for over 6000 years, with its 2000 ancient monuments dating from the Stone Age. So many customs of Ireland changed but this ancient place remained unchanged. On a clear day, the view was breath-taking and on a harsh day it was as if all the elements where fighting to be heard.

A little inland from this was an old cottage, made of stone and miraculously withstanding the elements. Two small outhouses ran alongside it. It had stood there almost two hundred years and had been vacant for a few decades until a June evening in 1946 when a woman arrived from nowhere. Nobody had seen her travel there or heard of her stopping in other villages along the way. She just seemed to appear. People were suspicious of her. She certainly wasn't Irish, yet she seemed to know the history of the place better than most. She moved into the derelict cottage and made it her home. She needed very little. A few blankets, some cooking utensils and her

41

books, which she had carried with her. At dawn she would sing a haunting tune that made some of the Kerry people think she was mad. But she meant no harm to anyone and in time they slowly began to accept the 'Fort Woman', as she became known. She'd been there ever since, a gentle person who lived alone as if guarding the ancient landscape. Many said that the area was steeped in ghosts and at night they travelled along the paths of the Fort and the Fort Woman communicated with them. Others said this was all codswallop.

Where she came from nobody knew. Her hair had been a pale-yellow blonde but now the yellow had changed to silver-grey. Her face was pale as milk. Her eyes were the lightest blue that anyone had ever seen. She had delicate hands and she wore a silver ring on her wedding finger. People said she talked to herself. Bessie said that if she lived up there all alone, she would talk to herself too. The Fort Woman walked the Peninsula collecting wild garlic, sorrel, bitter cress, comfrey and wild nettles. On the sea shore she picked rock samphire, periwinkles and wild mussels. She used them in a broth. Drying beside her little fire to add to her broths and elixirs were wild kelp, sea beet and wild sea kale. Unusual seashells and stones made a path to her door. She lived mostly on seafood, herbs and wild vegetables. But the locals often brought her food in exchange for her medicines.

Victoria could see her now. She was out washing some seaweed in an old pot, dressed in a black cape, with wisps of her white silken hair escaping. She looked up and smiled when she saw Victoria, as if she was expecting her.

Victoria had visited her before with her father. He had brought her up some honey from the bees and some bread baked by Bessie. He had a mare and the vet had tried everything, but she was still lame. Someone had suggested he try the Fort Woman. She made an elixir and told him to steep a cloth in it and wrap the leg in it. Her father swore that it had worked like a miracle. Her mother thought it was all nonsense and had no time for anyone who lived such a reclusive life.

There was a large barrel beside the hut filled with rainwater and the woman filled a pitcher as she beckoned Victoria to come in.

The smell of turf embers filled the air.

'Sit and rest.'

Victoria gave her a gift of some brown bread that she had taken from the kitchen at Kilbride House and some freshly churned butter. The woman took them graciously.

Victoria sat down in a threadbare armchair, with a soft cushion at her back.

The woman took her cape off. She wore a simple brown dress and hobnail boots. Her white hair was tied up with what looked like a nail from a horseshoe.

She put some water in a pot on the fire and began adding herbs and leaves to it. She gently stirred it with a wooden ladle.

Victoria looked about. There was a simple table and a chair in the centre of the flagstoned kitchen. On the table an old milk bottle with wild flowers gently scented the air. She looked at the thickness of the walls. They must be at least two feet thick. It was cosy and clean. The little fire lit up and threw golden light across the walls and the flagstone floor. There was a feeling of peace in the

43

cottage. She closed her eyes. She was so tired. All the deceit, the pretending and trying to hide her sickness. Her eyelids grew heavy.

The woman put a faded rug over her.

'You are not feeling well.' Her accent had a foreign lilt to it.

'No – I'm feeling sick all the time.'

She had no idea how she would tell her, but she had to get some help. Each morning she thought she was going to die with retching dark-green bile, but instead of disappearing it was now lasting all day. Although her belly was growing, she knew she had lost weight and her face looked like chalk. Her mother had wanted to take her to the doctor, but she had lied and said she felt better. The smell of food at dinner was the hardest thing and when she knew fish was being served, as it often was, she had to lock herself in her room until the aroma of it was gone.

'You are going to have a baby?' the woman asked kindly.

'How did you know?'

'I know. You have the sickness.'

Victoria could feel the relief flood through her. She could see the concern on the woman's face and the kindness. She had so wanted to confide in another woman. But she couldn't. This was too big. Besides, she had promised Canice she would say nothing to risk their plans being found out. He knew she planned to go to the Fort Woman who would not tell their secret.

Everything had changed now.

Edith had noticed she had stopped riding.

'Silver is lame, so I have to wait until she heals,' Victoria had lied.

44

She had longed to go on the cliffs on Silver. But she was worried about the baby. She could not bear to think of having to leave Silver. Leaving Kilbride was killing her. But she knew they had no choice. Especially now. Each day she tried to store images in her head. The sea that changed from blue to grey, depending on the light. The rowdy gulls nesting in the cliffs. The shifting fog over the bay. The distant boats at the dawn of day with prayers from the shore for their safe return. Kilbride House, her home that she cherished, its views overlooking the bay where she had looked out at the cliffs as they begged her to come dance in the wind on them. But there was a life now growing in her belly and she loved Canice, she was sure of that. Being apart from him would kill her and they could only do what so many had done before them.

They would run away to England and get married. Canice would get some work. Her father had left her some money which would be hers when she reached eighteen, so that would help.

'I feel so sick, all the time.'

The woman nodded knowingly.

'It will pass. You are worried and that is not helping.' She stirred the mixture in the pot and then ladled some in a cup and gave it to Victoria.

'Drink. It will help the sickness and not harm the baby. It's just herbs. It will help.'

Reluctantly she held the tin cup to her mouth and took a sip. Somehow the gentle taste of the herbs comforted her and did not make her retch.

It was such a relief to be honest with someone.

'You are from Kilbride House?'

Victoria was shocked that she knew who she was,

considering she had never left the Fort.

'Yes, but please don't tell anybody I was here.'

The woman smiled reassuringly.

'I was here as a child with my father – is that how you know who I am?"

'I remember him, and I remember you. He loved you very much. He had a strong passion for horses, a kind man.'

Victoria could feel herself crumble. How she missed him! Maybe he would have understood and somehow helped her.

As if reading her thoughts, the woman said, 'He is with you. Call him when you feel fear and he will walk with you. He loves you still.'

Victoria cried. She was tired of being strong.

'You now have a kind man too?'

'Yes, but ...'

'Not of your faith.'

'He's from the Island. I am a Protestant. My mother would never allow it. I'm sure of it.'

'Religion rules this island of Ireland. It has for centuries.'

Victoria caught the look that crossed the woman's face. It was one of fear.

The woman rose and fetched a small jar from some shelves against the wall. She sat beside Victoria and opened the jar which was filled with a greenish ointment. She rubbed a little on Victoria's forehead and said some words that sounded like Latin. She kept repeating them. It was soothing and the nausea seemed to ebb away and then disappeared.

'You must be strong, difficult times are ahead. You

will be tested. You must never lose faith in yourself and your own strength. It is inside of you. You must dig deep, but remember you are strong. Remember the love you have had, and the memories will keep you strong. You will live long. You and your baby will live in a land far from here. One day your hair will be as white as mine.' The woman's eyes were almost ice-blue yet there was a real warmth radiating from them. 'Now rest a while.'

Victoria looked around the sparse room. A pot, two tin cups, a tin bowl and plate on the table. Three or four pieces of cutlery. But there were lots of books on the shelves. She got up to look at them.

'May I?'

The woman nodded. Many of the classics were there. There were books of poetry and books in Greek and Latin. Some thought the Fort Woman was a nun seeking some type of hermit's life. But she never mentioned a religion.

'Come, child. I must speak further.'

Victoria sat again and the woman took her hand.

Silently, she gazed in Victoria's eyes again as if reading something in them.

'You must escape at all costs,' she then said abruptly. 'Go make your plans and never look back. Your road is far from here. You must leave.'

The urgency in the woman's voice frightened Victoria. They planned to leave soon but maybe they should leave even sooner. Fear gripped her heart.

As if reading her thoughts, the woman reiterated her warning. 'You must leave. *Now*.'

'Why? Why do you say this?'

She caught Victoria's hand. 'Trust me, please. I mean

47

you no harm. Leave, do not delay, do not spend another night in Kilbride. Go far away.'

'*Tonight?* I can't.'

'You *must*.'

'It's so hard. I love Kilbride. It is my home.' Victoria began to cry.

'Nobody will ever take that away from you. It is in your soul, the wind and sea, and your beautiful home will always remember you. But you must think of your baby now and go.'

'We had planned to go soon, but not that soon.'

The woman shook her head. 'You must leave now. To protect your baby. Remember: stay strong – you will be tested.'

With two bottles of the herb tincture in her basket she cycled to meet Canice. Tears were rolling down her face.

He was working on a currach near the cliffs. His eyes crinkled as he grinned at Victoria.

Then, as she dismounted and threw herself into his arms, he saw that she was crying.

'What's wrong – not the baby?' His eyes were full of fear.

'No, no, nothing like that – the baby is fine – but I was with the Fort Woman and she told me that I must leave Kilbride. *Now*. She told me not to delay.'

'What? Sure, we are leaving soon – we have all the plans nearly in place.'

Victoria shook her head. 'No, no – I believe her – we must leave *now*! She said to protect the baby. She said I must not stay in Kilbride another night. We must go, we must. I believe her! I am not staying another night here.'

48

He wrapped his arms around her and held her close. 'Calm down, my love – that's crazy. Leave because a strange old woman says so? How can she know this? Living in solitude as she does up there? She can't be in her sane senses living such a life!'

'Canice! I don't know how she knows – but she's extraordinary – like someone who can see into the future. I believe her – you have to trust me.'

'I do trust you – but –'

'*Canice! Please!*' She began to shake in her distress.

'Victoria, please calm down – if that's what you want, that's what we'll do. We have enough money to go. Alright, love, alright. We will leave tonight.'

They both looked around at the place that would stay with them a lifetime. The salty air of the peninsula was embedded in their souls.

'I wish we could take a piece of all this with us,' she sighed. 'Why does it have to be like this? I love you and you love me – why punish us for that?'

'The history of our land, love. Hopefully someday it will change.'

Victoria stared at the cliffs and the beaches that she so adored. 'I will never ride on these beaches on Silver again.'

He held her close. 'You will, in your heart. You will.'

CHAPTER 7

New York
2018

Many of Edith's friends had come back to the apartment after the service for lunch and drinks. Now most had left.

Catherine was sitting alone, looking out the window, sipping on a scotch and ice.

Lainey came and sat beside her.

'The house is so strange without Grandma in it,' she said.

Catherine nodded but didn't otherwise respond.

Lainey stared at her mother who had begun picking flecks off her elegant black suit. Her rich auburn hair was up in a chignon and delicate pearls adorned her ears. Her make-up was light but impeccable. Lainey had not noticed her cry at all. She knew that if her mother could have left after the funeral and returned to the theatre she would have. It wouldn't be long before she did just that and then she would see very little of her.

At least her father Travis was here. He had a calming effect on everyone. Smiling and chatting, making sure everyone had drinks and someone to converse with. It was just the easy way that he was. Thankfully, even though they were divorced, her parents remained on good terms.

Lainey looked out through the window over the trailing rosebush – a burst of bright pink, it looked so beautiful and full of life. On a normal day she would have taken her camera out and tried to capture it. Her grandma had given her a beautiful camera when she was very young and had taught her how to see the beauty in everything. The wonder of a dark winter's evening, when the clouds were full of thunder, an abandoned house with ivy trailing over it, a river with the colours of the rainbow echoing through. Lainey's fascination with photography had started from that first camera and all the trips to Central Park with Edith. Her camera always at the ready, she would snap as the seasons changed and the colours began a brand-new canvas. It was her profession, but it also helped her see the world in a different light. Always trying to see the beauty and capture the soul of something.

She followed her mother's gaze. The sky was full of candy-floss clouds mixed with a piercing azure blue. She could feel tears threatening.

'I'm sure she has left the apartment to you – we really must arrange to see her attorney,' Catherine said flippantly as she drained her drink.

Lainey flinched. This was the home that she had shared for so long with her grandmother. She knew the history of everything within the walls. A two-storey apartment in Carnegie Hill, noted by some as the most quintessential place to live in New York, Lainey adored it. It dated back to 1901 and despite its grandeur it was filled with soft homely touches, like a wood-burning stove, soft floral armchairs, curved coffee tables and on the walls a gold-embossed wallpaper. Pale-blue embroidered taffeta drapes hung from the high cathedral-style windows. When she was young and upset over something, she would hide behind them. Edith would gently pull back the curtain and try to figure out what had upset her.

'Well, today is not the day for discussing it,' Lainey warned.

'I am just saying it needs to be sorted and we need to know the contents of the will.'

Lainey stared at her. She knew how hurt her grandma would be to hear her only daughter sounding so cold. It was her funeral, for goodness' sake!

'We need time to adjust to Grandma being gone first, Mom. Maybe you don't but I do. We can make an appointment to see her attorney in a few days but today is to remember Grandma. In case you have forgotten!'

Catherine threw her eyes up to heaven. 'No need to be so tetchy. I just want to check that everything will run smoothly, and you know me – I like to get things sorted.'

Lainey took a deep breath. She didn't want to fight, not today of all days.

'Perhaps we could have dinner here tomorrow night – I can cook?' she suggested.

'I'm not sure,' Catherine said hesitantly.

Lainey shrugged. 'For goodness' sake, Mom! I have lost my grandmother – surely you can spare a few hours?'

'We can do lunch.'

'You are unbelievable!'

'What? I am merely suggesting we have lunch instead of dinner.'

'You know exactly what I mean – you can't wait to run back to the theatre.'

'Everything okay?' Lainey's father walked over and took a grape from the canapé tray.

'Fine,' said Catherine.

'I was just asking Mom to spend a little time with me, maybe even have dinner, but she is far too busy,' Lainey said.

'That is not true. I merely suggested lunch instead. You were always so sensitive.'

'Okay, Mom, you win. Let's just have a coffee some time – that way I won't take up too much of your time.'

'Keep your voices down,' said Travis. 'There are still some people here.'

'I wish they would leave – we have given them lunch and drinks, the party's over,' Catherine replied as she poured another scotch.

'Oh, for goodness sake, Mom!' Lainey said, exasperated. 'Dad, will you please talk to her?'

Catherine got up and walked away to air-kiss one of the guests who was leaving.

Travis put his arm around his daughter.

'Look, Lainey, everyone handles grief differently.'

'Grief! Mom is not grieving. I have no idea what she's feeling, but it certainly isn't grief. I just can't understand her. I know she wasn't very close to Grandma, but surely she could shed one tear for her?'

'As I said, just because she's not crying doesn't mean this is not affecting her.'

'Please, Dad, don't try to defend her. She is treating her death like a big inconvenience. She would much prefer to be back at her beloved theatre. How can she be so indifferent to the fact that Grandma is dead? I miss her so much – she was the best grandmother anyone could ever dream of having.'

'Yes, she was a fantastic grandmother and I owe her a great debt. She was always there for you. But your mother and her? Well, they just had a very complicated relationship, honey, but it sure doesn't mean there was no love there.'

Lainey knew that he could be describing his relationship with Catherine. Complicated! Yet a lot of love, from his part anyway. Catherine had many admirers over the years. But she liked to play with them, quite like a cat with a mouse. When she was done playing, she tossed them away.

She watched her now as Catherine kissed someone else on the cheek and then waltzed back over to them. She certainly looked much younger than her years. She could easily pass for being in her early fifties.

'Mom, did you let Grandma's brother in Ireland know that she died?' Lainey asked.

Catherine shook her head. 'No, I didn't. Considering they haven't spoken since she left Ireland all those years ago, there is hardly any need.'

'For goodness' sake, he is still her brother!' Lainey said. 'They sent cards every Christmas.'

'So does my banker! If that's the extent of their relationship, why bother? He was hardly going to suddenly fly over after all these years to see her dead when he never bothered a phone call in sixty years!'

'Seriously, Mom! She was his sister.' Lainey shook her head. 'I don't know why I'm wasting my time talking about this with you. I'll let him know. Do you have an address?'

'Suit yourself. I'm sure you'll get very little response. I don't even have to look up the address. I remember it from all those Christmas cards. It's Kilbride House,

54

Dingle, County Kerry. I wrote to him myself a few times when I was younger, but he never responded – just all those damn Christmas cards.'

'Actually, now that I come to think of it, there was an email address on the one from last Christmas. Was there something about him having a daughter? It's possibly her mail address. He must be in his late eighties by now. I'll look for it tomorrow. I know where Grandma kept them – in that hatbox beside her bed.' She looked quizzically at her mother. 'I never knew you had any interest in getting in touch with Ireland, Mom?'

Catherine pursed her lips. 'Believe me, I had my reasons, but my mother would not hear of it.'

'What do you mean, you had your reasons?' Lainey asked.

'Oh, nothing. Just a youthful curiosity.'

If Catherine was going to divulge anything, she had changed her mind.

'Did you ever consider going over?' Lainey asked, her curiosity stirred.

'Yes.'

'When?'

'I can't really remember.'

'Mom!'

'Okay! After college, I thought a trip to Ireland would be great. I even considered studying acting there – they have a great theatre legacy with Joyce and Yeats. But Mother would not hear of it, threatened to stop any allowance that she was giving me. She did everything to stop me, so eventually I lost interest.'

'Oh!' Lainey had never known her mother had wanted to visit Ireland. She believed that Catherine had always done exactly as she wanted. Her grandmother must have really put her foot down to stop her from going. But why on earth would she have done that?

'Strange that she never wanted any of us to have anything to do with Ireland.'

'I am sure she had her reasons,' Catherine replied, throwing her eyes up.

'How do you mean?'

'Nothing, Lainey. Stop with all the questions about Ireland!'

'But it was her home, where she came from. How could she turn her back on it so completely?' Lainey could feel a new interest in her grandmother's past stirring in her mind.

'There is no point in digging up the past,' Catherine said.

A few days later Catherine and Lainey met in the law firm of Fox and Jameson, on Park Avenue, for a reading of the will.

'Edith put a lot of thought into her will,' Alistair Fox explained in a soft New York drawl. He was a man in his seventies, dressed elegantly in a grey suit that matched his silver hair. He had a broad smile and gold-rimmed glasses.

Catherine crossed her legs and tapped the table with her manicured hand. She had disregarded any mourning clothes and wore a stunning red dress under a soft cream camel coat. Her hair was pinned up perfectly and her make-up as always flawless.

Lainey looked more like her father. Her blonde hair had red streaks, making it strawberry in the sun. Her long fair lashes and pale-blue eyes were make-up free.

'Edith has appointed her granddaughter Lainey Miller to be executor of the will. It will go to probate. Basically, when it passes probate the estate will be dealt with. But I had my accountant look over it and everything looks in very good shape. If there are no problems, the bequests will be dealt with quickly. The apartment is to go to Lainey. There is a substantial amount of money to go to you, Mrs Lee Miller. She has a request also.'

He paused and let that hang in air for a moment.

'Oh, for heaven's sake get on with it! What is her request?' said Catherine. 'Please tell me it's not to have some sort of religious blessing with lots of promising to repent?'

He looked at Catherine over his glasses. He held his pen mid-air.

'Her request is that you both go to Ireland, to the place where she was brought up.'

Catherine eyeballed him, scowling. 'You are kidding us?'

'It's quite clear – she requests that you both go to a place near Dingle in County Kerry in Ireland. A place called Kilbride. Kilbride House, to be exact. I gather you have never visited before?'

'No, we have not,' Catherine replied, 'and I can tell you I have no intention of doing so in the future either!'

'Eh … I called it a "request" but I am afraid it is a stipulation. The will cannot be finalised unless you carry out her wishes.'

Catherine slammed her hand on the table. 'Unbelievable! She stops us all our life from visiting Ireland and now she wants us to go!'

'I'm afraid it has to be done in order to execute the will,' Alistair stated. He leafed through the files in front of him and showed them a copy.

'*This is ridiculous!*' Catherine said, raising her voice.

'It does seem a bit odd,' said Lainey.

Catherine threw the document on the table. '*But why now?*' she all but shouted.

'She left no explanation but stated that you should go.' Alistair took a sip of water.

'I never heard anything so ludicrous. How dare she leave this mess behind her!'

'It's hardly a mess, Mom – she's left us a huge amount,' Lainey said, trying to calm her mother down.

Catherine eyeballed her. 'As long as we play by her rules. Well, forget it, I am not going!'

Alistair shuffled the papers. 'Well, in that case there is no more to be said for the moment. The will cannot be dealt with until you make the trip. You had better go and discuss your position.'

Lainey read the will again.

'Very well. I will certainly go to Ireland if that's what Grandma wanted. Mom, will you just think about it? It could be fun. I would love to visit Ireland and especially see where she grew up.'

'*No! Absolutely not!*'

'I am afraid it states quite clearly that you *both* must go,' Alistair Fox pointed out.

'How dare she dictate to us where we must go! I will get my own attorney to sort this ridiculous request!' Catherine spat.

'What is the big deal, Mom? It's just a visit to Ireland. It could be great. You wanted to go once, you told me.'

'Yes, but I couldn't because it would have upset your grandmother. Now, how wonderful, we have her blessing. She is controlling us from the dead. I can't stand it!'

Lainey lost patience. 'Get over yourself, Mom. We are just going to have to go and that's that. I will make plans as soon as possible.'

'Sorry, Lainey, but I refuse to go. For goodness' sake, this is absurd. I have no intention of finding some long-lost Irish relatives or trotting over to some wet, sleepy, backward village in Ireland, just to keep my dead mother happy.'

Lainey flinched. 'You have made your feelings perfectly clear, Mom. This is not just about you though. Try to remember that.'

'So you think we should carry out this mad plan of hers? Forget it. There has to be a way around it.'

'I am afraid I cannot see any way around it,' said Alistair Fox, 'but I suggest for now that you go away and let this information settle before you make any decision.'

Lainey got up and shook his hand.

'Thank you for your time, Mr Fox, and I will be in touch.'

'Very well. I would point out to you, Mrs Lee Miller, that it is very much in your interest to carry out your mother's wishes. In my opinion, spending money on unnecessary legal bills is a waste of money.'

'If I want your opinion I will request it,' Catherine retorted. 'Good day to you. My own attorney will be in touch.'

CHAPTER 8

Ireland
2018

All the holidays abroad and the travelling she had done over the years could not compare to the emotion of landing on Irish soil for the first time. Over sixty years ago her grandmother had left, never to return, but Lainey knew that Edith's heart was entwined in the country up to the day she died. She wished her mother had agreed to come but, regardless, she had decided to fulfil her own part of Edith's request. Catherine had refused completely and had asked her own attorney to see what he could do but, much to her annoyance, he had not yet managed to find a way out of the clause.

'How terrible can it be, Mom, to spend some time in Ireland? We could visit Dublin and the galleries and the theatres. You could see where Joyce grew up – we could even go to Sligo where Yeats wrote so much of his work.'

'It doesn't suit me now. I am an actress in the middle of a production.'

'That's not the reason. You have an understudy. It's just because Grandma asked you to and you don't want to honour her dying wish.'

'Don't be so dramatic, Lainey. I do think it's a

ridiculous request, but as I said it does not suit me now and that's just it.'

Lainey was freelance so could work anywhere. She was single and, although she adored New York, she quite often left for her work.

She had married for a short time, but it hadn't lasted very long. Douglas was a doctor who was working as a registrar in New York. He hated New York and had wanted her to move back to Nova Scotia in Canada with him. She felt trapped when he gave her such an ultimatum. So, in the middle of the worst winter in years Douglas left for Canada without Lainey. He had not returned and by the end of the fall moved in with his ex-girlfriend, another doctor, and began work in a hospital in Nova Scotia.

There had been a few relationships since, but nothing serious. She was enjoying her freedom and had begun a portfolio for a book of her photography that would be published in the summer. She knew Edith had worried about her. She had never really warmed to Douglas.

'When you know it's right, you would move to another world for the love of your life,' Edith had told her. 'Never settle for anything less, Lainey. Life can be difficult, but love can withstand everything. Your marriage was not meant to be. You have so much love to give, but you are like a wild rose – you need to feel free and not trapped.'

Shannon Airport was manic for the Saturday morning arrivals. She had decided to hire a car and drive as far as Tralee. Then she would sleep for the night in a hotel and awake refreshed (hopefully) to drive to Dingle the next day.

As Lainey drove down the dual carriageway towards

Limerick she felt exhilarated. She was in Ireland, the birthplace of her beloved grandmother. All the times she had thought about coming here but knew that it would upset Grandma! It now seemed ludicrous that she had never visited. She was well travelled and yet had never been here. She had tried to talk to her mother about it before she left.

'Why did you never go to Ireland after your studies, when Grandma couldn't have stopped you?'

'I may have had a very rocky relationship with Mother, but she was financially generous to me all my life. In the earlier years, she would still threaten to cut me out off if I went to Ireland.'

'But when you were young, were you ever close to her?'

'Yes, but when I got older we clashed constantly. I didn't doubt that she loved me but growing up she kept me on a leash that was so tight I almost choked. I resented it and never found my way back.'

'I can't imagine Grandma behaving like that. She was so different when I was growing up,'

'Well, as I said, she did mellow. You were the daughter that she wanted me to be.'

'Why are you only telling me this now? How come you never said any of this when Grandma was alive?' It wasn't that she didn't believe her mother, but why now when Edith was dead?

'Look, she was a wonderful grandma,' Catherine said. 'Maybe living in America changed her over the years and eventually gave her a different perspective.'

Strongly advised by the internet to bypass Limerick city and its traffic, Lainey took a turn-off for the

Limerick Tunnel. When she emerged from under the River Shannon, she followed the signs for Tralee and ended up on the M20 motorway. This took her almost as far as a wonderfully picturesque village called Adare where she stopped for a coffee and was tempted to linger. But the Dingle Peninsula lay before her and she pressed on, following a good two-lane road, the N21, which would take her all the way to Tralee. For someone who had driven in New York, it was all a delightful walk in the park – when she'd got used to the small matter of having to drive on the left.

Tralee turned out to be a handsome town, the 'county town' of County Kerry – more importantly, Lainey thought with a grin, the home of the International Rose of Tralee Festival.

She had booked a room in The Ashe Hotel, which was in the middle of the town. With the aid of the satnav she easily found it. She parked and went inside. It was very elegant yet understated.

She was welcomed by a dark-haired girl who led her to the reception desk. It was strange getting used to the Irish accent.

The receptionist whose name badge said *Claire* was checking her booking information on a computer.

'Just the one night?'

'Yes, that's all. And may I have some food to my room?'

'Of course. There's a menu in the room.'

'Terrific.'

The room was super-modern with a big comfy bed. She ordered a bowl of chowder and a green salad and washed it down with a glass of white wine. It was a bit early for wine but with the jet lag her body clock was mixed up. She took a long shower and then exhaustion overwhelmed her and she crawled into bed. It was still early but she had failed to sleep on the plane. The room was quiet except for the soft hum of a hoover down the corridor. It was her first time to sleep in Ireland, an Ireland she had heard so much about. The family who lived here, her own flesh and blood, she knew nothing about.

At first her mind would not settle. Images of her grandma, her mother, the images of Ireland that she had passed along the journey from Shannon to Tralee were flashing in front of her. She could feel herself eventually drift to sleep. It was like that half sleep, somewhere between waking and sleeping. She drifted into a dream.

In the dream it was raining, and she was running. It didn't look like anywhere that she knew and she looked around to see anything that she recognised.

But suddenly it became darker. There was a fog everywhere and there was no sign of anyone. She was alone. She felt the cold enveloping her. There was water everywhere and a sliver of a moon was her only guide through the thickness of the fog. She was flailing and lashing around in the water, screaming, her body gripped by the iciness and the frozen fear. But she could not see anything in the dark.

She could hear an urgent thudding.

'*Are you okay?*'

Her eyes flashed open.

'*Excuse me, are you okay?*'

Someone was knocking at the door.

Then the phone beside her bed began ringing.

Lainey sat up, startled and bewildered.

She had no idea where she was or what was happening. She picked up the phone, her body trembling.

The voice on the other end said: 'I am sorry to disturb you. This is Claire at the front desk. Are you in some distress? Our housekeeping alerted us. I am so sorry if we are intruding.'

'What?' The confusion was overwhelming.

'My colleague is at your door – she heard some sounds of distress coming from your room. We're just checking if you are alright?'

Clarity hit Lainey. She was in the hotel. In Tralee.

She'd had a nightmare – but it was so real.

'Are you okay?'

Lainey composed herself as quickly as she could.

'It's okay, I just had a bad dream. Thank you – I'm fine.'

'Would you like me to send something up – a hot drink perhaps?

'No, I'm fine, thank you. It must be the jet lag – sorry to disturb you.'

'Not at all, and if there is anything at all you need just dial 0.'

Lainey thanked her and hung up.

The person at the door had stopped knocking and must have left.

Lainey could feel tears flowing down her face. Shakily she got up and went to the bathroom. It may have been a nightmare, but it had been so real. She must have been screaming for housekeeping to hear her.

She took a shower and made some tea afterwards. She

had stopped shaking. What on earth was that about? It must be the jet lag mixed with the glass of wine she had with her meal.

She lay back after the tea and tried to read but her mind could not settle. She turned on the TV and watched a documentary about wildlife in Ireland.

She was glad she had booked the hotel before driving down to Kilbride. She had slept badly since her grandma had died and she'd been very busy tying up a few commissions before she left New York. It was good to just take time out.

Eventually she dozed off into a dreamless sleep and awoke in time for breakfast.

After breakfast she immediately packed her bag. She wanted to get on the road early. The road to Kilbride House.

CHAPTER 9

Kilbride House
2018

Ruby Chamberlain sat by the stove in a big comfy armchair. Thankfully the stove was working properly, which meant that at least the kitchen was warm. The plumber was meant to come today to try to fix the heating. Kilbride House was absolutely freezing. Ruby had forgotten how cold it could get. When she was a child, she remembered her parents constantly trying to heat the large house. A wave of guilt swept over her, thinking of her grandfather Edward living here on his own up to a few months ago. It was a cold autumn and winter was on the way. Winnie, who had lived in one of the stable cottages, had helped to look after the house but had recently got ill herself. Ruby was very fond of Winnie and felt responsible for her.

She had been shocked at the deterioration of her grandfather and of Winnie when she had first arrived home from London. She immediately found a lovely nursing home for Winnie in the village, where her two best friends were already living. Winnie was sad to leave the cottage but after a couple of days she had improved both mentally and physically and now was very happy with her new home.

Edward Goulding was eighty-four and had managed very well up till now with the help of Winnie. But Ruby had noticed how forgetful he seemed to be. She hoped it was the fact that he was just a bit under the weather but there were lots of obvious signs that her grandfather could not be left living by himself anymore, especially now that Winnie was gone. Winnie and Edward had known each other all their lives. He, the son of a well-to-do Protestant family, and Winnie whose family had moved to Kilbride from the Blasket Islands in the fifties. Winnie had never married, and Edward's wife had died very young. They constantly argued but nobody could deny that they had great affection for each other. They often had heated debates where Winnie would tell him a few home truths.

'Sure, what would you know and you a blow-in from across the water? My people are here since time began.'

'My family may have originated in England, Winnie, but that was centuries ago and I am just as Irish as you, born and bred here in Kilbride and my ancestors before me.'

But all this was forgotten when she visited twice a week for their card games, which were legendary. Kilbride House had a long history of card games. Edward's father had held many card nights and Edward had maintained the tradition.

Ruby noticed that the ceiling in the kitchen looked very dicey. The kitchen was originally in the basement but her own mother and father had redesigned the house a little to make it more liveable and cosy. The kitchen was now on the ground floor where one of the drawing rooms had been. A large leak had occurred at some stage.

A house like Kilbride needed huge maintenance. Her grandfather needed someone to look after him. But her life was very much in London where she worked in an art gallery. And now this long-lost cousin was about to descend on them. She wasn't sure how she felt about that. She had thought about cancelling her, but something stopped her.

Kilbride House, with all its flaws, its faded wallpaper and its leaking ceilings was a beautiful house. It had stood the test of time. It had a view of the rugged coastline with winding paths leading to the pier. The Blasket Islands could be seen on a clear day and the sunsets were like nowhere in Ireland. The demesne was planted with roses, trees, flowers and plants that brought a cornucopia of colour to every season. The Tudor-style house with separate wings was imposing yet architecturally beautiful. Drawing rooms, a dining parlour, a library, a study, a basement that had once contained the kitchens, eleven bedrooms, four bathrooms and the attics completed the residence. But to Ruby it was just home, a home that had been filled with love and memories.

And this was her cousin whose grandmother had also been brought up in this beautiful house, yet Lainey had never stepped foot inside the door. Perhaps it hadn't been opened for her, but Ruby had absolutely no idea why.

Edward was sleeping now, and the doctor had said that he needed lots of rest. He had got such a setback when he heard the news about his sister Edith passing away in America. Considering they had never seen each other in all those years, Ruby had never expected him to be so upset. He rarely if ever spoke of her. It was something that as a family they had accepted. Her mother Florence had never pried or suggested they look her up. Her own late father thought there must have been some family falling-out.

At first, her grandfather was very anxious when she had told him that Edith's granddaughter wanted to visit. He was normally so good with visitors and was very welcoming. But he seemed very hesitant about her arrival. Ruby was glad she had decided to get one of the stable cottages sorted out for her stay instead of putting her in the house. The cottage was cute and cosy, and she had fresh linen on the bed. John Hogan who looked after the horses in Kilbride had helped her cut back the ivy and the rose bushes. She had the inside painted and a lovely floral tablecloth covered a round table in the centre. A cream turf stove gave a gorgeous feel to it. She had even put in a proper shower and bathroom. So it was all set.

Lainey seemed happy with the arrangement and had thanked her in her last mail. She hoped she didn't mind that she had not invited her to stay in the house but, considering the way her grandfather was acting, she thought it wiser. Maybe this cousin could shed some light on the falling-out. She would arrive in a few hours.

Edward came down the stairs again, dressed and ready to pop in to his haunt in Kilbride village.

'Just going out for a while, Ruby,' he said, as he struggled into his overcoat.

'Will you just stay in bed, Grandfather, and rest, doctor's orders, or I will not be responsible for my actions.' Ruby was worn out with trying to keep him indoors.

'I was just going to go for something to help my

throat – a good strong hot brandy would see me right as rain.'

'Grandfather, Grandfather, just rest, please.'

'Very well but bring me up a hot toddy when you can. Unless that is banned too. Such a fuss over a cough.' He took off his hat and his overcoat and reluctantly stomped back up to bed.

Ruby couldn't help but smile. He was more like a teenager than a man of his years. She made a large hot brandy for him which she was sure wasn't recommended with his antibiotic, but she felt it was better than letting him off into the village to visit his little haunt, O'Rourke's pub, for the afternoon.

CHAPTER 10

Lainey slept late and after breakfast packed her bag and set out on the road from Tralee to Dingle. She was now only about 60km from Kilbride but decided to venture over the spectacular Conor Pass rather than follow the coastal road. The road was certainly not for the faint of heart – in truth in was quite nerve-racking and there were times she regretted her choice as she had to pull to the side of the narrow road, an alarming drop to the side of the car, to allow oncoming cars to pass. Or rounded a tight corner to have a hugely woolly sheep bound across the road in front of her. But the journey was a tapestry of scenes that made her photographic eye go into overdrive. A shifting fog gently drifted over the mountains, revealing a mystical Ireland that she had thought existed only in fairy tales. The sheer beauty of the landscape with its dramatic mountains and clear lakes astounded her. It looked like the purest place on Earth. Her emotions see-sawed as at times her heart was breaking, thinking that she had never really appreciated what her grandmother had told her. She remembered Edith saying that some people thought the Dingle Peninsula was the edge of the world. And she remembered that when she was a little girl her grandmother had told her that Dingle was the last place created – but being the last it had to be the finest, the most perfect.

She got out of the car at various points and took photographs. She saw a tour bus and a feeling of melancholy overwhelmed her. That is what she was. A tourist, an American tourist. But somehow it didn't sit right with her. Part of her was very Irish and it was time she discovered that part. She was feeling a connection that she had never felt before, a sense of place that was embracing her.

She stopped in Dingle town for a coffee and walked around taking photographs and soaking in the atmosphere – the boats, the sea, the quaint little shops and streets selling all sorts of delights. Listening to the voices, the people of Ireland, her people, the people of her grandmother. Not for the first time since her grandmother passed, she questioned so much. Why? Why forbid them this? What on earth had happened to make her grandmother leave and never set foot on this beautiful land ever again?

She drove next towards Ventry, a place of textures, colours and images that held the story of Dingle's past. Ruins remained of an existence of so long ago. Her camera was out again. The images were too good to pass. She took a shot of an old creamery can with weeds growing all around it. Another of an ancient cottage with only part of the four walls remaining.

Eventually she set out on the road to Kilbride village. It was between Ventry and Dunquin and now she was approaching the tip of the peninsula which was like a jagged finger pointing out into the Atlantic. She stopped many times to admire the rugged coastline and look out at the Blasket Islands. To think a whole settlement of people had lived there not so long ago! She had read about them and how they had moved to the mainland. She tried to imagine what it must have been like, living somewhere that was so dependent on the elements.

It was everything Edith had described. Steeped in an ancient beauty, the sky was purple with indigos and blues. The Atlantic, wild and crashing against the cliffs, the foam from the waves floating across the strands like bubble bath. The gulls swooping in and out. The view of the Great Blasket, barely visible with a descending fog that made it ghostly in the most beautiful sense.

Lainey could feel the tears threatening out of nowhere. She wished she had seen this with Edith. How she must have loved it! Edith who had shown her the beauty in everything. What on earth had prevented her from coming back to this majestic place? When she left, did she know that the memory of it would remain in her heart, the smell of the sea, the sound of the gulls and the vison of the islands? This beautiful mystical land must have haunted her dreams. New York was home and both she and Edith dearly loved it. Vibrant, diverse and home to so many cultures. But being here on the Dingle Peninsula, staring out at the islands, Lainey had never felt more alive, as if she was coming home.

The salty Atlantic air was like a rocket to her senses. With new enthusiasm, she drove on into the village of Kilbride, like a child on Christmas morning, waiting expectantly. She took the first turn right as Ruby had instructed in her email.

The Kilbride village that she entered was nothing like the village that Edith had described. As she parked and walked around she tried to see something of the village that was held in her grandmother's memory. Where was the shop that sold the bonbons? The old creamery? She could see the small church which held the Protestant community and the large Catholic church where most of the inhabitants went. Edith had described it as a village divided by faith like any other village in Ireland in the early fifties, yet both faiths living in an agreeable peace. As long as they knew their boundaries! She tried to picture it as Edith would have left it, perhaps with a few motor cars, some ponies and traps. A market every Thursday. But now it looked totally different, with quirky shop fronts, a couple of pubs advertising authentic Irish Cuisine and a small art gallery.

Reluctantly she drove out of the village, to find Kilbride House.

The road was narrow and pot-holey which made her slow down as she turned a corner – then suddenly she saw it: her first glimpse of Kilbride House. She could see the chimneys, all eight of them. Two with smoke coming out. A large stone wall surrounded the estate. She drove to the entrance where two black iron gates were open. Slowly she drove up the wide avenue lined with chestnut trees. As the avenue turned right, she could see the house in all its splendour. Imposing. Wisteria growing on the sandstone walls. The glass from so many windows looked dark. She could see a pond in the garden to the left and on the right another avenue leading to what looked like a stable yard.

She stopped and looked up at the fourth window on

the third floor. Edith's bedroom. Imagining the ghost of her youth staring back at her. She slowly drove on, barely looking where she was driving, she was so taken aback at the pure grandeur of Kilbride House.

Lainey wasn't sure what she expected her cousin to look like. There was an attractive young woman, perhaps in her thirties, smiling and waving at her. She was dressed in old jeans and a chunky jumper. Her long dark hair was plaited. She certainly didn't look like the lady of the manor. Could this be her cousin?

She pulled up and stepped out of the car.

'Lainey, you are very welcome to Kilbride,' said the young woman, giving her a brief hug. 'I'm your cousin Ruby.'

Lainey noticed her accent was very English. There only a trace of an Irish accent from her.

'It's lovely to meet you,' said Lainey. 'And what a beautiful house!'

'My grandfather, your Great-uncle Edward, is waiting for you in the drawing room. Winnie, who was our housekeeper, is out of the nursing home for the day, so she is keeping him company. Come in, come in.'

Lainey walked into a marble-floored large hall. There was a magnificent staircase that reminded her of *Gone with the Wind*. A chandelier hung from the high ceilings. The walls were half-papered in a blue textured paper and the bottom half painted in a deeper blue.

'I half expect Rhett Butler to be at the top of the stairs,' Lainey said, smiling.

'Afraid not – only Grandfather,' Ruby said with a grin. 'Here, let me take your coat.'

Lainey handed over her coat and tried to settle herself.

Every emotion was engulfing her. How on earth had her grandmother left all this behind? Her great-uncle was scarcely twenty-one or two when Edith left. Edith was only eighteen. The mystery of her grandmother's past was becoming much more intriguing.

When she walked into the drawing room, sitting beside a blazing fire on a soft leather sofa was an elderly man dressed in a brown suit, a colourful waistcoat and a neck-scarf. He had a cup of tea in his hand. He was chatting earnestly to a small little lady who looked like she had just got a perm in her soft white hair. She was sitting opposite him in a tall hard-backed chair and she was the first to spot Lainey.

'Edward,' she said, 'there she is.'

Edward put his teacup down and slowly turned towards Lainey. He went to stand up but suddenly he staggered. Ruby helped to steady him and handed him a black walking stick to aid him.

Edward was silent as he stared at Lainey's face.

'Grandfather, this is Lainey,' Ruby said reassuringly.

But Edward just kept staring at her.

Winnie too gaped at her, mouth opened.

'It's lovely to meet you both.' Lainey smiled, aware of the strange reception she was receiving.

'Grandfather, are you okay?' Ruby asked anxiously.

Winnie seemed to compose herself and replied instead.

'*Mr Goulding, it's your sister's grandchild come to see you!*' she almost screeched, as if to bring Edward back to reality.

His blue eyes were full of wonder but, also, Lainey sensed she could see fear in them. Why? She had absolutely no idea.

He took her hand and held it tightly.

'Welcome home.' His voice was hoarse.

Ruby helped him to sit back down.

'Where are our manners? Would you like a cup of tea?' Winnie said with some composure.

'I would love a cup, thank you.'

Ruby poured her a cup and asked her about her drive from Shannon. Lainey could see that she was trying to cover up for her grandfather who was still staring at her.

'So, you are Edith Goulding's grandchild?' Winnie asked, her eyes taking in every feature of Lainey's face.

'Yes, she talked so often of Kilbride and especially the beautiful landscape. I am sorry it has taken us so long to meet.'

'It has certainly been a long time – a lifetime, you could say,' Winnie offered, her eyes watching Lainey's every move. 'Some cake? Although it's a bit heavy. I always used free range eggs for my sponge cakes, but I don't think Cecilia uses them, does she, Ruby?'

'I got them from the shop that you told me to get them in,' Ruby replied as she took the plate from Winnie. 'Cecilia helps in the house, Lainey. But Winnie ran the house until recently.'

'Tell Cecilia that I will have a chat with her about sponges. That sponge will sit in my stomach until tomorrow. It could kill a horse. Would you like a slice, Lainey?'

'Thank you, Winnie, but no thanks,' Lainey said with a smile.

'Wise decision. I will be up all night with indigestion after that.' Winnie proceeded to give Lainey a rundown of her indigestion troubles while Edward sat in silence.

Ruby stood up. 'Lainey, I'll show you the cottage and get you settled.'

'That would be super – I'm beat from the drive from Tralee.'

Edward had still said nothing else.

'You can see Lainey again at dinner, Grandfather.'

Lainey took the cue and bid them farewell.

'I will show you the house later if that's okay?' Ruby said. 'Cecilia is cooking dinner. Hope you like roast chicken?'

'Make sure she cooks it well,' said Winnie. 'I don't want a bout of food poisoning and neither does your grandfather. Tell her not to put too much fat in the gravy either and not too much butter in the potatoes. Real butter, mind, not that horrible margarine stuff. Plenty of salt on the vegetables.'

'I'll tell her that, Winnie.'

Ruby grinned at Lainey as they walked out of the room.

'Winnie likes to make sure everyone knows their place. Poor Cecilia is always on edge when Winnie arrives. I hope Winnie doesn't scare her away. I do apologise for Grandfather. He is normally full of chat.'

'No need to apologise. But they did seem very taken aback when I arrived. Hopefully he will be okay with me staying here?'

'Of course he will. It must be the shock of never seeing you before. I am sure they will be fine by dinner. Come on, you can drive over to the cottage. I hope you don't mind that I put you up there? It might just work out a bit better.'

Lainey smiled in agreement. 'It's perfect.'

They drove the short distance to the cottage. There were four of them. They were all stone and attached to each other in a row. They had red half-doors and shutters on the windows. There was smoke coming from one of the chimneys.

'John lit the fire earlier. He looks after the horses around the estate. Cecilia put a few things into the cottage for you in the fridge – just in case you need some time alone – but please have all your meals with us.'

Lainey was glad that she was staying in the cottage. Her great-uncle obviously needed some time to adjust to having her here.

The cottage was full of quirky pieces and very cosy.

'Thank you, Ruby, this is beautiful.'

'I am just glad to finally meet you. I will let you settle in and we can have dinner about seven.'

'Okay, see you later.'

Lainey was glad of the time on her own. She needed time to gather her thoughts. There was something strange about Edward's reaction. Kilbride House was full of secrets. She was sure of it. Well, sixty-three years was long enough to keep them.

CHAPTER 11

Ruby was opening a bottle of wine when Lainey arrived in.

'That smells delicious.' The aroma of oregano, rosemary and thyme hit her senses. 'I thought I wasn't very hungry, but I certainly am now.'

'Good, because Cecilia has cooked enough for half of Kilbride. I don't know who she thinks she's feeding. I'll have to have a chat with her. Here, take a seat at the stove. A glass of red or white?'

'Red would be lovely, thank you.'

Ruby handed her a glass and poured one for herself.

'I thought we would just eat in here,' she said, then added apologetically, 'It's only the two of us.'

'Oh, are the others not joining us?' Lainey asked, surprised.

'Afraid not. Winnie has gone back to the nursing home and Grandfather is having a lie-down. Cecilia brought them some dinner earlier. Look, it's all a bit much for him, you arriving like this. I suppose it brings back so many memories for him. Grandfather is acting a little strangely and, to be honest, so is Winnie. He is normally the most welcoming man you could meet. Please, don't let it get to you, it's not personal – in fact, ever since I told him Edith died, he's not himself. It's all so weird, especially as he never talks about her and they have never bothered to meet all these years. Well, let's say, it seems to have knocked the stuffing out of him.'

'I guessed as much. The last thing I want to do is intrude or cause any ill feeling,' Lainey said worriedly.

'Look, whatever is going on with him, it's to do with the past and not us. I am thrilled you are here and hopefully Grandfather will come around. But, while we are on the subject, why did they stay estranged all these years? Grandfather will never talk about it, so I am at a loss. I was hoping you could enlighten me?'

Lainey shook her head. 'All these years, it must be the only thing I could never talk to my grandmother about. She refused to talk about her family here. She often talked about Ireland and I know she missed it terribly. But it was always the sea, the islands and of course Kilbride House that she talked about. I feel I know every room in this house to be honest. She used to describe it to me when I was little. The wallpaper that was shipped from America. The chandeliers that caught the light. The kitchen was downstairs then as far as I recall? But she never talked about her family. It's funny but I didn't think about it that much. I suppose we were just used to it. I am sure I must have asked her lots of questions when I was small but when I was older I knew not to go there. My grandmother's apartment in New York is so different, but I can see definite similarities. Being here, I feel close to her.'

'What was she like?' Ruby asked, intrigued.

'I have photos of her when she was young, shortly after arriving in New York. She was beautiful. She was beautiful up to the day she died. She had that magical way of making you feel you were the only person in the world that she wanted to spend time with. I went to Grandma with all my worries. Her relationship with my mother was quite strained though. She tended to keep my mother on a very tight leash when she was young, and it left them a bit distant in the end.'

'I am so sad I never met her. It seems ridiculous. I have often visited New York and yet we never got in touch until now,' Ruby said sadly.

'I know, and the weird thing is that only for Grandma requesting that I come here, I probably would never have come. I would have missed so much, seeing where she came from, meeting you and my great-uncle. I feel in some strange way I have come home.'

'Let's raise a glass to that, Lainey – to Kilbride House and coming home! You are so very welcome!'

They clinked their glasses.

'Let me just check dinner. Cecilia is very much into simple home cooking, but it does look yummy. She has a chocolate fudge pudding for afters. I can feel my waist expanding already.'

'It looks and smells delicious.'

'So, you have no idea why Edith left?' Ruby asked, her curiosity building.

'None. She was eighteen and arrived alone. But she had money to get by on, so she was not like so many other Irish who arrived in the fifties. She met my grandfather and married him. He was Canadian but was very much accepted into the elite of New York society.

Then so was my grandmother and my mother. But unfortunately he died. He had very little family. My grandma inherited everything, so she never really had to worry about money.'

'Was she happy, in New York?'

Lainey thought about it before she answered.

'She had many interests but, even though we had money, she tended not to mix in the higher circles. Although according to my mother, when she was first married and after my grandfather died, she did. She had some close friends and she was really involved in looking after the homeless. She was forever organising fundraisers. My Christmases were always at homeless shelters helping. But to answer your question, she was wonderful at seeing the beauty in things – it could be a squirrel in Central Park that she would watch for ages, marvelling at it, or the colours of autumn. She bought me my first camera and I believe it was her influence that made me become a photographer. But there was a grief there – not a depression, just a loss that I could never reach. She tried to hide it, but it was always there. It was difficult to explain to be honest.'

'Did she run away, do you think?' Ruby asked.

'I really don't know.'

'Maybe she just wanted a new life and was fed up here?'

'But the way she talked about Ireland, it was as if her heart was here, so why run away? And there was nothing stopping her coming back all those years. But she wouldn't entertain the idea and practically banned my mother from coming here when she was young.'

'Well, obviously there was something stopping her,' Ruby said.

'But what?'

'Somehow, I think your grandmother felt it was time we all know and that is why she sent you home. However, Grandfather doesn't seem to feel that need to share the past with us. We must tread carefully. He's not in the best of health. I get the feeling there was no bad blood between them though.'

'I agree – on the rare occasion that she mentioned your grandfather there was nothing to suggest a falling-out. The obligatory Christmas card arrived from Ireland. It simply said, *All at Kilbride.*'

'Same here – but I haven't thought about it in so long!' Ruby poured more wine. 'Isn't it funny what becomes acceptable in a family? So many times I should have contacted you, but I didn't. I feel terrible now – all those wasted years and now I will never get to meet Edith. To be honest, I don't even know what she looked like.'

'Even up to the time she died, she still looked lovely – the high cheekbones, the fair skin. Her hair was completely white, but it suited her. But are there no family photos? I would love to see my grandmother as a child.'

'I'm afraid not. There was a fire years ago. Before I was born. They were redecorating, and all the photos and documents were in a room and loads of them got destroyed. Any of Edith are gone. There are some portraits still hanging in the hall, but only of ancient ancestors.'

'Your father died recently?'

'Yes, he died a few years ago and my mother is a doctor with a charity working in Africa. I love her dearly but rarely see her. So, Grandfather means so much to me

– he is always here in Kilbride. Having no siblings, most of my Christmases were here with Grandfather.'

'It's funny – it's very coincidental – you have been almost reared by your grandfather and me by my grandmother. We both have, let's say, distant relationships with our mothers.'

'Yes, I suppose it is very similar.'

'You had an unconventional upbringing then?'

'Yes, my mother wasn't into playing Happy Families. I did learn to be independent. I spent so much time in London since I first went there to boarding school. I'm divorced. My ex has remarried recently. So, when I heard that Winnie was unwell and needed care herself, I didn't really hesitate in coming back. It's years since I spent any time here, so I forgot how much Kilbride means to me. There is something so beautiful about this part of Ireland. It is almost hauntingly beautiful.'

'I wondered about your accent. There is an Irish lilt to it, but it's quite English.'

'I suppose I was in London so much more than here. I do love it here. I am a curator of an art gallery in London – they are very kind and giving me some time off, but I think I will have to decide what to do soon. Grandfather is not well enough to be left alone anymore.'

'What about your mom? I gather she's not coming home to care for him?'

Ruby spluttered her wine. 'Mum come home? No chance of that. I haven't seen my mum in over a year. She has spent years in Africa. My dad was a doctor too and that is where they met. To be honest I don't think she will ever live here again. I admire her terribly and we are really close even though I rarely see her. Skype is great when she has internet. Now she is in the wilds of Africa and I don't get to talk to her so much. She suggested that I investigate a nursing home, but there is no way I am doing that. Winnie has really settled into the nursing home, but Grandfather would just die if he had to leave Kilbride House. I think I am going to have to hand in my notice. I will have to decide in a month or two.'

'Would you mind terribly having to give up your job, your life in London?'

'Grandfather is my priority. If that's the next path for me, I can deal with it. I do love London, but it will be there again. Grandfather won't always be there. He means the world to me. On the flip side, Kilbride is beautiful, so I don't mind spending some time here. I can only imagine as a photographer you will think you have died and gone to heaven. The islands are beautiful – you can take a boat out and explore them.'

'I took some shots on the road from Tralee to Dingle and of course in Ventry. The islands look so mystical.'

'You will have to take your camera there.'

'I read that they were evacuated in the fifties.'

'Yes, the government evacuated everyone. There was a boy who got sick and with the weather they couldn't reach the mainland to get help. He died. It was shortly after that that they moved. Some of them still speak Irish – and some of the mainland locals too – you will hear it in certain parts. There are books and biographies of the people that lived there. It really is a life that is part of a vanishing Ireland. Winnie was born there, and her family was one of the last to move to the mainland. She still talks about the islands. She says once an islander, always an islander.'

'Do you think we could try discreetly to find out a little bit about my grandmother's leaving without upsetting your grandfather? Is there anyone else who could help? I feel she sent me here to find out about the past, though why I have no idea. But I can't shake the feeling that that is the reason why I am here.'

'Let me think about it. There must be someone else that knows something. Winnie is very loyal to Grandfather, so she is not going to say anything indiscreet. She was very young when Edith left but I have a feeling she knows more than she is letting on. I spent so little time in Kilbride that I don't really know that many here. I know that there was a vicar who was a great friend to Grandfather – he always said that he was the best friend he ever could have. The vicar died a few years ago. But the vicarage would keep all the records of the families, I think. Who knows, maybe we might find out something there? The new vicar and his wife are very friendly.'

Lainey got up and walked around the room.

'You mentioned that there was a fire and all the photos were burned. Look, maybe I am totally overthinking all this, but I can't help but ask. Do you really think there was a fire? For some reason that we are totally unaware of, could there be something in those photographs that reminded the Goulding family of the reason my grandmother left?'

'It never crossed my mind, to be honest. I remember being told about the fire when I was young. I never thought to doubt it. But with all this secrecy it does seem a bit farfetched.'

'Here, I have some photos on my phone – it's in the

cottage. There are lots of photos of her after she arrived at New York but nothing earlier. She was beautiful. She had these amazing gold flecks in her eyes that seemed to sparkle and dark curly hair.'

Ruby glanced at her, noticing her strawberry-blonde hair colour.

'My mother's hair is lighter, more auburn,' Lainey said. 'Not sure where I got my strawberry blonde!'

'I can see you miss your grandmother so much. Look, when Cecilia gets here in the morning we'll go off to do a little bit of research. She can keep an eye on Grandfather. He will be down to his little haunt in the village if he thinks he can get away with it. The doctor has told him to rest. That reminds me, I'm going to take him up a hot drink. Purely medicinal, of course.' She winked.

Lainey watched while she made a large hot brandy and laced it with oranges and cloves. It smelt divine.

'Right, I'll pop this up to him. Pour some more wine and we'll make some plans over dinner. I will be down in a few minutes. Let's see what happened in 1955 to make Edith Goulding leave Ireland forever.'

CHAPTER 12

The pitter-patter of rain on a nearby galvanised roof woke Lainey. She needed coffee. She'd had the dream again. It seemed so real she'd found it hard to sleep afterwards. She had heard of recurring dreams but never remembered experiencing one. She tried to push it out of her mind. The wine from the night before had given her a headache. They had stayed up chatting for hours and eating Cecilia's delicious fudge pudding which was lovely at the time but made her tummy feel queasy now. She got up, put on a robe and went into the pretty little kitchen. The wood cabinets were painted in a duck-egg blue. A small round table with a vintage-style tablecloth and four chairs covered in the same fabric was in the middle of the cream wooden floor. A window seat in a pretty flower fabric was the perfect place to sit and look out at the vast gardens of Kilbride House.

She popped on the electric kettle to make a cup of instant coffee – she missed her coffeemaker that normally came on by itself and woke her up. The cottage was warm and toasty. She was about to sit on the window seat and drink her coffee when she noticed a blue envelope on the floor. It must have been shoved under the door. She put her coffee down and picked it up.

There was no stamp or name on it. Inside was another envelope, frail and worn, yellowed and frayed at the corners. It was open. In this envelope there was an old black-and-white photograph. She delicately picked it up and held it up to the light of the window to see it better. It was a photo of a man. With a sense of shock she saw that it was the same man she had seen in the photo her grandmother had hidden in her jewellery drawer. He was wearing dark trousers and a white shirt open at the neck. He was handsome and had piercing light-coloured eyes. He was standing beside a Morris Minor car.

She turned the picture around. *Kilbride 1954* was written on the back in large sprawling handwriting. There was no more information.

So Ruby had been down earlier. She must know who this man was.

There was a knock on the cottage door, startling her.

'It's only me!' Ruby called. 'Come up to the house for some breakfast when you're ready, Cecilia has enough breakfast on to feed an army!'

'Hold on, Ruby!'

Lainey unlocked the door.

'Good morning,' she said with a smile.

Ruby came in, closing the door behind her. She had a coat over her head.

'It's miserable out there now, pouring down. Hope you slept well?'

'I did.'

'We can head off for the day and see what we can find out about the family history. Believe it or not, it's supposed to clear shortly. The weather here can be a bit bizarre. Just wrap up well – it's freezing out there.' She paused, looking at Lainey. 'Is everything okay?'

'Fine – just puzzling about the photo.'

'What photo?'

'The one you pushed under my door.'

'What?' Ruby looked perplexed.

Lainey held out the photo.

Ruby threw her coat on the back of a chair and gently took the photograph.

She stared at it and then at Lainey. 'I've never seen it before. It wasn't me.'

'What? So who?' said Lainey, confused.

'I can't imagine.'

'Thing is, I found a photo when my grandmother was dying. It was hidden in a drawer. It was a photo of my grandmother standing with a man. It looks like the same man in this photo. I can't be sure, but I think it is. Who he is I have no idea. But it looked like it was taken in Ireland – they were standing outside a thatched cottage.'

Ruby squinted in thought. 'So she knew him. Or was he a relative? But who could have left it? Who would have such a photo? And why on earth not just give it to you?'

'I know, it's weird. It was after we went to bed. Otherwise I would have seen it when I came back last night. Granted we had plenty of wine, but I still surely would have noticed it. Well, I think. But, in any case, why deliver it in such a way? Do you think it could be your grandfather left it?'

'Why would he do that? Why not give it to me to show you? Makes no sense. In fact, he's not that well this morning – he's staying in bed – he's not himself at all.'

'It's me being here that has upset him,' said Lainey.

'Look, I told you – whatever happened in the past has surfaced for him since your grandmother died. But you or I have nothing to do with it.'

'I suppose. I still feel guilty somehow …'

'Don't.'

Lainey sighed, studying the mystery photo again, wondering who would have kept it for over sixty years. Treasured it, perhaps. She looked up.

'Ruby, could it have been Winnie left it?'

Ruby pulled a face. 'Winnie rambling around here in the middle of the night? Don't be daft. The nursing home doesn't let its inmates wander off like that. Besides, the gates are normally locked at night. I'll ask John if he saw anyone around after the gates were opened this morning. Oh! It could have been him – I mean, someone in the village could have given it to him to deliver.'

'What about Cecilia?'

'Yes, that's possible – she could have been asked to drop it in – in fact, that's very likely. I'll go ask her. If she and John – and Grandfather say no, we could drop into the nursing home and ask Winnie. I'm sure she might know. There isn't much that she doesn't, but whether she will tell us is another thing.'

'Great.' Lainey was excited at the prospect of finding out who the mystery man was.

'Okay, see you up at the house.'

'I'll grab a shower first and be up to the house in a little while.'

'But hurry – breakfast should be ready now. You know, in London I have a tight schedule with work and my diet is fairly good. But since I came back to Kilbride I seem to be eating much more and drinking buckets of tea. I think Cecilia is trying to fatten us all up and unfortunately it's succeeding.' She pointed to her waist. 'My jeans have gone so tight. We can walk up to the nursing home, just outside the village, so we can work off the breakfast.'

'Oh brilliant – I'll be with you as quick as I can.'

'Great, put on some walking boots or shoes. But, first, after breakfast, I'll show you the house properly. Grandfather is asleep, so we won't disturb him.

'I hope he's better soon. I can't help feeling bad.' Lainey hoped that he would give her a chance to get to know him. He was another link in the chain to Edith.

'Ah, don't worry, Lainey – look, we can always get Doctor Doyle to check him out. See you in a few minutes.'

'Okay, see you shortly.'

The big kitchen was warm and cosy, and Lainey shocked herself by eating loads at breakfast – the most scrumptious brown soda bread and creamy scrambled eggs, crispy bacon and fried mushrooms she had ever tasted. She managed to forget for a while the nagging questions about her grandmother's past that were besetting her. Ruby had already asked Cecilia and John about the photo, but they knew nothing about it and neither of them saw anyone around the house that morning or the night before.

Sipping her third cup of tea, she gazed around. 'The kitchen used to be in the basement, right, if I remember what Edith told me correctly?' she said, looking at the high ceiling with its cornices and mouldings. 'This was obviously a drawing room of sorts?' She looked up at the stained-glass window that illuminated the room with spirals of light.

'Yes, this was the drawing room up to about thirty years ago. My father tried to make the house more modern and family friendly. The kitchen was originally downstairs in the basement which has been shut up for years. I don't think I was down there in about fifteen years. To be honest, it's a bit ghostly down there. There are loads of rooms in the house that are not used – they all need so much repair.' She sighed. 'It's a very old house with so much history. Did you know it was built in the sixteen hundreds?'

'My goodness, I had no idea!' Lainey exclaimed.

'Your grandmother certainly kept things to herself. All those scary-looking portraits are our ancestors. They had a huge amount of land, almost ten thousand acres at one stage. We are very much one of the last Big Houses surviving in Ireland.'

'Big it sure is,' Lainey replied, smiling.

'*Big House* was a term used to describe this type of house. Their inhabitants were nearly always of English Protestant origin with a lot of difficult history where the "Anglo-Irish" family were landlords and the local people were tenants. It all changed over the years and in the 1920's some of the houses were burned to the ground. This house was lucky to escape. The nationalists had enough, I suppose. They were trying to reclaim Ireland. But anyway, Kilbride was not targeted.'

'There is so much history between the British and the Irish and of course the Catholics and the Protestants, but

I never heard about the burnings,' Lainey said.

'During the War of Independence in the 20s, these so-called Big Houses represented all that was wrong with Ireland to the Irish people. Our great-grandparents were good people and tried to reverse some of the ill feeling with the Catholics. Over seventy per cent of all the land is now owned by the people of Kilbride. It was bought back by what was called the Land Commission and given back to the Irish People. We still have about one hundred acres that surround the house. Ten acres of that is gardens. It was so much more. All sorts of ornamental gardens, but some of the gardens were reclaimed and Grandfather and his father before him reared horses on it. Thoroughbreds. Grandfather still does. John Hogan looks after them now, Grandfather likes to go down and give advice and make sure everything is as it should be. He's mad about John though. They get on great. John is a man of few words, but he has great time for Grandfather. They can talk about horses for hours on end.'

'I must go to the stables and have a look. I love horses – always did since I was a little girl.'

'By the way, I had a sneaky look on the internet about your mum. But I had heard about her as a much-acclaimed theatre actress. She's very striking. Can't believe I have such a famous aunty.'

'Ha! Mom does not exactly do fame. The theatre is her life, but she hates any celebrity stuff. I think that's why she's never done TV or anything – terrified she would be recognised. Finds it vulgar.'

'That's refreshing in a culture where everyone wants to be famous.' Ruby grinned. 'Come on, I want to show you something.'

They walked out of the kitchen and up the stairs, stopping at various portraits of ancestors including their great-grandparents, Edith's parents. Lainey noted the likeness to Edith, the high cheekbones of the woman in the portrait, the elegant neck. The man looked very much the Lord of the Manor but there was something very engaging about him, as if his stern appearance could easily break into a smile. Again, she had never heard anything about either of them. Then up another stair where the walls were papered in a moss-green paper with wooden panels halfway up the walls. The ceilings were decorated with ornate mouldings.

'We don't use this floor at all,' Ruby said when they reached the landing. 'Come on.'

Ruby brought her into a bedroom to the back of the house which had an open fireplace and a four-poster bed. The bed had a canopy overhead. The pattern on the wallpaper was of roses.

'This was your grandmother's room,' Ruby said. 'Edith's room.'

Lainey was puzzled. She looked out the window. In her mind, she could hear her grandmother's voice. *'On a harvest moon, the light from it would illuminate the bay and make it shine like silver.'* Lainey knew her grandmother's room overlooked the sea. This room was beautiful, but it overlooked the grand gardens and the vast orchard.

'Are you sure?' she asked.

'Yes – well, almost. Winnie said that it was Edith's room.'

Lainey walked around the room. 'It's just that Grandmother always described her room as being to the front of the house. There were daisies and daffodils on the wallpaper. And she could see the ocean. I am sure of it.'

Ruby looked perplexed. 'Gosh, Winnie obviously got it wrong. Come on, follow me.'

They walked down a corridor and turned to another corridor. Ruby opened a door and Lainey walked in. She knew immediately. The daisy and daffodil wallpaper was peeling but it was still there. She walked over to the window. The rain was clearing and there was a thick fog, but in the distance she could see a glimpse of the sea. She could just imagine how beautiful it would look at night, when the stars were out.

'This is my grandmother's room,' she said, almost to herself.

'This room has not been used as far back as I can remember. We live on the first and second floor. It's not been used since my grandfather was quite young.'

'It's definitely her room.' Lainey touched the dark wooden bed, the large porcelain jug and dish. Could the room be untouched since Edith had slept here? It was here that she had looked out of the window and saw the silver stars. Here that perhaps she had contemplated a different life in a place that would never remind her of Kilbride. She touched the wallpaper, crumbling and faded. Something made her grandmother leave forever this place of family, roots and privilege, and Lainey was determined that she would find out what it was.

CHAPTER 13

As the rain cleared, shards of golden sunlight shimmered through the lacy trees that lined the road into Kilbride village.

In the village itself, Lainey could almost feel Edith's presence guiding her, pointing to where the old mill was, the creamery, the drapery store. She could hear her voice as she told her tales of her own life as a child.

'Every spring Mrs O'Hehir and her neighbours whitewashed their cottage walls and it brought the village up like a new pin. In May they decorated either a hawthorn tree or a holly tree with eggshells and ribbons and set it in front of the house. It was believed to bring good luck to the household, a remnant of their pagan past. Then in the winter of 1945, the rain arrived like never before. We thought we were going to be swept away by the Atlantic Ocean. The bridge in the village flooded and you would need a boat to cross it. Sure, I thought it was the end of the world and we would need an ark, like Noah in the Bible. I was going to bring my kitten and my dog. It rained for five days without stopping. But eventually it did stop, and the sun came

out as if saying "What was all that about?"

We had a market on a Tuesday and supplies were bought for the week. There was a butcher, a baker and a tailor. There was a little church where we gathered every Sunday – the Catholic congregation gathered on the other side. In the middle of the village was the little Protestant school that had only twenty pupils including myself attending and the larger Catholic school that the rest of the community went to. Miss O'Flaherty, our teacher, was kind and we would put our bottles of milk near the fire to warm them.

I had a beautiful Crolly doll that I called Miss Sparrow. I had a dress for her made of red velvet, with a white lace collar and lace cuffs. Dainty little daisies were embroidered on the edge of her dress. She had a black-velvet hairband with gold flowers stitched on. She had a silken underskirt and bloomers. On Fair Day, I would take Miss Sparrow and we would get some hard-boiled sweets in the grocery shop ...'

How different Edith would find it now! A large bright supermarket was now in the centre of the town. There was a coffee shop called the Old Schoolhouse Café. Lainey knew it must be the old Protestant schoolhouse that Edith had described so well. A tantalising smell of baking and coffee was coming from it. The cottages were still there that she had described and each one looked prettier than the next, with spirals of smoke coming out of their chimneys.

'Some of the cottages are used by artists as little retreats – they like to come and spend time here capturing it on canvasses. I will have to take you into the Old Schoolhouse Café. The coffee is to die for, and they do a lemon-and-chocolate cake that tastes like nothing you have ever tasted. It's an unusual décor too, very vintage, like stepping into the 1920's with china cups and saucers. The nursing home is just up this road.'

They walked out of the village and up a treelined avenue. A big bright purpose-built nursing home came into view. A carer let them in and told them that Winnie was in her room watching a rerun of the soaps. Winnie adored the soaps, Ruby told Lainey, and God forbid if anyone disturbed her.

'*Whisht!*' Winnie warned when they arrived, putting her finger to her lips to be quiet.

She was watching the TV programme as if her life depended on it and not happy at all at being disturbed. A man and a woman kissed on the TV and then the credits and music started.

Winnie turned to them at last. '*I knew it!* That lad with his auld moustache, that poor wife of his is the best old soul ever. She's lost her daughter and her dog and even her cat and now he's going to have it off with that – that *floosie!* Well, I say she's welcome to him. Poor Karen is better off without him – I would burn him if I was her. He's not worth spitting on.'

Ruby grinned at Lainey. 'Just in case you're confused, Lainey, it's the characters in the soap that Winnie is talking about!'

Lainey laughed. 'Oh, I wasn't quite sure there for a minute!'

'It's no laughing matter,' said Winnie. 'A disgrace that lad is – he's after having relations with everyone in the town. They should run him out of it. I have a good mind to write to RTÉ – it's a disgrace! I know what I would do with him – it's far from running around he would be doing if I got my hands on him, the scoundrel. I've changed my mind – burning is too good for him.'

Ruby sat down beside her and pointed to another chair for Lainey.

'I hope you don't mind that we called in, Winnie. We were just having a chat last night and we thought it would be lovely to know a little about Edith before she went to New York.' Ruby was treading carefully with the conversation. 'We were trying to figure out a few things about the past. There's so much we don't know about her. If it's not asking too much, we were hoping you might be able to help us.'

Winnie folded her arms. 'Has it ever struck you that you might be as well leaving the past where it is? There are reasons why people keep quiet about things and you going around asking questions, dragging up the past, is not going to help anyone.'

Lainey was taken aback at Winnie's retort. She glanced at Ruby and shook her head slightly. Clearly it wasn't Winnie who had left the photo at the cottage – or asked anyone to deliver it.

'Well, the last thing we want to do is upset anyone, Winnie – we are just curious,' Ruby said cautiously.

'My grandmother adored Ireland, I know that,' Lainey explained, 'but for some reason she never came back here. I would just like to know why?'

Winnie shook her head. 'There were lots of reasons why people left Ireland – it was a different place in the fifties. Maybe there was no reason and she simply left for no reason, have you thought of that? If she had wanted you to know she would have told you.'

Lainey was not giving up that easily. 'But she specified in her will that my mother and I should come here so I think she wanted us to find out about her past.'

'That's a strange way to carry on – why did she just not tell you then?' Winnie asked.

'I don't know, I suppose that's what I need to find out,' Lainey replied.

'I don't know why you think I can help you. I barely remember her. I was young, very young, maybe ten years old when she left.' Winnie shrugged.

Just then the tea lady arrived. She cheerfully greeted them and distributed tea and biscuits. After she left, they drank and nibbled their biscuits in near-silence.

Then Ruby looked enquiringly at Lainey who nodded.

Ruby leant towards Winnie. 'Winnie, Lainey is staying in the cottage, as you know – well, last night someone pushed an envelope under the door, we have no idea who or why, but there was a photograph of a man. It's an old photo with *Kilbride !954* written on it.

We were hoping you could tell us who the man in it is.'

'Who would have done that?' Winnie asked, holding her biscuit in mid-air before dipping it in her tea and eating it.

'We have no idea,' said Ruby.

'It must have been your grandfather,' said Winnie. 'Did you not ask him?

'No, not yet – he's not the best this morning, he's sleeping.'

Winnie nodded knowingly. 'I knew he wasn't great yesterday. Don't be asking him questions about the past. It's upsetting him.

'We won't,' said Ruby, 'but … maybe you might recognise the man in the photo?'

'Look, I have no idea if your grandmother had a boyfriend if that's what you're asking me. She left but there was never any talk of a man. To be honest I don't think she ever courted. She was a fine-looking lady, but I remember her as quite prim and proper. She certainly kept herself to herself and Gertrude Goulding, her mother, was a sore one, a good-looking woman but she would turn milk into buttermilk with the sour look on. She had certain standards for her daughter – it would be hard to find someone to measure up, if you get my drift. And of course, they would have to be Protestant, that goes without staying – Gertrude Goulding was as staunch a Protestant as ever lived. To be honest, I rarely saw the mother after that until I came to work at Kilbride House and she never mentioned Edith to me in all the years that I worked there. She talked very little. Rarely came out of her room. All the lovely gardens, yet she hardly ever walked in them. Edith left about a year and a half after your great-grandfather died, I think. As I said I was young, it was years later that I began work in Kilbride House. There was only Edward there, his wife had died years earlier and of course your mother Florence when she was young, Ruby. Sure, they sent her off to boarding school when she was only twelve. I missed her terribly. But it was the way of the family. When Edith left they were possibly still in mourning for your great-grandfather. Your grandfather never talked about her though. But I did hear in the village that everyone was shocked when she left as she was always with the mother.'

'Look, do you mind having a look at the photo to see if you recognise the man?' Lainey asked. Winnie might prove to be the only link to her grandmother's past as most of the village people who had known Edith were dead.

'Oh, go on then, show it to me. Give me my glasses. There they are on the table'

Ruby fetched the glasses while Lainey took the photo out of the envelope, careful not to mark it. She passed the photo to Winnie.

Winnie put on her glasses and began studying it intently. She looked up after a few minutes with a puzzled look.

'Well?' Ruby asked. 'Do you recognise him?'

'Yes, I do. I barely knew him, but I heard him sing a very long time ago – his voice was like no other in Kerry. He was known far and wide for his singing.'

'Who was he?'

'He was Canice Meagher. He was originally from the Island but settled on the mainland in the fifties like our family. A big young man, a gentle kind if I remember well.'

'But what did he have to do with my grandmother?' Lainey asked.

'Nothing that I know of. But there was talk about him alright.'

'What kind of talk?' asked Lainey eagerly.

'Well, if I remember correctly, he disappeared to England and died soon after while still very young. I forget how he died. Maybe it was an accident – there were lots of accidents in those days on the building sites in England.'

'Oh,' said Lainey. This was very disappointing. She looked despairingly at Ruby.

'But why then did someone shove the photo under your door, Lainey?' said Ruby. 'If this Canice had nothing to your grandmother? And, hey, didn't you say you saw another photo with your grandmother and him together?'

The tea lady arrived back in to clear the things away, this time saying little as if she sensed the tension in the air.

When she left Winnie asked, 'What's this you're saying? About another photo?'

'I'm afraid it's in America,' said Lainey. 'A photo of my grandmother with this man. A photograph she had hidden away, what's more.'

'Are you sure it was him?'

'Well, no, I'm not … I wish I had brought the photo with me. I really should have.'

'It couldn't be him,' Winnie stated.

Lainey sighed. There seemed to be nothing more to be said.

Then, after a small silence, Ruby asked, 'There's nothing more you can tell us, Winnie? Anything at all about Edith as a young woman?'

'Not much, really. To be honest, I remember more about her sister Victoria.'

'*What?*' Lainey and Ruby exclaimed together.

'Yes, I remember her quite well. She was a real beauty. Edith was too but there was a wild free spirit in Victoria that, as young as I was, I recognised as something rare. You would stop to look at her. She was forever on a horse too, had a lovely big grey mare. She would ride

106

bareback sometimes, I remember that. Oh, she used to spend hours down on the beaches!'

Ruby looked astounded. 'But never in my life have I heard that there was another sister in my grandfather's family. I only ever heard of Edith. Are you sure?

'Absolutely certain. There were two girls. Edith was older than Victoria. That is all I can tell you,' Winnie said adamantly.

Lainey could hardly take it in. So, she had another great-aunt that she had never heard of! What on earth was all that about?

'But what happened to this Victoria?' Ruby asked.

'She left of course, but I don't remember how or when. Oh, it's time for my bath. Here's Helen to take me.'

One of the carers walked in with a wheelchair and helped Winnie into it.

'Be careful of the past, Ruby,' Winnie warned. 'Look after your grandfather – he does not need any shocks.'

'Of course – we'll take care,' Ruby said worriedly.

'The past may be better left there, in the past. That's all I am saying,' Winnie replied as her carer wheeled her out of the room.

CHAPTER 14

'What on earth was all that about?' Ruby asked when they walked out of the nursing home. Lainey was quiet. They walked for a few minutes before she spoke.

'Do you believe Winnie? It can't be true. Another sister?'

'Well, she seemed pretty positive. Winnie might be physically laid up but as far as I know there is very little wrong with her memory.'

'Your grandfather or my grandmother never mentioned that there was another sister. Why would they do that? It doesn't make sense!'

'I agree, it sounds ludicrous. Grandfather rarely talks about his family, but he would certainly have mentioned it if he had two sisters. And Mum would have known about it. No, she must be mixed up. I can ask Grandfather, but I would rather not today. There is one other person though who might help us shed light on this. Remember I told you about the vicarage in the village? He actually telephoned earlier to say he would call to see Grandfather later. I am sure he has lots of records going back.'

'That would be great.'

Ruby was looking at her iPhone. 'Look, I have the vicar's number – how about I give him a call?'

'It's worth a try,' Lainey replied.

The vicar told them to come by, adding that there was something he wanted to talk to them about.

Intrigued, they set out.

The vicarage was a pretty house down a winding avenue. It was just about to rain as they rang the bell.

His wife answered the door.

'Come in! Hello, Ruby! So this is your cousin?'

'Yes, this is Lainey.'

'Lovely to meet you, Lainey. I am Pierce's wife Olive.'

Olive was a small lady with bright-blue eyes and two rosy cheeks. She wiped her hands in her clean bright-pink apron which she wore over a very flowery dress. Her grey hair was cut short and feathery.

She ushered them in and shut the door behind them.

'Thank you for having us,' said Lainey.

'It's a pleasure! Peirce was telling me that you want to search some old records. He'll be with you in a jiffy – he's gone to bring some files over from the church. Most of them are on a database now and of course everyone's births are recorded in the national registry. But Pierce likes to look at the old records too.'

They walked into a bright warm kitchen with a large cream range taking pride of place. Although there were jars and jars of ingredients lining shelves, all labelled and placed in order of size, it did not look cluttered. It was like something out of a cookery programme with Delia Smith all homely and inviting. It certainly looked like

Olive bought nothing readymade. A large pot of marmalade was simmering on the hob, with crystal-clear jars waiting for it to be poured into.

'What a lovely home you have!' said Lainey.

'Thank you, Lainey. I loved it instantly when we moved here from Dublin. It feels very much like home now. As you can see, I like to cook.'

Lainey looked at an array of baking. There were two apple pies cooling on a tray as well as two trays of muffins.

'You certainly do! It smells divine.'

There were three china cups with plates and cutlery already laid on the table. Olive brought over a coffeepot and poured. She then placed a gorgeous coffee-and-walnut cake, already sliced into wedges, in the centre.

'Wow, that looks delicious,' Lainey commented.

'I love the baking – it's trying not to eat it all is the problem.' Olive laughed as she began to serve them generous wedges of cake. 'Now you must excuse me – I'm heading out on a quick errand.' She gestured towards the window. 'There's Pierce coming in now.'

Pierce arrived into the kitchen, carrying some boxes of files. A large Persian cat followed him in.

'Good afternoon, Ruby, and this must be your American cousin.' He put the boxes down and held his hand out to Lainey. 'Pierce Richfield. It's very good to meet you.'

'I'm Lainey. Thank you for having us at such short notice.'

'To be honest, I was intrigued – and by a strange coincidence I also have something to ask you ... but first coffee and some cake.'

'I'd better be off,' said Olive. 'Hope you find what you're looking for, ladies.'

'Thanks again,' Lainey replied warmly as Olive left.

Pierce sat and served helped himself to some coffee and cake. He was a tall man of about fifty with dark-rimmed glasses pushed up on his head, dressed casually in a shirt and trousers.

'So, ladies, you are looking for any information that might help you understand why Edith Goulding left Kilbride and never returned?'

'For starters!' said Ruby. 'But it has become much more complicated than that. Lainey, go ahead – tell him about the photo first.'

'Alright,' said Lainey and she launched into the story of the photo with all its details.

When she paused for breath, Pierce said, 'I suppose the easiest thing to do is ask your grandfather?'

'Grandfather is under the weather, so now is not the time to tackle him about the past – or the photo,' Ruby offered worriedly. 'Though, in fact, he could be the one who slid it under the door – but it seems altogether unlikely.'

'Okay, very mysterious and mum's the word.' Pierce gave them a reassuring smile, then spent a few moments looking for his glasses which he eventually found sitting neatly on his head. 'But I have a mystery of my own. These are the old records from the vicarage. I had them out recently. I came across something recently that made me go searching.

'Did you find out something about my grandmother?' Lainey asked.

'Not quite. But I did find something else. It's just that

we are cleaning up the old graveyard down at the church. Most of the graves are so old that there are no relatives left alive and it is falling into terrible disrepair – we don't even know who the people are. Of course, there is a new section too. Anyway ... this is a bit sensitive ...' He cleared his throat. 'We have some people from the local employment centre trying to clean it up a little and, while they were working there, they came across this grave. There was a small metal cross on it. They could barely read it. But I had it cleaned and now, although faint, I can read it.' He paused. 'It says: *Baby Goulding, Kilbride House, 1955.*'

Lainey looked at Ruby who shook her head.

'The same year that grandmother left Ireland never to return,' said Lainey. 'And the year after the photograph was taken.'

'So I'm wondering if your grandfather knows anything about it,' said Pierce. 'But, to be honest, it looks quite forgotten. I'm not sure whether to mention it or not to him.'

Lainey was quiet. Part of her felt like leaving it all in the past. Just like Winnie suggested. Why did her grandmother hide all this? She had always talked to her grandmother about everything. That was the thing about her. How could this big part of their life be hidden all these years? Walking around Kilbride was like stepping back into her grandmother's shoes all those years ago. Was the baby hers – is that why she ran away? Or was she driven away? One thing was for sure, late in life her grandmother had decided that whatever happened was not to be hidden any longer and that was why she wanted them to come here. All she could think about was

Catherine, her mother. She should be here. But Catherine always did as she pleased. She wanted to bury her head in the sand and not deal with this. Lainey now knew that she would drag her to Ireland if she had to. It was her grandmother's wish. She had no idea how she would but, somehow, she would get Catherine to come to Kilbride.

'Can we see the grave?' Ruby asked.

'Yes, but first I need to show you something. To be honest, I was a bit shocked when you called because I was planning to look through these records today anyway. It's all a very strange coincidence.'

Lainey looked at the vicar. He was a nice man and she knew he was treading carefully, so as not to alarm them.

'I think we need another coffee first.' He refilled the cups and then said he had to get something from his office.

'This is something else, I can hardly believe it,' Lainey said to Ruby.

Pierce arrived back in with a brown envelope and took out a death certificate. He explained that he had gone searching for it when they found the grave of the baby. The girls read it.

Name: Baby Goulding. Place of Death: Marlborough Asylum. Sex: Female. When registered: February 25th, 1955. Person to whom issued: Gertrude Goulding, Kilbride House.

Lainey felt a wave of nausea. 'What? Marlborough *Asylum*? An asylum? As in a mental hospital?'

'I looked it up,' said Pierce. 'It's a couple of hours from here. It was closed years ago. Gertrude Goulding was your great-grandmother, Edward's mother.'

'How awful! That's horrible.' Had her grandmother

113

spent time in an asylum? Her head was spinning. She couldn't think.

'I took the liberty of searching to see if I could find a baptismal certificate,' said Pierce. 'But no luck. However, I did come across a baptismal certificate for the other sister.'

'The other sister?' Lainey exclaimed.

'Yes. Victoria Goulding.'

'So there *was* another sister?' Ruby gasped. 'As Winnie said!'

Pierce looked confused. 'What? Are you telling me you hadn't heard of her?'

Ruby shook her head. 'Never.'

'Nor had I,' said Lainey. 'My grandmother never mentioned her. Winnie just talked about her but we could hardly believe her. That was what we really came here to ask you about.'

'How extraordinary!'

'Where is she now? This sister?' Lainey demanded.

'I'm afraid I have no idea,' Pierce said. 'She may have died as a baby. That would account for the silence about her. Did Winnie not say?'

'No – she didn't die,' said Lainey. 'Winnie remembers her as a young woman – well, a teenager.'

Ruby was very quiet.

'Ruby, are you okay?' the vicar asked. 'All this is quite a shock.'

'I'm just worried about Grandfather. There is obviously a lot we don't know – but, it's just that he is so feeble – I can't risk dragging all this up.'

'I totally understand,' said Lainey. 'We can investigate it, without letting him know. Maybe for now we shouldn't show him this or mention the grave. My arriving here was a big enough shock for him.'

'Right,' said Pierce. 'Let's hop into the car and I'll show you the grave.'

They spent a few minutes admiring a large Persian cat that was sunning herself in a window while he was looking for his keys.

'Okay, I have the keys – follow me.'

The graveyard had an old iron gate that had been recently painted but also a little stile with some stone steps. They used the stile.

It was a small graveyard adjacent to the old church. Lot of the gravestones were falling and there was no legible inscription on many. Then there were tombs above ground with rusted chains outlining the plots. There was a separate area for the vicars who had once presided over the village, dating back as far as the late 1700's.

Pierce continued to an area which was sheltered by a willow tree. Then he got down on his hunkers and pointed to the small metal cross. It was hard to read but if they studied it, they could read it.

Baby Goulding, Kilbride House, 1955.

They were a solemn little group standing there in silence for a few minutes, not looking at each other. A few seagulls flew overhead and began to chatter.

Lainey was overcome with a feeling of dread. Was this Edith's baby? Was this the secret so deeply buried for so many years, as this poor baby was? All the clues pointed in that direction.

'Can you keep all this quiet for the moment, Vicar?'

115

Ruby asked. 'And we can get back to you when we decide about letting grandfather know or not?'

'Of course. I'll pop up later to see him, but I won't mention any of this. Olive has baked some apple pie for him. I have to be off now, ladies, I have some calls to make, but we will keep in touch about all this. Can I drop you anywhere?'

'Let's go for some lunch?' Ruby suggested to Lainey.

'Sorry, Ruby, but I'm not very hungry.'

'Well, I think we could do with a drink. Could you drop us to O'Rourke's, Vicar?'

'No problem.'

There was a welcoming turf fire in the old-fashioned pub. A few men were sitting at the bar, chatting and reading the papers.

The barman looked up at Ruby in recognition.

'Two glasses of white wine, please, Brian,' Ruby said.

'Take a seat and I'll drop them over, Ruby How is your grandfather?'

'A bit under the weather actually.'

'Give him our regards.'

'Thank you. I am sure he will be in as soon as he can – it's hard to keep him away from here.'

They found a table at the fire. They were both lost in thought for a few minutes.

'There are so many possibilities my mind is racing,' Lainey said then.

'Look, let's stick to the facts – there's no point in trying to figure it all out yet.'

'I'm going to insist my mother comes over, Ruby. But I think I will book her into a hotel. There is one outside of the village, I think – what's it like?'

'It's a gorgeous boutique hotel called Carrigmore. Lots of American stay there. It's beautiful, very ornate.'

'Great, I'll drag her over if I have to, but whatever we find out I want her to be here.'

CHAPTER 15

New York
2018

'Well, what do you think?' Juniper Hynes leaned against the dressing-room wall. She was dressed in Chanel jeans, a dark-blue silk shirt and tailored jacket. Her hair was cropped and silver, her creamy skin flawless without a hint of make-up.

Catherine admired Juniper's style – it suited her personality. She hated it when people followed trends. Juniper Hynes certainly never followed trends – she was very much her own woman and took no crap from anyone and Catherine loved her for it. They had the opportunity to take the play to London to the West End. But Juniper wanted to know if she would have Catherine on board. Although the play had the critics running wild, to have Catherine would be like adding gold dust to it. Catherine had a history of only working with female directors and when she worked with Juniper Hynes, a critically acclaimed director with many accolades, it was always a triumph.

While Catherine had lots of attention from men, the truth was they bored her and when it came to her art she felt that women understood the human soul more than men and made better directors. She trusted Juniper as much as she could ever trust anyone.

'I'm not sure, Juniper. Can you leave it with me for a little while?'

'Of course – we can talk again before there is any decision made.'

Catherine had played the lead many times in the West End and had received an Olivier Award and several nominations. She had loved London, but the older she got the less she wanted to travel. When she was younger, she had worked with the Royal Shakespeare society and had lived in Stratford-Upon-Avon while working with them. It had been an extraordinary experience. She had the privilege of playing the lead in many productions.

'Is everything okay, Catherine? You seem ... distracted. Will you have dinner with myself and Laurie later? There is a new Japanese and Laurie is fit to be tied because we still haven't tried it out. She has a few of New York's elite to come with us. Please, you know how they irritate me.' Laurie was Juniper's partner.

'Thanks, Juniper, but no, not tonight. Everything is fine. I'm a little tired perhaps, that's all, but I think I need an early night.'

'If you need some time out, you know you only have to say the word.'

'I know.' Catherine smiled.

'Okay, you know where I am if you need me.'

After Juniper left Catherine reopened her email. She had just received one from Lainey, practically ordering her to come to Ireland. She reread it. Lainey had discovered some news about another sister that Edith had, but they had no idea if she was still alive or not. A sister called Victoria. She was full of chat about Kilbride House and how it was everything Edith had said it was. The beautiful staircase, the portraits and the stained-glass window. She had seen the bedroom that Edith had grown up in. The wallpaper of daffodils was still there and even the bed. The view of the bay.

Then she came to the part where Lainey explained about a grave of a baby in the churchyard. She shook her head in irritation.

She liked her life just as it was, she had no interest in unearthing the past and finding some long-lost aunt or whatever other grim discoveries were lurking in a village in Ireland that she felt absolutely no connection to. Her mother may have been born there, but she had the good sense to leave and never look back. If only she had kept it that way, instead of stirring things up when she was dead. It was unbelievable that she could do this.

There was a knock on the door and her assistant Lucille appeared, looking polished with a pair of designer glasses on her head. Catherine loved having Lucille. She was very different to most of those who worked in the theatre. She looked more like a banker. She was super-efficient and knew everything she needed to know about how to make Catherine Lee Miller's life more comfortable. She set about making a tea of echinacea, honey and hot water for Catherine.

'I just want to confirm some promotional interviews with you, Catherine. I have also had a call about somebody offering to write your memoirs?' She looked at Catherine as if she already knew what her answer would be.

'*What?*'

'Your memoirs. An editor from a very reputable publishing company rang to know if you would be interested. I told him I was extremely doubtful.'

'Tell him that I have no interest whatsoever. My private life is just that. Private! I have no intention of changing that. Anyway, most people have never heard of me. The theatre is not exactly the stuff of gossip columns. Why on earth would they want my story?'

'No worries. I will tell him absolutely not. But regarding interviews for the next few weeks – can I go ahead and schedule them? There is one for *The Stage* and one for the *New York Times*.'

'Very well, but be careful who you schedule me with – no little snippet who knows nothing about the theatrical world and wants to know why I never went to Hollywood!'

'Of course.'

'Tonight, after the play, can you have a car ready? I am so tired, I just want to go home straight afterwards.'

'Of course. Is there anything else I can get you?' She was checking the make-up and costume that Catherine would wear that night.

'No, that's all,' Catherine replied as she began to clean off her day make-up.

'Okay, I'll see you later to zip you up.'

This was the time of the evening when all the hours of rehearsals, the learning of lines, dialect, the choreography of movement on the stage and the mood of the play must all come together for the performance. It was what inspired Catherine about the theatre. It made her feel more alive than anything in the world. There were no second takes. No close-ups or best angles. It was a transformation into the character that had to be sublime and real. The connection to the audience was like no other. It was alive and needed everything for it to be successful.

Catherine would transform herself into the character that she was playing. One critic remarked after a performance: **'When Catherine Lee Miller takes to the stage it is almost a spiritual transition for this actress, making her one of the finest theatrical performers of her time.'** She had offers of TV and movies, but she always declined. The theatre was what she was born to do. Nothing less or more.

The tea was for her throat and her vocal cords. She put on some meditative music and lay down on a yoga mat and did some light stretches. Afterwards she began her make-up. Then she dressed in a white silk underskirt and then a rich silk dress and robe that was embroidered with gems and embellished with jewels and pearls. A hairdresser had put her hair up earlier and now she fixed a velvet headdress studded with jewels on her head just as Lucille arrived back to help zip her up. She finished applying her make-up, which was quite a creation. She had mastered the art of theatre make-up many years ago, not trusting many of the young artists that the theatre often employed. She had researched the character and knew exactly how she should look. She stood up and examined her appearance and then began her throat exercises. When she was finished she closed her eyes as she brought everything she could into the character that she was playing. She remained in that position for about half an hour, until she got the call to go backstage. Her character was Empress Vilma of Russia, whose husband had drowned, leaving her to try to figure out if it was an accident or if he was murdered. Her performances to date were described by the critics as 'compelling and brilliant'.

When she exited her dressing room, she walked and held herself as her character would. It was as if she had left Catherine Lee Miller behind. When she stepped on stage all else was forgotten and she had become the Russian Empress, through her voice, body and soul.

After the final curtain, she was drained. She took off her make-up and undressed, showered and got back into her own clothes. Most of the cast went for a late dinner. But Catherine never did what most did. Lucille arrived with some tea. They left the dressing room immaculate, putting the costume carefully away. Then Catherine wrapped herself in a cashmere cloak and slipped out the back-stage door into a waiting car.

She watched New York from her window. She was so committed to the role that she usually needed time to walk away from it. But tonight her mind was muddled. It had hit her as she was taking off her make-up earlier. Lainey's mail had really unsettled her. It began to rain as she stepped out of the car at the entrance to her apartment block. She took the elevator to the top – her apartment was the penthouse. She kicked off her shoes as soon as she closed the door to her stunning home.

The décor was all soft blues and brocade wallpaper, with dark furniture and floors broken by lots of opulent cushions and Persian rugs. Chandeliers hung from all the ceilings, even the bathroom.

She filled the bath that stood in the middle of the large

room that was completely gold-embossed and poured some French lavender oil in. While it was filling up, she poured a glass of chilled white wine and brought it in to sip on. She drank very little but tonight she needed something to take the edge off. The luxury of the lavender water soothed her mind and she tried to put Lainey's mail out of her head.

But afterwards as she twisted and turned in the finest Egyptian cotton sheets, her mind could not rest. She got up, put on a silk dressing gown, sat at her laptop and reread the mail again.

She had heard of a sister. An aunt. But only once. Her mother's sister. Her mother had told her about her when she was only a child. It was so long ago now that Catherine had almost forgotten the conversation. It was Christmas and Edith had told her of Christmas in Kilbride House. Then she had begun to cry and when Catherine had asked her why, she had stared out at the New York Skyline.

'I had a sister,' she said. 'She was so beautiful and wise, and I owe her everything.'

'Where is she?'

'I can't talk about it, Catherine. I'm sorry.'

She had never talked about her again. The years had almost erased Catherine's memory of it. She had tried to talk to her about it when she was older, but it seemed to upset her mother so much that she never did again. She had never spoken of her to Lainey and obviously neither had Edith. What on earth was this about the grave of a baby? Whatever it was, she wished that they knew nothing about it. Why on earth had her mother left this mess behind her? Catherine wanted to have nothing to do with it. But then she thought of Lainey. Lainey had been so close to Edith. It had suited Catherine to almost allow Edith to rear her. It left her to devote her time to the theatre. Lainey's father, although close to his child, spent long spells away. Edith and Lainey had formed a strong bond. Lainey adored Edith – so much so that if there was some terrible secret uncovered about Edith, Lainey would be devastated.

Catherine went to a bureau and took out a cigarette and a lighter. She opened the balcony door and lit up. She had given them up years before but kept a packet for emergencies. She fought with her conscience. The last thing in the world she wanted to do was to go to Ireland. Perhaps that was because it was what Edith had wanted her to do. But now her daughter was there, and she wanted to protect her from any grim discoveries. The cigarette made her head dizzy.

She stepped back inside and sat down at her laptop. Edith was not here to protect Lainey. Is that why Edith had asked for both of them to go? She opened the laptop and began to write a reply to Lainey. She wanted to order her to come back to New York and tell her that she would book a flight. But she knew that was useless. Lainey needed her, that was the thing though. Catherine was never good when anyone needed her, especially her daughter.

Dear Lainey,

Against my advice you have gone to this backwater in Ireland. I really wish you would just come home. However, I know you have no intention of doing so. I have no choice. I will come to Ireland for one week only. Expect me Sunday.'

CHAPTER 16

'This is the hotel I told you about, Mom – it's so pretty – what do you think?'

Catherine did not have the heart to quench the enthusiasm of her daughter even if her first impression of Ireland was one of wishing she was back in New York pronto. It had rained in Shannon when her plane touched down. She was assured by her neighbour on the plane, an Irishwoman, that it would be 'only a few showers'. Despite this prediction it had rained all the way down to Kerry. They seemed to be travelling for hours. They had taken a few breaks and could hardly get out of the car without getting soaked and when it did briefly stop, they could barely see out of the window with the dense fog. Ireland so far was horrendous.

Lainey picked her up. Now they had arrived at the hotel that she was staying in for the next week and it was still raining.

'I'm sure it is pretty if I could see it. If it has a bed, I will be quite happy. I am utterly exhausted. Do you mind if I just have something to eat in my room and then I will sleep – you can show me around tomorrow, darling.'

'Okay but no complaining about the weather – it's beautiful here even in the rain.'

'Sorry, but I need a little more convincing. Right now, I'm tired, hungry and cold and it all looks miserable. Maybe with some sleep it might all not look so *wet*!'

Lainey grinned at her. 'Thanks for coming, Mom. I know it was hard for you.' She reached out and hugged her.

Catherine inhaled the smell of jasmine from her hair. She was not the hugging type. She knew her daughter had lots of issues with her. Bur for that one moment, she was glad she had come.

'I couldn't let you have all the fun, running around like Miss Marple, finding out all the dark family secrets.'

'Don't worry, we have lots more to find out. Grandma certainly kept things to herself when it came to Ireland.'

'Well, she has got her way, we are here now,' Catherine said with a touch of sarcasm.

'Go on, grab some sleep. I want you well rested to meet your relatives tomorrow.'

'Oh God! I had forgotten about that. I am not good with small talk.'

'It will be fine. Ruby is really lovely, and Uncle Edward is just trying to come to terms with the fact that we are here.'

'Hmm ... we'll see. Did you let the hotel know about my allergies?

Lainey grinned. 'Don't worry – they are well warned that a diva is in town.'

Lainey had given the hotel a full rundown of her mother's dietary requirements.

After checking in and saying goodbye, Catherine

ordered a gluten-free, meat-free, sugar-free and dairy-free organic roasted vegetable wrap with an organic green salad and organic green tea to be delivered to her room. It was of course not on the menu, but she was assured that her order was fine.

The bedroom suited her, opulent with a touch of old glamour. The walls had a vintage floral wallpaper and the windows rich green velvet drapes. The inviting four-poster bed with cream organza canopy and crisp white bedlinen looked fit for a queen.

It was getting dark and to her amazement it was still raining, pounding against the window. She ate her meal and had a shower, then pulled the drapes, changed into some silk pyjamas and fell into a deep sleep.

When she awoke it took her mind a few minutes to adjust to where she was. Her body felt better and she knew she must have slept all night. The journey had been so long. She hated long-haul flights and the added journey to Dingle was dreadful. But she felt rested now.

Juniper was a bit shocked when she told her that she was taking some time out. Her understudy would play the role. She was excellent but, as the reviews said, 'She was not Catherine Lee Miller.' But when Catherine decided something it was hard to change her mind.

She hoped she had made the right decision to come here. But for Lainey's sake she knew she had needed to. God knows there were lots of times that she had not been there for her and with Edith gone she felt she had better try a bit harder. It was dark in the room, but she could hear birds singing so she went over to the window and pulled the heavy drapes. It was almost dawn and to her surprise it was not raining. She made a cup of tea, put on her robe and watched the dawn arrive.

As the blanket of the night disappeared, the sky shimmered with hues of pinks and lilacs. She wrapped her hands around her cup as she watched the glimmer of sun send shards of golden light into the horizon. The beauty of a new morning. The mist of yesterday washed away. The sky was alive with shimmering shades of light. It was utterly beautiful. Her first morning in Kilbride. This was the dawn that her mother had described to her. Her beautiful Kilbride dawn that had never left her memory. As she clutched her teacup, she was shocked to feel tears rolling down her face. She could see her as she did when she was a child. When she had adored her, and her world was only Edith, before her teenage years took her away from her mother.

Within minutes the moment was gone, and she was getting ready for her first full day in Kilbride.

'How was breakfast?' Lainey enquired.

'Fine – you had them well prepared, darling.' Catherine grinned at her daughter.

'I know what you're like, so I thought it only fair to warn them.'

'It was fine.'

'Praise indeed.' Lainey grinned as they drove off.

The poor waitress had nearly lost her life when Catherine had arrived down for breakfast, immaculately dressed in a cream tailored trousers and cream cashmere jumper and a designer scarf, with full make-up on. She ordered a table by the window and proceeded to ignore the menu and instead ordered a freshly squeezed organic green vegetable juice and some freshly ground coffee.

'Ruby is expecting us for coffee at eleven, but I thought I would show you around the village first,' Lainey said.

'Fine, although you know me – I am not much into sightseeing.' Catherine sighed

'Mom, this is Grandma's home, where she grew up.'

'Okay, no need to be so sensitive. So, what have you been up to other than fishing for all this information about Edith?'

'Believe it or not, I have been riding.'

'Oh! Where?'

'At Kilbride House. Apparently it's really in the family. Can you believe it? You always wondered where I got my love of horses.'

The day after Winnie's revelation, Lainey had taken a walk down to the stables. Lainey knew her horses and recognised five Arabian thoroughbreds. They were stunning. Then, in another section there were two Appaloosas. She adored this breed and of course it was native to America – she had often taken one out riding. She had some great shots of them too. In another stable was the most majestic draft chestnut she had ever laid eyes on. He whinnied and when she nuzzled him she could see he was a gentle giant. Outside were two lovely chestnut cobs grazing in a paddock near the stables. Lainey walked over and one came up to her. She nuzzled his nose and the horse whinnied in delight at the company.

Then she noticed her Uncle Edward walking towards her. She knew that Ruby would be cross with him as he was meant to be resting, but he was not the best-behaved patient. She was certainly not going to tell on him.

He nodded at her. 'You have a way about you. Horses can sense people out.'

'I love horses, I always have. It's funny but growing up in New York all I wanted was a horse. I've done quite a lot of riding over the years – it's something that I have always loved.'

'That's not surprising, it's in the blood. Come on – I'll show you around and see what kind of a horsewoman you are.'

She had linked his arm as they walked around. It had started as simply as that. They both had a deep love of the horses and somehow there and then it bridged a gap of generations.

Now she told her mother, 'Uncle Edward has some beautiful horses. I was blown away by his knowledge. He has bred some real winners too on the race track and had one of the best jockeys in Ireland ride his horses. He also has a gorgeous chestnut called Prince. So, I saddled him up and I've been riding every day and helping with the horses. Uncle Edward comes down every morning and makes sure everything is as it should be. We're so near the beaches here and they're utterly gorgeous. There is a man called John who looks after them – he was very reluctant to let me ride out, but he has relented now after Uncle Edward persuaded him – as long as I am not alone. So sometimes I go out with John or one of the girls that help John out from time to time.'

'I think Edith used to ride – well, all the privileged young women used to in those days.'

'Victoria too. Winnie mentioned it.'

'There is so much we don't know about your grandma and her life here.'

'I know – and to be honest it's not easy finding out much about her. Uncle Edward is saying very little about her.'

After driving around the village, they set out for Kilbride House.

Lainey watched her mother take it all in as they drove up the avenue.

'Well? Impressed?'

'Edith did not lie when she said it was grand – it's beautiful,' Catherine replied with a touch of sadness.

'It reminds me of *Gone with the Wind*.'

'I'm assuming Rhett Butler is not waiting up there for us?'

Lainey laughed. 'I said the same thing to Ruby about the staircase in the house the first day I came here! No, no Rhett Butler but Uncle Edward has agreed to see you.'

'That's big of him.' Catherine threw her eyes to heaven.

'He's an old man, Mom, give him a chance. It's not easy on him, all this being brought up. By the way, we haven't mentioned the grave or the fact that we know he had another sister yet. Ruby is planning on talking to him tomorrow. Let him get over the shock of you arriving first.'

'I had no idea he would need time to "get over" me arriving,' said Catherine acidly.

'Mom, just be nice!' Lainey implored.

'Okay, I'll be nice!'

Lainey watched her mother walk into Kilbride for the first time. Catherine never dressed down and she looked every inch the glamorous theatre star from New York.

Ruby met them in the hall and held out her hand to Catherine in welcome, greeting her warmly.

But there was no embrace, Lainey noted.

Edward was waiting for them in the drawing room. He stood up when Catherine walked in. He was visibly shaken. He didn't speak.

'Grandfather, this is Edith's daughter – your niece Catherine,' Ruby said.

He shuffled over to Catherine, catching her hand as if checking if she was real. Staring at her. Then it was as if it was all too much for him. He swayed on his feet. He sat down with the help of Ruby. Tears glistened in his eyes.

'Are you okay, Grandfather?' Ruby asked worriedly.

Lainey went over to him. 'We don't want to upset you, Uncle Edward. We know it's hard after all these years.'

He looked at Lainey and took her hand.

'I am sorry, but the past has a way of catching up and grabbing you when you least expect it,' he said. He looked over to where Catherine was now sitting. 'You are welcome to Kilbride, Catherine. Welcome home.'

Catherine felt extremely awkward. Welcome home? It all made no sense to her. He had never met her, had never tried to meet her and here he was looking as if she was his long-lost daughter or some sort of apparition. As inexplicable as Edith's behaviour – never returning to Kilbride, preventing her from coming to Ireland and then stipulating she must in her will. She looked at Ruby. She was very attractive – but as for her dress sense? Torn denims and a chunky jumper with big boots more suited to a man. But her face was all high cheekbones and creamy skin. Her hair was like Edith's. She had half expected her to have reddish hair like her and Lainey.

'Lovely to meet you, what a beautiful house!' Catherine smiled. She knew how to charm people and for Lainey's sake she decided to be nice.

Lainey was looking extremely anxiously at her. She obviously wanted this little meeting to go well. Why bother? Why now after all these years? Edith was dead. Did it all matter anymore? All this business about graves and lost sisters. She wished they could get it all sorted and she could go home to New York. Good grief, she was only here a day and already she wanted to go home. Welcome to Kilbride indeed. It was a little late for that. She was over sixty years of age. A Christmas card every year from her precious Irish relatives. Never a visit or an invite over. Why could Edith never visit here? What had happened that she could never come back or allow her only daughter to come here? She was terrified at the thought of her coming here.

She looked at Edward. This old man knew something about her mother that had kept her away for over sixty years. So, it was a little late for coffee and tears. A little late for big welcomes and false talk. This house held secrets and this man did too. He was no relative of hers, she felt nothing towards him. Why should she? She wanted to get up and walk out.

Then she looked at Lainey who was giving her a pleading look.

'Mom, would you like to see Grandma's bedroom?'

Catherine gave one of her brightest smiles. She was an actress after all. She was not inclined to go to her mother's bedroom and she noted Edward looking uncomfortable at the idea.

'Is that okay, Uncle Edward?' Lainey asked.

'Yes, of course.'

'I would love to see it,' Catherine said, getting to her feet.

'I'll stay with Edward – you can be your mom's guide,' said Ruby to Lainey.

But Catherine would need no guide to the house – unless of course it had changed radically since Edith's day. She had described it all so lovingly. She knew the first floor consisted of the large drawing room, the library, plus the formal dining room. The guest bedrooms were on the second floor. The basement contained the kitchen and sculleries, pantry and storerooms. The attic was the living quarters for the servants. The family bedrooms were on the third floor.

She admired the sweeping staircase, the grand cathedral ceiling and immense window which illuminated the hallway. She stopped to look at each portrait. She touched the beautiful wallpaper that she knew had been shipped from America when Edith was a child.

They bypassed the second floor which, Ruby told her, now was used by the family and mounted the stairs to the third floor which lay dusty, untouched and abandoned.

Lainey led her into Edith's bedroom. Catherine was immediately drawn to the window.

The view of the bay was every bit as breath-taking as Edith had described it. Today was a beautiful day after all the rain and the view was for miles, drawing you in. But instead of feeling overwhelmed with the beauty of it, she was overwhelmed with the anger of it. The room her mother grew up in. An old doll sat on a worn stool. Her hair covered in cobweb and her once ruby-red lips peeling. Why now? Why now when she was dead? What on earth was all this about?

'Are you okay, Mom?' Lainey asked worriedly.

'Yes, I just wish it had been different. Why now? Why send us here now?'

'I know – but Grandma loved us – she never sent us here to hurt us or upset us. I am sure of that.'

Catherine gathered herself together. And nodded in agreement.

'I know how much you loved her, and she loved you too, Lainey. I just hope we don't regret coming here. Whatever secrets this house holds, I hope we can cope with them. I do know that Mother adored this house. Even when she was old, she referred to it as home. Come on, I want to see the rest of the house.'

She closed the door on her mother's room, leaving the memories contained in it for now, as for the first time in her life she walked around Kilbride House.

CHAPTER 17

Kilbride House
1954

Victoria held her breath in case she awakened the house. She had waited in bed until she was sure everyone was asleep. She had her clothes on under her nightdress and dressing gown and carried her boots in one hand. She tiptoed out of her room and down the corridor. The moon was shining through the windows on the stairs. She didn't dare light a candle. It was as if the sheer act of breathing could give her away. Tiptoeing down the stairs, through the hall, taking the steps down to the basement and the kitchen and into the pantry. Yes, the window was still slightly ajar. Not enough to really notice, just like she had left it, before she went to bed earlier. She had got back up when everyone was in bed and sneaked downstairs to open the latch on the window and fill a satchel with a loaf of bread, some cheese and a bottle of milk, all wrapped in a clean tea towel.

Now it was time to leave.

To her family it had been an evening like any other. She had taken some of the herbal tincture that the Fort Woman had made for her and it had settled her belly a little – and thankfully there was no fish for dinner. Bessie had made a roast, potatoes and vegetables. Victoria managed to keep some potatoes down by eating slowly and trying not to inhale the smell of the roast. Any type of meat tended to worsen the nausea. Edith kept looking at her of course, watching what she was eating.

'There is a tea dance on in Dingle next week – run by Reverend Wilkinson. I think you should go and wear that blue dress we got in Dublin on our last trip, Victoria. It has such beautiful crystals on the collar. It's such a shame never to wear it.' Gertrude Goulding was dressed in a black gaberdine skirt and a black blouse with a stiff high collar. Her grey-black hair was pinned tightly on her head. Her face was thin and pinched and her high cheekbones more prominent because of the loss of weight on it. She had lost an alarming amount of weight since her husband died. She picked at her food, barely touching it

'But what about our black mourning clothes?' Edith asked.

'It's time you all stopped wearing black. I know I kept you all in mourning. But I feel it may be good for you to get out. Especially you, Victoria. You are not yourself. You look the colour of chalk. You spend far too much time walking alone on the cliffs. Edith, will you go to the dance and look after Victoria?'

Edith looked at her mother and nodded her head. 'Of course, Mother – but isn't it too soon to come out of mourning?'

'No, I can't keep you in mourning forever. Life has to go on. Doctor Ford has advised me to stop too.'

'He seems to have a lot to say for himself,' Edward remarked gruffly.

'What do you mean by that?' Gertrude asked.

'Well, what is it to him what Edith or Victoria wears? It's none of his business as far as I am aware. He seems to be forever sticking his oar in. Our father never trusted him, and I often wondered why, but I think he was right.'

Gertrude put her knife and fork down now as if trying to find the words to answer her son.

'Mother, are you alright?' Edith asked.

'I am as good as I can be. I miss your father terribly, but I know we must try to continue on. It is my only wish to see you all in good marriages and settled down.'

'Victoria, you look unwell, take some water.' Edith passed it to her.

Victoria took a sip of water. 'Sorry, Mother,' she said, 'I don't feel well. I think I should go and rest.'

'Of course,' said her mother. 'But we will need to get Doctor Ford to look at you tomorrow – you are so pale – perhaps you need a tonic.'

'Yes, it probably is better to see the doctor.' Victoria was afraid she would throw up the potatoes that she had just eaten.

'I wish there was a different doctor,' Edward piped up.

'Please, Edward, enough! There is nothing wrong with Doctor Ford. He is simply offering his help because your father is not here.'

'I'm here,' he said. 'You don't need him for advice. I don't believe that man would do anything unless there was something in it for himself.'

'Why, may I ask, would you think that?' Gertrude raised her voice slightly.

'Ever since our father died, Ford is forever around the place. He drives me mad. He arrives in here like Lord of the Manor, and there is something about him that I don't trust. I can't put my finger on it. But every time I look around he seems to be here with you.'

Gertrude shook her head in annoyance. 'Edward, your father was the best husband I could have ever wished for and I have absolutely no intention of having another husband if that's what you are worried about. I only appreciate Doctor Ford's advice during this difficult time, this very difficult time.'

'Edward, you are upsetting Mother,' Edith said.

'I just need to say how I feel. He annoys me no end. He seems to look down on everyone in the village, thinking he is above them, and he clearly would just love to get a foot in here at Kilbride House.'

'Well, he will be getting no foot in here and I never want this matter mentioned again.'

There was silence for a few minutes.

'How much did the village fête make?' Edith asked then, trying to change the subject.

'I have no idea,' Gertrude said. 'Victoria, why don't you go upstairs now?'

Victoria looked around, knowing that this was her last dinner with them. She bit her lip.

'Are you alright, Victoria?' her mother asked.

'Yes, Mother, but I'll go now if that's all right.'

She took a last look at them as she walked out the door.

She had no idea when she would see them again.

Victoria took the satchel from the cupboard where she had hidden it. The window creaked as she opened it to its full extent.

Henry, the huge Irish Wolfhound who was meant to prowl outside in case anyone decided to call by night, came up and wagged his tail with delight at the prospect of some company. Once safely on the other side Victoria patted him and begged him to be silent.

'*Shush!* No barking, Henry! Sit!'

Henry did as he was asked.

She slid on her boots, then pulled off her nightdress and stuffed it in the satchel.

Henry just gave a whimper and lay down when she told him 'Stay!' as she crept out of the yard.

The path was barely visible with the moon almost hidden except for a small slice peeping from behind the clouds. But she knew the way. She could possibly go blindfolded if she had to. Past the gardens, past the pond, past the tree where the owl nested every year, past the one where Edward fell and broke his arm when pretending to be a monkey.

Mother would be so disappointed in her. But she seemed to be disappointed in her no matter what she did. No, it was better this way. Her stomach churned – she would need to eat some bread to settle it.

It was as still a night as anyone could imagine, with only the call of the night owl or the scurrying of a rat to break the silence. Something jumped in the ditch and she stifled a cry. What was it? Only a rabbit. A tiny rabbit that ran and hid as fast as it could.

She jumped again as there was a rustle in the trees. There was someone behind her. Her heart leapt to her throat.

'Where are you going, Victoria?'

Edith.

Victoria swung around.

'Why are you following me?' she asked curtly.

141

'I will ask the questions. Where on earth are you going – it's well past midnight?'

'I can't tell you, Edith. Anyway, it's none of your business. Just go home. Please.'

'You are obviously doing something that Mother would not approve of. If you think I am going to turn on my heel and allow you to continue you have another think coming.'

Victoria felt nauseous and exhausted. Now here was Edith on her high horse, going to ruin everything. All the days of planning, the secret meetings.

'Are you going to tell me where you think you are off to in the dead of the night?' Edith demanded again.

'Just go, Edith, go back to the house and pretend you never saw me.'

'You know very well that I have no intention of doing that. I demand that you tell me where you are going.'

Victoria remembered the time they used to play treehouses in this very wood. Edith had a wonderful imagination. They had bears, lions, elephants and always unicorns. Edith loved unicorns. She said that when they were all asleep the fairies of the woods would get on the backs of their silver unicorns and ride through the woods with their golden hair flying in the air behind them.

'What happened to you, Edith? You were always so much fun – now it's like having some cross aunt living with us, always ready to get us into trouble. I wish you were like the Edith that loved to play here in these very woods for hours with me. Our very own make-believe world. I barely recognise you.'

'I grew up, that's what happened, Miss Wild and Free. Somebody must be responsible. You are far too wild and

142

this is a new level. Come back to the house this instant!'

Victoria tried to think. How on earth could she get out of this one?

'Very well. I just wanted to see what the night was like – it's a beautiful night.'

Edith looked at her in disbelief. 'Really? What's in the satchel?'

'Some food. A picnic. A midnight feast like the ones we used to have. Do you remember?'

'I remember. But we were children then. Victoria, come home now. Mother has enough to worry about without you giving her more. She has already sent for Doctor Ford to come see you tomorrow. You're looking very sick and here you are gallivanting in the middle of the night.'

'Very well, stop fussing, I'm coming home.'

They started to walk back with Edith leading the way and telling her how silly she was and how she must start acting more maturely.

'Edith, I know we fight a lot now, but it wasn't always that way – you know how much I care about you.'

'Don't be so maudlin. Look, I know you are going through a difficult time. It's been so difficult with Father gone. I know how close you two were.'

'I miss him, Edith.' Suddenly tears rose to her eyes and she sobbed.

'Hush now, it's alright.' Edith kept walking. 'Now what on earth do I tell Mother if she's awake when we get back? I'll have to tell her you were sleepwalking or something. But she'll hardly believe that, will she? What should I say? Victoria? What am I to tell her? Victoria?'

But Victoria was gone.

CHAPTER 18

She had hidden an old bicycle at the bottom of the woods, quite close to a small gate that led onto the road – it was a place where she had often met Canice. She had thought it better to use an old bike rather than her own which might be missed. Moving aside branches, she retraced her steps to where it was hidden. It was still there. But the small green Samsonite suitcase was gone. Good. That meant Canice had been to collect it.

She hastily put her bag in the basket, rolled the bike onto the road and cycled off. It was so late there was little chance that there would be anyone to see her. Unless the priest was out if someone was ill or had died. He tended to drive so slowly that he missed nothing. But no, the real danger would come from behind. If Edith betrayed her.

Her stomach lurched. Oh, please God, no! She just couldn't stop to be sick.

She had planned to ride steadily at a normal pace, so as not to attract attention should she encounter anyone on the road, but now that she had been seen by Edith she threw caution to the wind and cycled as fast as she could.

She focused on thoughts of Canice to stop herself from panicking. She couldn't wait to see him. She knew he would swoop her up in his arms. They would drive to the boat and go to England to get married. She even had a makeshift wedding dress in the suitcase. She had wrapped it in a pillowcase and put it at the bottom of the case. It was a lace dress that her mother had made. There were tiny crystals, beads and pearls at the waist. A sweetheart neckline. Bessie would say she shouldn't wear white of course. But she wanted to look pretty. She had also put in a cream half hat with pearls encrusted on it, cream low-heel shoes and a cream shawl.

She couldn't wait to see Canice's face when she changed. He said that they would get two strangers as witnesses. Two people off the street. Imagine. With all the people she knew, two strangers would be her witnesses for her wedding! She just wished it didn't have to be like that. He had told her of London – there was nothing easy about it. Island life was in his blood. He knew every nest of the gulls and could name all the plants and flowers that grew on the rocky soil. He knew the safest time to take the boat out and fish. He had lost his father and brother to the sea and as there was only him, his mother would be heartbroken at him leaving. She would be looked after at least, living as she now did close to her sister and her family. Victoria felt guilty for taking her only son away from her. But there was no other way. Canice had put some money in an envelope for her and would leave it for her tonight. It would see her by and they would send her more money when they were settled.

Canice had brought her to visit his mother. She was a

kindly woman who almost curtsied when she met Victoria. But Victoria could sense the fear she felt knowing what her son was doing. She only spoke in the Irish tongue. Victoria knew some Irish from school and could make out bits of what she was saying.

'They will destroy you, son, you have to leave. You are everything that they do not want for their daughter.'

'It's so unfair – I love Canice!' Victoria cried.

The woman began to lament in Irish. Now Victoria could not make out what she was saying. She looked at Canice.

'She says that it's a story as old as time. Religion is in the way. When your family find out, there will be no way back. They will never accept us.

His mother was crying and crooning – it sounded like a lullaby in Irish.

They had made the plan like so many before them. They would escape to England and once they were married there was little anyone could do. Victoria guessed that Canice's mother knew she was pregnant. Woman's instinct. She hugged her and cried with her. She wished she could get to know this lovely island woman, but she also knew that she was right, they had to get away. She had listened to enough from her parents about marrying the right kind. It was one thing to be pregnant without marriage but when the man was the wrong religion, well, that was a far worse story.

She cycled on, looking back compulsively now and then to see if anyone was behind her, though she knew that if she were pursued she would hear the sound of a car. Please, Edith, just this once. Don't tell Mother. She should have been more careful. How did Edith hear her?

It was as if the sky was full of tiny pieces of silver glittering, guiding her. The smell of the sea air, the soft low of sheep. When she was in her bedroom earlier, she had tried to take a mental picture of it. She loved everything about it and especially its window which at night was like a gateway to the stars and shimmered with light when the sun rose in the morning. The great stairs that she would creep down and sit and listen for her father when he was working late. When she was little he would chase her up the stairs and tickle her until she cried with laughter. She would so miss Silver. She had hugged the animal for the last time, taking in her aroma to last a lifetime. She would write to Edward and ask him to look after her.

She put her hand to her stomach. God knows what her mother would say if she knew she was going to have a baby. This was the only way. She had played it out in her head so much. There was no looking back. Perhaps in a different time, but not now, not in Ireland. They had not followed the rules set out for them.

Poor Edith, who was always trying to do the right thing! She wished she could have confided in her. But there was no way. Now Edith would tell her mother that she had disappeared. They had to go as fast as they could. If they started searching for her and found her all hell would break loose. She tried to concentrate on the road, terrified that her mother and Edith or Edward would find her. She would miss Edith so much and Edward. They quarrelled like all siblings, but there was also great love and friendship. Maybe one day, when she was married and the baby was born, they could all be reunited. She prayed that they would.

She felt her stomach lurch again and this time she had

to stop. It was as if all her insides were turning inside-out on her. She threw up and took out a handkerchief to dry her mouth. She knew she had to cycle on before anyone found her. The sickness was making her weak. Hopefully it would pass soon. She took a little of the tincture the woman at the Fort had given her and mounted the bicycle again.

She made it to a gap just before the village and, just as they had planned, Canice was there. He had arranged for his friend Freddy to give them a lift to Cork. There was a sailing at five thirty the next evening on the *Innisfallen* at Penrose Quay and he had tickets. They would travel to Swansea in Wales and then they would get a mail train into London.

He hugged her tightly. 'You made it, my girl! We're on our way!'

'Oh Canice, Edith saw me. I managed to lose her and run but she will have told Mother and Edward by now. I'm certain of it. We have to go as quick as we can.'

Freddy gave her a big grin and lost no time in getting on the road. The car shook and Victoria feared that it could break down at any moment.

She kept obsessively checking to see if anyone was following them. After an hour had passed she could feel herself calm down. Perhaps Edith hadn't told on her? After all, she didn't know that this was an elopement. She probably thought it was just a romantic encounter with some boy and that she would soon be back home. And even if she had told, her mother and Edward would assume the same, and just send the servants out to search the woods and the grounds.

Some hours later they arrived into the village of Ballycotton, about thirty miles east of Cork City. Canice had a cousin who lived near the village and they would hide out there for the day and allow Victoria to rest before the ship sailed that evening at eight. Canice had got a message to his cousin earlier that day to expect them. It was a small cottage by the sea.

It was dawn when they arrived. Declan, his cousin, had kept a fire going and an oil lamp was lighting. His wife Deirdre looked about thirty and kindly. She made them welcome and showed Victoria into a small bedroom.

'You are poorly. I have some broth made.'

'Thank you. I will try some and hopefully it will stay down.'

The broth was comforting and miraculously stayed down.

'Thank you. You are very kind.'

'You've had a long journey, pet, and more to come. Rest now.'

Rest she did. Tiredness overwhelmed her and she slept for most of the day.

Eventually the evening was upon them and it was time to catch the boat. Freddy had stayed around and now took them back to Cork city and the quays.

As they drove along the River Lee and onward to Penrose Quay, Victoria could feel her stomach retch from the sickness and with nerves. She still feared pursuit but they had got this far without any problem. Hopefully all would now go well. Even if her mother suspected they had eloped, she wouldn't know which port they had headed for – they could equally have sailed from Dublin to Liverpool or from Northern Ireland to Scotland.

Canice reached from the passenger seat into the back

of the car and grabbed her hand in reassurance.

'We're in luck. It's a calm night so it won't be too rocky.'

She retched again and she shouted at them to stop the car.

Bile came up as there wasn't anything in her stomach. She felt she could die. She gulped some of the elixir again, then grabbed some bread from her bag and forced herself to eat it.

'We are almost there, pet,' Canice said worriedly.

They could see the ship in full view now, with its black hull and white top.

There was no turning back.

They drove on until they reached Penrose Quay. There they got out, thanked Freddy, grabbed their bags and made for the boat.

The ship was looming above them when they had to stop again to give Victoria a chance to allow her stomach to settle.

Then, as they picked up their bags and turned to continue, a squad car pulled up beside them and two gardaí got out and confronted them.

Victoria grabbed Canice's hand. He held it so tight it almost hurt. It was as if her legs had turned to jelly. She leaned into him and he put his arm around her in support. She could feel how tense his body was.

'Are you Canice Meagher?' the older of the two gardaí demanded.

'Why?'

'Answer the question, boy.'

'Yes, I am.'

'And you are Miss Victoria Goulding of Kilbride House?'

'Yes,' she said, and her voice came out as a whisper.

KILBRIDE HOUSE

'You are both taking the boat?'

'Yes,' said Canice defiantly.

'We are arresting you, Canice Meagher, for the abduction of Miss Victoria Goulding.'

'No!' said Canice. 'You've got it wrong! Ask her!'

'He is not abducting me – I am going of my own free will!' Victoria protested.

'You are not yet seventeen, Miss, so this is abduction.' He turned to Canice. 'Hands behind back, Meagher, if you know what is good for you.'

The younger garda handcuffed Canice.

'*It is not abduction!*' Victoria shouted.

The first garda eyeballed Canice. 'You should have been more careful making your plans, Meagher.'

'*Please!*' Victoria cried. '*He hasn't done anything wrong!*'

'He can tell that to the judge,' the younger garda quipped.

They were shoving a struggling Canice into the back of the car when another car pulled up. Victoria recognised it instantly.

Doctor Ford and her mother got out of the car.

Victoria's heart sank. How on earth did they know where they were?

Gertrude Goulding was dressed immaculately in a black velvet coat and hat. Her face would have been beautiful except for the dark scowl on it.

'*I have not abducted your daughter, Mrs Goulding! I love her!*' Canice shouted.

'How dare you!'

Victoria froze as she heard her mother's voice like ice in the air.

'How dare you even suggest that my daughter would have anything to do with you! Victoria, come here now!'

Victoria felt like she would throw up. This could not be happening. Then her stomach churned even worse than before when she saw Edith climb out of the back of the car.

'*How could you?*' Victoria screamed at Edith.

She turned to her mother and composed herself.

'I am not going home with you, Mother, and I am not being abducted,' she stated, sounding a lot more together and mature than she felt. 'I am in love with Canice and we are leaving because we knew what your reaction would be, so tell these men to take their hands off him.'

'Victoria, let me remind you that you are not yet seventeen years old and as my child you are under my care. I have no idea what this man has said to you, but if I find out that he has touched a hair on your head, he will spend his days paying for it.'

'*Stop it, stop it! Leave him alone!*' At that she retched worse than ever. She tried to hold it back but fell to her knees and threw up.

Gertrude stared in horror. 'My god, what has he done to you?'

'*He has done nothing to me except love me! Yes, I am going to have his baby. Do your worst, Mother, but it won't stop me!*'

The older garda addressed Doctor Ford. 'Do you need our help to get the girl in the car, sir?'

'No, no. Thank you for your help. You may go.'

The Garda car drove off and before Victoria knew what was happening her mother and Doctor Ford had pulled her to her feet and shoved her into the car.

'*You cannot do this! You cannot, Mother! Let me out!*'

'*I can do a lot worse!*' her mother roared at her. '*You are a disgrace! Now sit still and do not speak!*'

Edith was looking distraught. 'Mother, Victoria is ill – stop treating her like this. She's obviously in love with this man whoever he is.'

'*In love!* How childish you sound, Edith – you have no idea what you're talking about. She has shamed us beyond belief. I am just glad your father is not here to see what she has turned into.'

'He wouldn't react like this, Mother, you know he wouldn't!' Edith cried.

Victoria's eyes were wild and her face snow-white from shock. '*Let me out!*' she screamed.

Gertrude turned to her. 'Shut up, you stupid, stupid girl!'

Edith was crying now. 'Victoria, I am so sorry. I had no idea this was going to happen. I should never have told on you. I was just worried about you and didn't know what to do when you disappeared.'

'Edith, stop them – don't let them take him, please – he never wronged me! I am begging you to help me!'

'Shut up, Victoria, or you will only make it worse for that vagabond,' Doctor Ford warned.

'He is no vagabond! And we were going to get married.'

'Well, it's lucky your sister alerted your mother to your disappearance, as there is no way you can marry him.'

'No way in hell!' Gertrude interjected.

'You can't stop us, Mother. I'm having his baby.'

'Just watch me stop you,' Gertrude replied calmly.

Victoria felt like a trapped animal.

'If Father was here he would never allow you to treat me like this!' she sobbed.

'It's true, Mother, he would not allow this!' Edith cried.

'Your father would be shocked and ashamed at what you have done. At least he is not here to see it.'

'You're *lying*!' Victoria shouted.

'Stop it, your insolent girl. You should be begging my forgiveness.'

The journey back was torturous as Victoria threw up several times and almost fainted with shock and sickness. She was so weak by the time they got back to the house that Doctor Ford easily led her to her room which was locked soundly afterwards.

Edith was beside herself at what had happened.

'You cannot lock her in there, Mother!'

'I have absolutely no choice. Edith, go and rest. I will deal with this and do what is best for your sister.' And she walked away, leaving Edith a crumpled mess outside the door of Victoria's room.

When Victoria awoke it was dark. The events of the day flashed before her. She could hardly believe what had happened. Her heart ached as she thought about Canice.

She tried the door, but it was locked. This was worse than she could have imagined. Surely her mother did not plan to lock her up here?

Someone had left in some water and a sandwich for her. She tried to eat but the sickness was too bad. She lay down on the bed again and sobbed in despair.

She heard a faint knocking. There was someone at the door.

'It's me – Edith. Are you alright?'

Victoria began to cry – it was all too much.

'It's alright, Victoria. I have told Edward and he is going to help you. I am so sorry. I felt you were my responsibility – but I had no idea Mother would react so badly. But what could I do? I will do everything I can to help you. She can't lock you up here. I promise.'

But Gertrude did not plan on locking Victoria up in her room. She had other plans.

CHAPTER 19

Her body ached and the nausea was making her feel wretched. She thought for a minute she must be on the ship with Canice. She would need some dry bread to settle her stomach or some of the tincture. Then reality hit her like a stab. She was still locked in her bedroom.

She awoke now fully, still in the clothes she had on the day before. Her stomach was churning – it felt like her whole body was turning inside out. The sandwich from the day before was gone. Now there was some bread and butter and a glass of milk. There was also another glass and a jug of water. She tried to eat some bread and take a sip of the milk. Hopefully it would settle it.

She should be across the sea by now, ready to start a new life with Canice. All the plans. They were so careful. How did it all go so wrong? She cried to think of Canice.

'Please, God, don't let them hurt him!' she prayed.

A thought came to her. The Fort Woman was right. She had warned her. What had she seen? She had said she was in danger. That she must protect her baby. What did she mean by that? It was worse than a nightmare. The way they had shoved Canice in the car like an animal. If she could only see him, talk to him, tell him that it didn't matter what they said or did, they would be together again, somehow.

How could her mother do this? She always knew her mother would not approve of her relationship and the fact she was going to have a baby out of wedlock was of course a terrible shock – but to go to this extreme! Did she really believe that she had been abducted? She would never have believed her mother could act like this.

Her father would never have allowed it. He was so kind. He could not treat anyone like this. Her mother was so different since he died as if he took a piece of her too. How on earth had she known all about them leaving? Edith hadn't known where she was going, or even that she was going anywhere – so how did they know where she was headed? Perhaps someone had seen them in Freddy's car heading off on the road to Cork.

Poor Edith! Victoria knew she was feeling so bad about everything. She never meant any of this to happen. She accused her of interfering and bossing her but in her heart she knew that Edith was forever worrying about her – she wouldn't harm a hair on her head or allow anyone else to either. Even when they were young, Edith would worry when Victoria climbed the highest tree she could find. Edith was always more careful, making sure the tree was safe and telling Victoria not to go so high, constantly looking after her.

When they were very young, their father had made a makeshift camp in the garden and the three of them got ready all day for their big night camping. Dragging out blankets, lighting a campfire, getting provisions, they were so excited about sleeping outside they could not wait until nightfall and left the house when it was still light. But as soon as the dark came, Edith began to think she heard wolves and got so upset that Edward had to run and get their father. There was no calming Edith and she had to go inside, leaving Edward and Victoria to camp under a beautiful night of stars. But then Edith couldn't sleep because the wolves might get to Victoria and Edward, and much to Victoria's annoyance they all had to come in because Edith was so worried.

And Edward! When he had discovered what had happened she had heard an unmerciful row downstairs. She had only spoken to him through the door. She told him and Edith everything, how she had met Canice and fallen in love, the fact that she was going to have a baby and how they had decided the best thing to do was go to England.

Edward had asked her why she had not told them before – had she not trusted them?

'I thought it was for the best, Edward. I wish now that I had told you.'

Then he said he would go and find Canice and vouch for his good name, try and get him released. And Edith would try to talk to their mother, get her to see sense.

Edward hadn't yet returned – or he might have come home while she slept. She was desperate for news of Canice.

The nausea was making her feel wretched. She lay down again and prayed that it would ease. She couldn't think. She closed her eyes and prayed to her father that somehow he could help her. Eventually she fell back into a deep sleep.

At first she thought she was still asleep and dreaming. There was a large woman standing over her. She was dressed in a long black coat and hat and she had a sickly smell of perfume that made Victoria want to retch. Her large red face had a big purple vein at her forehead. Startled, Victoria pulled the blankets closer to her.

Then she saw her mother. The look in her eyes frightened Victoria.

'Victoria, Doctor Ford is here, sit up like a good girl,' her mother said.

Victoria didn't move.

'Come on now, missy.' And then the large woman was dragging her out of the bed.

Victoria could hardly believe what was happening.

'*Get off me! Who is she? Get her out of my room, Mother!*' she shrieked.

'Calm down, Victoria,' her mother said.

Victoria tried to push the woman away. She had dragged her to a sitting position at the side of the bed.

'Who is she, Mother? And why is the doctor here? It's not even morning.' It was barely dawn – she could see the light in the distance. 'Oh God, I feel sick, I'm going to throw up.'

Her mother grabbed a basin and Victoria threw up the bread from earlier. She was so tired, she just needed to sleep. She tried to lie back down

'*Come on now, missy – get up!*' the woman said sharply, jerking her back into a sitting position.

Victoria pleaded with her mother. 'Mother, I beg of you! Stop her! Please. Who is she, Mother – what is she doing?'

Now the woman was grabbing her and lifting her from the bed as roughly as if she were a bag of potatoes. Victoria pushed her away with all the strength that she had.

'*Get your hands off me!*'

Her mother tried to stop her from struggling. 'Stop it, Victoria! Stop fighting us! This is Kitty, she works for Doctor Ford. They have come to help us. Stop it – you have done enough damage as it is. I need you to get dressed, Victoria. *Now!*'

'Just put her dressing gown on, it will suffice,' came Doctor Ford's voice.

He came forward and looked down at Victoria as if she were a spoiled toddler having a tantrum.

'Put your dressing gown on, there's a good girl,' her mother said, holding out the dressing gown and ignoring the look of terror on her daughter's face. 'Victoria, listen to Doctor Ford – he is here to help us, help you – come on now, put your arms in.'

'Mother, what's happening? Why are they here? Why won't you tell me? You're frightening me.'

Victoria recognised the coldness and deep disappointment on her mother's face – it was as if she was disowning her.

'I am doing what is best for you. Your father is not here, so I must do what I think is best. I never imagined you would ever put me in this position, but you were always wild, it was never going to lead to anything good. And now look at you! *Ruined!*'

'Stop it, Mother, stop it! I haven't murdered anyone – all we wanted to do was leave. If that's how you feel about me, just let me go! And for God's sake let Canice go! He is kind and gentle and would never hurt me in any way. Just let us go and I promise that you will not have to look at me ever again. Just let me go.'

'Don't you understand? You have disgraced us all.

160

Something must be done to protect the family. And protect you and your future. Now the arrangement is made. Doctor Ford is taking you somewhere – it's for the best, he has assured me – it's all arranged.'

'What's all arranged, Mother? What have you done? *Get away from me, all of you!*'

The doctor shook his head and checked the time on the pocket watch attached to the waistcoat of his pinstripe suit.

'I would like to get on the road now,' he said. 'It's a good journey there and back. I will call to you later and tell you how it went. Just get her to the car. I can see you have your hands full. You are making the right decision, Mrs Goulding. There is absolutely no doubt there.'

'What decision, Mother? *Tell me!*'

Gertrude's face had the pallor of chalk. It was as if all emotion had left her.

The doctor grabbed Victoria and pushed his face close to hers. His eyes were bloodshot and his forehead glistened with sweat. 'Don't shout at your mother, or you will feel the back of my hand!'

Victoria pushed him away and he almost fell over. Then she felt the bile hit her mouth and she threw up on the bed.

'Look what he has done to you,' her mother said coldly.

An unbearable fear made Victoria almost choke. Her body was shaking and she could barely stand with the fright of what was happening. She began to scream for help. Like an animal screeching in the wild at being caught in a trap, she screamed for all she was worth. The doctor and Kitty dragged her downstairs and within minutes they had her kicking and screaming in the car. Kitty was almost sitting on her to keep her from jumping out, but the doors were now locked.

The doctor started up the engine as Edward and Edith appeared at the door in their dressing gowns, their eyes wide with shock at what was happening.

Edward ran to the car. 'Mother! What on earth are you doing?' he shouted, trying to open the door of the car. 'I demand you open the door, doctor!'

'Get away from the car, Edward,' Gertrude said. 'Doctor Ford is taking your sister for some help.'

At that point Bessie arrived for her day's work. She gaped at the scene before her.

'Mrs Goulding, what is happening?'

'*Bessie, help us!*' Edith cried.

'Bessie, stay out of it,' Gertrude replied sharply. 'Doctor Ford is taking Victoria to get her some help.'

'*Help?*' Edward yelled as he tried the other door. '*Well, why is she screaming like a wild animal, if he is trying to help her?*'

'I am sending Victoria somewhere, Bessie, where she can be helped,' Gertrude responded with vigour. 'We cannot do anything here – she is beyond our control.'

'Is this because of Canice Meagher?' Bessie asked.

'This is family business, Bessie – none of yours,' Gertrude said sharply.

'Please, ma'am, we can look after her capabilities, don't send her away!' Bessie pleaded, tears now falling down her face.

'Bessie, I am at the end of my tether. This is exactly what I was afraid of happening – she is out of control as you can see – she would just run away if I leave her here.'

'Canice Meagher is a decent man, Mrs Goulding. His family are good island people. There is no malice in the Meaghers. He stepped above his station, that was his only crime, but it does happen and we can deal with it. They could move away – but not this, anything but this – please, ma'am.'

'Bessie, I think you should know your place and keep out of this matter. My decision is made. That man will never see my daughter again, and he will rue the day that he ever did. She needs help now and the doctor has assured me I am doing the right thing.'

'*The right thing?*' Edith screamed. '*What do you mean? You are treating her like a criminal. She is our sister, for God's sake! Let her out! Now! Mother, what have you done?*'

Edward went and stood in front of the car, his arms on the bonnet. His mother and Bessie dragged him away, afraid the car would drive over him, emotions were so high.

The doctor reversed and swung the car around, narrowly missing Edith, accelerated and drove down the road.

Victoria could hear Edith and Edward running down the drive after the car, shouting. But it was useless, the doctor was going too fast. She tried again to get the woman off her, but she was no match for her. She felt weak enough to faint, she could barely breathe.

'You imbecile of a girl, stop fighting with me!'

'*Get off me! Why? Why?* What have I done that is so terrible that I need to be trapped like an animal and treated in this way?'

'You crossed a line when you had anything to do with

163

that lad. He's in prison and he will get his due too. You imbecile of a child! That is what you have done. His poor mother will hardly be able to live here, the way he has disgraced her. And you should bow your head in shame and ask forgiveness for what you are putting your poor family through.'

'*Doctor Ford! I beg you! Take me home! Stop! Stop!*'

'*Stop it now!*' he roared, shocking them both. 'You are going to a special hospital and they will look after you there until the baby is born. It will be a long drive. Now I don't want to hear another word from you until we get there.'

'What –'

'*Enough!* I mean it, be *quiet*, Victoria. Or you'll regret you've spoken.'

CHAPTER 20

Marlborough Asylum
1954

They seemed to be at the edge of the world to Victoria. She could see the sea, but it was stark and lonely, not beautiful like it was at Kilbride, where the mountains overlooked the bay and the water looked like blue silk. Here there was a grey fog over the sea. They had passed villages and towns earlier. Life was continuing. She had wanted to scream and break out through the door and run to find Canice so that he could tell her that it was all right now. They were safe. But she was trapped.

The journey seemed an eternity. Kitty chatted to the doctor, ignoring Victoria, but if she made the slightest struggle, she grabbed her by the forearm. Kitty was a large woman and Victoria was no match for her. She almost lost her breath when she grabbed her. She could feel the bruises from her grip.

Her stomach churned as the nausea almost made her faint. The smell of car polish and some sickly flowery perfume off her jailor made her even more nauseous than usual.

They drove further on and came to a river. The fog was shifting. It was then she felt fear, fear like she had never felt it before. There was a drawbridge down over a narrow part of the river and the doctor drove over it. Then on to an entrance with a man standing at two iron gates. Connected to the gates was a high limestone wall. He opened the gates and allowed them in.

It was then she saw it: an imposing redbrick building with a winding treelined avenue, stacks of chimneys and what seemed like hundreds of dark windows.

Her throat went dry as a large sign met them. In large black writing it read: *Marlborough Mental Asylum.*

'*No! No!*' she gasped, her breath leaving her body. How could her mother have agreed to this? Did she even know where they were taking her, a lamb to the slaughter? This place, this terrible place. How could her mother have betrayed her like this? Her baby, what would become of her baby? Terror almost overpowered her.

Kitty was pushing her down, holding her arms. 'Now, now, Victoria, be calm. That man has your poor mind tricked. We are going to get you well.'

'Your mother cannot handle this by herself,' the doctor soothed.

'They'll be well able to handle her here, doctor. That's for sure.'

'I am sure they will. She'll be a different girl after her little holiday here.'

'*My baby, what about my baby?*' she cried.

He shook his head. 'No more questions now, be quiet now like a good girl. You don't want to give the wrong impression straight away, isn't that right, Kitty?'

'Unless you want to be locked up for good,' Kitty sneered.

Victoria threw herself at Kitty and clawed at her.

'Oh no you don't, you little demon! I will have to put manners on you!' With that she slapped Victoria across the face.

As her cheek burned Victoria could feel herself retch and green bile came out of her mouth and onto Kitty's coat and the car seat.

'*She has me destroyed!*' Kitty shouted as she pulled Victoria's head up by the hair. '*Oh no!* Doctor, the little bitch has just gone and vomited all over me! Your car will stink!'

The car stopped and they pulled her out.

'I can handle her from here, Kitty – let Mrs Burns know that we have arrived. Thanks, Kitty, I could not have managed her on my own. I'm sorry about your coat.' He twisted Victoria's arms behind her back and held her hands tightly together.

'It's not your fault, doctor – it's that little whelp. I will get Mrs Burns straight away.'

Then she turned to Victoria who was struggling to get away from the doctor's grip.

'You are a fiery one, Miss Victoria Goulding. Well, see how fiery you are after your little spell in here. I will ask one of the cleaners to have a look at your car, doctor. Though we should be getting this weasel here to clean up her own mess.'

The expansive hallway was tiled in black and white and gleamed with cleanliness. A young boy of about thirteen was sitting in a wheelchair. He smiled a toothless smile, putting his hand out to try to grab Victoria.

'*Sweeties, sweeties, please, sweeties, yellow marshy sweeties!*' he called, holding his hand out and shaking his head back and forth.

A tall woman met them and grabbed Victoria just as she struggled from the doctor's grip.

'Hello, Mrs Burns – this is Miss Victoria Goulding. Thank you for taking her at such short notice. Mrs Goulding of Kilbride House is most grateful, and we of course know that her stay here will be handled very discreetly.'

Mrs Burns was as thin as Kitty was stout. She wore a black serge dress belted at the waist with a snow-white collar and white cuffs. A white cap showed a widow's peak of grey hair. A thin line for a smile and eyes that looked at Victoria as if she had crawled out of the gutter.

'Now, Victoria, I am Mrs Burns and I will not tolerate any behaviour like this. You are only making trouble for yourself. We will get her admitted straight away and get the paperwork sorted afterwards, doctor. Come along, Victoria. I believe you have been very difficult on your journey here. Make no mistake, it will not be tolerated here. Step out of line and you will be very sorry. If you want to see Kilbride again, do exactly as I tell you. *Do you hear me?*'

Victoria was terrified. They walked down what seemed miles and miles of corridors, some empty and some with patients wandering aimlessly up and down.

'Any baccy?' a little woman asked. She had steel-grey hair cut like spikes on her head. Her brown shoes dragged on her feet.

'Go on with you, Maggie. I'll give you some tobacco later if you're a good girl.'

'Baccy now, ah baccy now, me good, me good,' the little woman whimpered.

'Later, Maggie – back to your seat now.'

168

Maggie touched the softness of the dressing gown that Gertrude Goulding had struggled to put on her daughter. Victoria flinched.

'*Off with you, Maggie!*' Mrs Burns shouted.

A blind man walked up, waving his head from side to side, holding a cane. He was crying as if in terrible pain.

'Sammy, go to the day room *now*! I will have you chained there if you move again, do you hear me?'

He hung his head but kept crying as he slowly turned around and headed back.

A nurse walked up the corridor and said hello to the doctor and Mrs Burns, not acknowledging Victoria.

They arrived at a small office. Two attendants came out, one around twenty and the other in her sixties.

'Victoria Goulding here for you,' said Mrs. Burns. 'I need to sort her paperwork. Can you get her sorted and I think for now we need high security?'

The younger one of them looked like she could take on a boxer, she looked so strong, the other scowled at Victoria. As the doctor held Victoria by the shoulders, she kicked and tried to get out of his grip. Mrs Burns held her hand up to strike her, but Victoria ducked and the blow missed her.

'You insolent girl!'

'Now, Victoria, you must behave,' said Doctor Ford. 'There is nothing you can do. You must stay here until the hospital is sure that you are cured. I will come back myself to fetch you. Your poor mother would not be able to see you like this. It would break her heart. Be a good little girl and do what you are told, and you will be as right as rain in no time.'

'*No! You can't leave me here!*' Victoria cried as she

grabbed his coat. '*I'll do anything you or my mother wants but don't leave me here!*'

'Come on, missy, none of your whinging – into that washroom with you,' the Boxer said.

The two attendants grabbed her and with the help of the doctor they managed to shove her into the washroom. She tried to escape and received an unmerciful clout across the face from one of them.

'They will take good care of her, doctor,' Mrs Burns said. 'Come on now, I have some tea and sandwiches ready in my office. I sent Kitty down to the kitchen – they will fix her something there and Johnny is gone out to sort out your car. You must be exhausted after that journey.'

Victoria could hear her shoes clip-clopping down the hall, as they chatted as if they had just left her in to have her hair done. She could hear him thanking her.

'You are too good, Mrs Burns. She is a handful – her poor mother is beside herself.'

The scowling attendant shut the door.

'Take off your clothes and get into the shower. There is some soap there. Make sure you wash every part of yourself, or we will,' the Boxer instructed sourly.

Victoria was shaking with fear and with the cold.

'*Take them off!*'

Slowly she began to peel off her clothes. She was terrified of what could happen if she didn't. She put her hand protectively to her stomach.

'You foolish girl, could you not keep the lad off you? Well, he won't get to you in here.'

The water was almost cold and Victoria thought she would faint with the shock of it – her body was completely numb by the end of it.

'Right, put these clothes on now.' The Boxer threw a faded nightdress and slippers at her and shoved her own clothes into a bag.

'How long will I be here for?'

The smaller one scowled at her. 'It will depend on how you behave. I would advise you to stop struggling and accept your fate, missy, if you ever want to see a blue sky again. It is very easy to shut a door and keep the problem under lock and key. You will get nothing for fighting. Already we've been told to lock you up in a cell. Take my advice and stop struggling.'

'What about my baby?'

'What about it?'

'Will it be okay? They're not going to harm it?'

'You will stay here till 'tis your time. When the baby is born it will be taken from you. They will find a home for it or send it to Tralee to St Joseph's. Either way, you can wash your hands of it.'

Victoria stared at her in horror and disbelief.

The attendant then took a scissors and cut off Victoria's hair in one big swoop. It fell to the floor.

Victoria was too shocked to say anything.

'If you play by the rules you can return and leave all this sorry business behind you,' said the Boxer. 'I am sure your family will have a good story to cover it up. You come from a well-to-do family – Protestants, I believe. I am sure there will be a match of your own creed, that is if they manage to keep this quiet. If people find out about you though, you will have no hope. So, button that trap now. Your mother has control over what happens. She could decide that she doesn't want you home at all, plenty leave the problem here forever. I have seen girls locked up here until they go out to that Cross on the hill, no coffins needed. One size bag fits all. So, do as you are bid, or this will be your home for good or you might be bussed up to Saint Joseph's and, believe me, this will seem like heaven to that. Don't worry, they will give you tablets to help you forget about this baby business. But be warned and stop fighting. Now follow me and stop struggling or I will give you something to knock the fight out of you and I certainly can't promise that it is safe for that baby you're carrying.'

The small bed almost took up all the room in the windowless cell. A fading orange bulb hung from the ceiling. There was a canvas-like material on the walls. Tea and bread were left in and then the cell was bolted until the following morning.

No one could hear the retching of her insides, how she cried for her mother to come for her, how she cried for Canice and most of all how she cried that her baby would not be stolen from her. The smell of the insides of her stomach filled her nostrils, there was no getting away from it.

She eventually fell asleep into a dark nightmare. Canice was shouting for her. He was in a boat. She could see a baby, she was running towards the baby and trying to reach it – she almost made it and then she saw her mother – at first, she looked kindly at her but when she saw Canice her mother turned into a witch with different heads. Then the baby and Canice were gone and there was no one left. Victoria was shouting for someone to help her. She was somewhere dark and grey and then she awoke, cold, frightened and very much alone.

CHAPTER 21

Kilbride
2018

'I found some old files down in the basement yesterday – there may be something about Victoria in them,' Ruby said as Lainey and Catherine got into the car. 'Call over later and we can go through them, when nobody is about.'

'I think I'll have a lie-down after lunch, Lainey, so go ahead,' Catherine said.

'Surprised you went down to the basement, Ruby – thought it was a bit scary down there?' Lainey said.

'It was, but needs must and all that. There is so much stuff down there, a bit of a treasure trove, as long as you don't mind dust. Grandfather is heading out for lunch to a friend, so he will be gone for a few hours.'

'Great, see you then,' Lainey replied.

They drove away.

'Well, what did you make of all that?' Lainey asked Catherine who was putting on dark glasses.

She sat back in the car as if thinking about her answer. 'Ruby seems nice, but what is the story with her clothes? My goodness, she lives in London, where shopping is to die for. She looks like a college student. A poor one! She must be at least in her thirties.'

173

'Not everyone dresses up, Mom. That's not what I was asking you. What did you make of Uncle Edward?'

'Whatever secrets he knows, he sure is keeping quiet about them. I have no idea why Ruby does not just ask him straight out. Did he have another sister? Who is the baby in the grave? It's not that complicated. It shouldn't be all such a mystery.'

'Ruby is worried she will upset him.'

'Same old story – we could never ask Edith all these years in case we upset her. When will it all end?' Catherine shook her head.

'Look, Ruby is going to talk to him – we just wanted him to adjust to having us here first. He is pretty weak-looking, Mom.'

'I am just tired of it all. We have come halfway across the world – the least we deserve is the truth. Why did Edith leave and never come back? Simple! Maybe she was just not bothered and that's all there is to it.'

'You know that's not true! You heard her talk of Kilbride and Kilbride House, it meant so much to her. Something stopped her from coming back.'

'Maybe I don't care anymore. I'm sorry, Lainey, but I think this is a mistake. Yes, I grew up hearing about this mystical land and a house that sounded like an enchanted fairy tale, but rather like any fairy tale we couldn't go there. It was a story that she retold and retold. It is a beautiful house, more than just beautiful. My whole life I wondered what it would be like to see Kilbride House – now, well, it doesn't really matter anymore. While we are on the subject, I really don't want to have to sit through any more niceties with an uncle that I have nothing to do with. I refuse to. I will stay for a few days but then I am

174

going back. That's all we had to do, as was stated in the will.'

'Is that all you care about?'

'That's not fair, Lainey – the last place in the world I want to be is here in Kilbride. For whatever reason it shut the door on me and my mother as much as my mother shut the door on it. But you are my daughter and I did not want you to be here alone – that's why I came, if you really want to know. Also, I wanted to tell you something. I should have told you years ago, but we were all so long living a lie that we never did. But no more lies.'

'What are you talking about? Lies? What lies?'

Catherine took a deep breath. 'I never knew Claude my father – he died when I was only two. But he left us everything. Because of him I had a wonderful and privileged upbringing in New York. But here's the thing. Claude was not my biological father. Edith had me before she came to Ireland. I was a baby when I arrived in New York with my mother.'

'*What!*'

'I know. I have no idea why we kept all this from you. It seems silly now, but Mother did not tell me until I was twenty-one.'

Lainey stopped the car.

'Why on earth did you not see fit to tell me?'

'Look, we didn't – there's no point in crying over it now.'

'I am not crying over it, I am just mad as hell about it! Why on earth keep it such a secret? Well, now we know why Edith left Ireland. Because she was pregnant out of wedlock. Who the hell is my grandfather then and your father?'

'I don't know.'

'What do you mean, you don't know? Did she not tell you?'

'She met a boy who was travelling through Kilbride. He was a singer. She lost touch. I don't think he was even Irish.'

'And you're telling me this almost casually! I feel sick. What the hell else have you all kept from me?'

'Look, yes, she left Ireland because she was a single mom. Maybe that was the only reason, but I always thought that that was only part of it, to be honest. I have no idea what, but that old man knows. I don't even know if I want to know. Claude gave us respectability ever since. As far as I'm concerned, he was my father. I don't need another.'

'All the years that I lived with Edith! How could she keep all this from me?'

'Oh, Lainey, get over it, it happened a lot in the past. Edith was lucky she met Claude.'

'But times changed – surely she could have come back here?'

'Well, as I said there is more to it, I am sure of it, but I am not sure I care to know what.'

'Do you think that is why she wanted us to come here, to find out something about your father?'

'I have no idea why she wanted us to come. I was so mad when I heard what she had asked of us. For Christ sake, why now? I am over sixty years of age – if she wanted me to have a connection to Ireland, it's just a little late.' She looked at Lainey. 'Are you okay? I'm sorry I never told you before. Sometimes things are buried in the past and it suits everyone to leave them there.'

'It still does not explain the other sister and the grave.'

'Oh God, it's all so eerie.'

'Look, I am going to head back to Kilbride House,' said Lainey. 'Let's have dinner later and try to just enjoy being here.'

'Of course, but no more visits to Kilbride House for me. It's too late. That door is closed.'

As promised, Lainey arrived over to Kilbride House to go through the documents that Ruby had found. She had them all laid out on the large kitchen table.

'You look tired, Lainey.'

'I am, to be honest. I keep having a recurring dream ever since I arrived in Kerry. Since that first night in Tralee actually. In the dream there is a river and I am frightened and trying to get out. It's possibly something to do with the long-haul travel. It does feel a bit weird.'

'Possibly the change of air. Hopefully the dreams will pass.'

'We'll be forever going through all these documents,' Lainey remarked. 'I thought lots of stuff got burnt in some mysterious fire years ago?'

'Well, that's what I was always told. Very convenient when you think about it. But yesterday, I braved it down to the basement. Lots of old remnants of years ago, even some wine would you believe? Anyway, amongst the clutter, I found all these documents. I went through a few – they seem to belong to Grandfather's parents, my great-grandparents. They date back as far as 1930.'

'Wonderful.'

'I have also trawled the internet looking at data, but without some dates it's hard to find out much. We can manually try and find the old records – there is a place that holds them all. But we might look here first, see if anything turns up.'

'I gather you have not said anything to Edward?'

'No. He was so shaken when he saw your mother, it was as if he could hardly believe it. He offered no explanation. He was not even going to go out for lunch as arranged, but eventually I persuaded him. His friend will take him for a drink afterwards and then he will come home and go for a nap straight away, so we have the kitchen clear until evening, when Cecilia is due in. I had planned on having dinner here and asking your mum, but with Grandfather acting all strange ...'

'To be honest, he's not the only one. Mom is peeved with the whole situation. I doubt she would ever have come here, only she was worried about what would be uncovered and how it might affect me. She has very little time for our hidden past. The theatre is her life.'

'I kind of gathered that. She is incredibly elegant. I can see her as an actress.'

'I was shocked when she did agree to take leave from it and come here, but I think she will cut her holiday short. If she had her way, we would be on the first plane back to JFK.'

'You feel differently?' Ruby asked.

Lainey thought about it. It was difficult to articulate as she didn't particularly understand it herself. She felt drawn to Kilbride, the village, the house, the peninsula. She needed to absorb what her mother had told her about her grandfather too. It was all very intense.

'There is something within me that connects to this place – perhaps it's from listening to all of what

Grandma told me and maybe what she didn't tell me. Even the islands, the Blaskets. I really want to see them and photograph them.'

'Do you know that there is a great body of literature from the island people and about them? They were poor in many senses but rich in other ways. I will get you some books. There are some biographies and autobiographies written too.'

'I would like that. Come on, we have lots to get through.'

They made some tea and got to work.

There were tons of receipts and invoices and other papers to do with the estate – some of them were fascinating and it was difficult not to linger over them, but the two women tried to be disciplined and press on.

'*Bingo!*'

'What is it?' Ruby asked, excited.

Lainey held up an envelope.

'This is addressed to Gertrude Goulding – wasn't that Uncle Edward's and Grandma's mother?'

'Yes, it was.'

Lainey took out a letter.

'What do have you there?' Ruby asked.

Lainey went white as she read the contents.

'What is it, Lainey?'

'It's an admissions letter for a Victoria Goulding. It is sent from Marlborough Asylum for the Insane. It's dated 1954.'

'Oh my God! So that's what happened to her! The baby in the graveyard was hers.'

'I don't like where this is going, Ruby.' But she realised she felt some relief. It looked like the baby wasn't Edith's after all.

'We have to find out. Keep looking.'

They rummaged through all the files, now even more motivated, but found nothing else.

Ruby switched on her laptop and looked up the asylum.

'It says here that the name was changed to St Ita's Psychiatric Hospital in the eighties and it was closed completely a few years ago. It's about an hour-and-a-half drive from here.'

'You have to ask Edward. He obviously knows.'

'Okay, I will. This is what he is hiding. They hid her away. It often happened, even in the fifties. The baby was hers and it obviously died. She was not married. It was a different country.'

'But they hardly locked her in a mental institution because she was pregnant!' Lainey exclaimed.

'It used to happen – it really did.'

'But maybe she was unstable. There must be more to it.'

'Gosh, I never expected this,' said Ruby. 'She was admitted the year before the baby was buried.'

'It's all getting very dark and horrible,' Lainey said.

Ruby's phone rang and she answered it. She looked shocked when she finished speaking.

'It's Grandfather. He's had a bit of a turn and they have taken him to hospital.'

'Oh no! Is he okay?'

'I think so, just a bit shaken. I have to go to him.'

'Look, I'll tidy everything up. And don't worry, I won't say anything to anyone about what we found. But should I go with you?'

'No, I'd better go alone. I'll ring you as soon as I know how he is.'

180

'Oh, Ruby, do you think all this has been too much for him?'

'Look, maybe it was. We'll just have to leave him out of it for now anyway.'

Ruby grabbed her coat and keys and left.

Lainey tidied up all the documents as best as she could and had another cup of tea. She really was tired. These dreams were starting to drive her crazy and it was having a huge effect on her sleeping pattern. The previous night it had taken her ages to calm down afterwards.

Ruby later rang to say that Edward was fine. He had felt weak and his neighbour was worried and had called an ambulance, but they were keeping him in for a few hours just to be on the safe side and Ruby was going to stay with him. Catherine was happy in the hotel, she was reading a play that Juniper had mailed over to her.

So, Lainey was free for the afternoon.

She knew there was one place she could go. She googled it on her phone and searched up Google maps. She could be there by about quarter to four if she left now. Without even thinking any more about it, she grabbed her keys and left. She headed for what was once Marlborough Asylum.

CHAPTER 22

Marlborough Asylum
1954

Days turned to weeks and to months. She was moved out of the cell to a dormitory. At first, she wished she was back in the cell, but slowly she adjusted. It was the crying at night that was the worst. Women crying into their pillows and screaming. Usually it was well past midnight when she might catch a few hours' sleep. She needed it for the day ahead. She had the job of making all the sixty beds. If they had urinated on the sheets, they had to be washed and put out to dry.

Some of the patients were deranged and some lost, beyond help. Others seemed perfectly normal yet like her they were here, trapped. Some were having *treatment*. This terrified her. They arrived back disorientated as if a piece of them died every time. A bus arrived every so often and randomly patients were loaded up, bussed to a different asylum. Some were released and their families took them home. Some that were released were readmitted shortly afterwards.

The long corridors were where Victoria could see the real sadness of the people there. They constantly walked up and down, going nowhere. She liked Ciarán, a farmer from Kenmare who had never been out of his own village in his lifetime. He had developed dementia. He had no children and his relatives could not care for him, so he was committed. Seamus was born there – at sixty-five years of age, he had never witnessed a different world. It was his home and the fear of leaving it kept him there.

One day a young girl who could only have been about fifteen was put in the bed beside Victoria in the middle of the night. She was so upset that Victoria had got out and knelt by her bed.

'It's okay, it's okay,' she soothed. 'My name is Victoria.'

She had never seen a face that looked more like what she imagined an angel to look like. The girl was so pale that her skin was white. Her pale-blonde hair, now cut short, was all soft and curly. Her big frightened blue eyes under long fair lashes were full of tears as she looked out at Victoria. She tried to speak, but she couldn't. Eventually she calmed down.

'What's your name?'

'Alice.'

She spoke so softly Victoria could barely hear her.

'Hello, Alice. I know how frightening it all is. But I am here, and I will try to help you, I promise.'

Alice grabbed her hand and held on to it as if her life depended on it.

Luckily, they gave her the job of making the beds with Victoria. At mealtimes she sat with her and followed her every move. She was taken away for treatment and Victoria knelt and prayed that she would survive. Afterwards, it seemed they had killed part of her. She stopped crying all the time and instead stared into space.

Victoria tried to get through to her, but she knew she was losing her.

'I am not like you, Victoria, I'm not strong like you.'

'Yes, you are. I will get out some day and I promise I will come back for you. I promise.'

'I see things. That's why they put me in here.'

'What kind of things?' Victoria whispered.

Alice looked up and stared at the ceiling. 'I see a light, a beautiful light. I know it's the angels guiding me – they are so full of love and wonder. I should not have told anyone. That is why they put me here. Now the light is dim, but I can still see them.'

Alice looked upwards as if in a trance.

Victoria's heart broke for her. She was like a little angel herself and here she was being treated like a criminal.

'Keep looking at the light, Alice – remember there is beauty in the world, outside there is a place of wonder and we will see it again, I promise.'

Patients worked. There was a large vegetable garden, a farm, a launderette, a bakery and a kitchen. It was like a small town for the many patients.

Victoria knew she was lucky so far. Other than locking her up, they had not given her any treatment because of the baby, but she knew that once the baby was born that could change – they had talked about making her forget. She could not sleep with worry about what would happen to the baby. They would not tell her any more than the attendant in the washroom did on that first day. That the baby would be taken from her. This gave her nightmares that made the sheets that she slept in

184

so wet that they looked like they had been steeped in a river in the mornings.

She had no visitors from that first day that Doctor Ford had brought her there. This part overwhelmed her – how could her family forget her? Where were Edward and Edith? Her mother had never visited. She had no idea if Canice was still in jail. She had no contact from her former life – it was as if she had no family. Sometimes she had a dream that she was back in Kilbride House, snug in her bed listening to the lambs in the early spring morning. She could take a ride out on the cliffs, lash across the beaches and feel the wind beneath her. Then she would hear a bell that signalled breakfast, work hours or sleep and her reality became almost unbearable.

At times she felt it was all too much, she couldn't take it anymore, but then she got a kick in her belly reminding her of this other life. How different to what they had planned! Canice, where was he? She feared what they might have done to him? She couldn't bear to think about it. Edward had spoken to her through the door that last night in Kilbride. He had said he was going to go to the gardaí and he would try and have Canice released. He said he would do everything he could to help. Yet she had never heard from them. Did they even know where she was? How could her mother do what she had done?

The baby came early, kicking and screaming, a girl. She thought she would die, her body in pain beyond belief. The baby was perfectly healthy. She only saw her for a short while, a tiny baby with a tuft of silken red hair. She tried to breathe in her smell, the curve of her perfect rosebud mouth, her tiny hands. The woman who had helped with the birth was kind and told her that she would look after the baby. She was not allowed to give her a name. In that precious half hour, she tried to memorise everything about her – she wanted to always remember what she looked like, her beautiful baby. When they took her she wanted to die. She screamed and pleaded with them to bring her back. When she awoke the next morning, panic overwhelmed her. She tried to get out, but her feet were tied to the bed. She kicked and screamed to see her baby. Her breasts pained her. They gave her more medication.

'Please bring her back to me, please, I beg you, don't take her!' she implored.

She was put back in the cell with the canvas on the walls. She had no idea how much time elapsed before she was let out. It could have been hours, days or even weeks. At times she wondered had it all been a dream? Was there a baby at all? She accepted the tablets that they gave her. They could kill her if they wanted to.

More time elapsed. Eventually she was taken out of the cell and brought back to the dormitory. She barely spoke to anyone except Alice who seemed to have faded like a flower that was never allowed any light. Alice held her hand and got a wet cloth for her head when the bad dreams and the sweating became too much.

Victoria made the beds and in the late morning she was put to work in the kitchen washing buckets of vegetables brought in from the farm.

'Work is the best therapy for the mind,' the psychiatrist told her on her next consultation.

'When can I leave?'

'When we are sure you are well. I am not convinced that you are yet.'

'My baby? Where is my baby?'

'You must trust us, Victoria. Your baby is fine, but you must try and forget that you ever had a baby. Put it out of your mind. I will have to prescribe more treatment for you if you don't.'

'Is my baby still here? Please just tell me that.'

'I think it's best that we don't discuss the baby anymore. It's for your own good. I am due to write a report for your mother about how you are doing. I am disappointed to hear that you still have a long way to go.'

She learned to numb her pain when she was talking to anyone to try and avoid any more treatment or medication.

At times she had started to believe them – perhaps she was mad, and this was the best place for her. Her mother was protecting her. They could not do this to her if she was sane, she must be mad. She was in a madhouse after all. They wanted her to forget. Had her poor mind made it all up? Canice? The baby? Was it just part of her mad mind? A hallucination? Edward and Edith – did she even have a brother and a sister? If she had, surely they would come and visit her, but it seemed she had nobody in the world to care whether she lived or died. The doctor talked of her mother protecting her. Could this be so?

But it was Kilbride House that saved her from believing she was mad. She remembered everything about it. How the ivy wrapped itself around the walls, how the staircase looked at Christmas with garlands of red holly

tangled around it. The basement that was the best hiding
place in the world. The kitchen where Bessie always
spoiled her with sweet cake and hot milk. She knew there
was a house called Kilbride and she knew it had been her
home. Slowly it came back to her. She could see the
silken water at Slea Head. She dreamed of Canice.
Sometimes just before she awoke she could see the baby
and almost feel her warm little body close to her, then she
would awake delirious and she would receive more
medication. But even with the treatment, part of her
mind remained strong. There was hope in her that she
was not mad.

She watched the stars at night through a small
window and marvelled at how the world was still the
same beautiful place despite what was happening. If Alice
was awake, she would drag her over to the tiny window
to look at the stars and the moon. How beautiful they
looked!

She started to do everything that they wanted her to.
She never mentioned the baby and obeyed all the rules
without question. She gave no trouble. The therapy
stopped. They continued with the drugs but secretly she
avoided them as much as she could, mashing them up in
her pocket and mixing them with the water as she
washed the vegetables, then throwing them out unnoticed
in the dirty vegetable water. Slowly, her mind began to
come back to her and with that the realisation of what
had happened. She had been captured and locked up like
an animal and her baby stolen from her.

A new girl called Mary arrived into the kitchen one
morning. She was employed by the hospital.

188

'That witch Mrs Cashman need not think I gave up a good job to come skivvy here for her. She may be the boss of the kitchen but I am meant to be a trainee cook not a vegetable-scraper,' Mary complained.

Normally the staff would not dream of talking to the patients. The patients were under strict instructions not to talk. Just work. But Mary was ignoring all the rules. Luckily, they were not overheard. She had begun work that day as a new employee and was working alongside Victoria.

'Where did you work before?' Victoria was thrilled to talk to someone who was free.

'Oh, in one of the big houses in Kenmare. Decent people but I wanted to learn more, and this job sounded promising, but I have my doubts.'

'To be honest, I can't see why anyone would willingly come here to work.'

'Well, the money is much better, and they have promised me good training. My employer has told me to come back if I don't like it. So that was good of her. I will give it a couple of weeks and if things don't improve I'm out of here.'

'I wish I could say the same,' Victoria whispered.

'No chit-chat, Victoria, concentrate on your work!' Mrs Cashman shouted.

Mary grinned and made a face behind the head cook. Victoria had to stifle a giggle. It felt good to giggle – she had forgotten how to.

Mary had a round face with a big smile and was forever singing as she worked. Victoria liked her. Unlike some of the other kitchen staff she did not use her superiority over them. She looked forward to the late morning when there was a chance to have a whisper with her.

One afternoon when they were washing buckets of turnips alone in the scullery, Mary discreetly slipped a tiny note into her hand.

'Destroy it after you read it,' she whispered. 'Do *not* on *any* account let anyone see it.'

It was almost two hours before Victoria had a minute on her own. She took out the note, wondering what it could be about.

Victoria, I am from Kenmare. I used to work for Ingrid's family, the girl who is courting your brother. Your brother and your sister want me to help you to escape with your daughter. She is still here, but probably not for long. I will give you instructions tomorrow. We are planning it for tomorrow night.

Victoria could barely breathe. They had not forgotten her.

CHAPTER 23

She went through her duties the same as any other day. She dared not do anything different in case anyone suspected. She had not slept all night trying to imagine how on earth they would escape. She lay awake for hours, listening to the rain pounding down incessantly outside. She wondered if it would be dry for her escape the following night. Would rain make it difficult or would it be a mercy, shielding her from being seen?

Her baby was still here. She had tried to imagine for so long what she would look like. The memory of her was embedded in her mind. The sweet baby smell that had stayed with her and woke her up in the middle of the night, imagining she was close and the unbearable heartbreak of knowing that she was gone. She could hardly breathe with longing to see her. Would she remember her at all? What had they called her? They had not given her away, not yet. She was still safe.

How would they escape? How on earth would she manage to escape this prison with her baby? It seemed unimaginable, but she had to believe that they would.

It rained all day and Victoria worried about taking a

very young baby – *her* baby – out in it. She prayed for the rain to stop. She prayed for God to rescue her and her baby from this hellish place. She prayed that she would not fail – because, if she did and lost her daughter, it would be the end. She would not be able to continue to live.

True to her word, when Victoria was washing a bucket of carrots in the scullery, Mary came up to the sink beside her and shoved another note into her hand.

'Quickly – put it inside your clothes before anyone can see it,' she whispered.

Victoria pushed it inside her dress, finished washing the vegetables as quickly as she could and returned the kitchen.

'When you finish there, you can help with the washing-up – some of the patients have come down with some sickness and I am short,' Mrs Cashman instructed Victoria. 'I have no idea how I am meant to run a kitchen on so little staff. Mary, you will have to do extra hours tomorrow. I know you asked for the day off, but I am too short-staffed.'

'Very well, Mrs Cashman, but don't forget you owe me a day from last week too,' Mary replied.

'I'm sure you will remind me. Come on now, girls, no slacking today. We have loads of work to do.'

Victoria was exhausted by the time she was finished and asked if she could go sit in the day room for half an hour before dinner.

'Very well, off you go,' Mrs Cashman replied.

'See you tomorrow.'

'Tomorrow will be another long day if I am short, so make sure you get a good sleep and that goes for all of you.'

Victoria took off her apron and folded it, then put it back neatly on the apron pile. She was terrified that Mrs Cashman would hear the crunch of paper underneath her brown dress. She slipped away as quickly as she could.

There were only a few in the dayroom and they were asleep. There was a little woman called Statia from Tralee who sat for hours with a doll she spent all day holding as you would a baby. She rocked it to and fro and sang a lullaby. Hours could go by and Statia would still be rocking the doll. Her hands were so bad with arthritis that they pained her terribly, but she would never put the doll down. At times she slept, as she did now, but her little hands never let the doll fall, cocooned beside her as she slept.

One attendant was slouching around, keeping half an eye on the inmates, obviously bored.

'What are you doing here?' she asked Victoria.

'Mrs Cashman agreed that I could, as I have worked since morning in the kitchen. I might read a book if that's alright?'

The attendant shrugged her shoulders. 'Suit yourself.'

Victoria picked the largest book that she could and sat far from the attendant. She was desperate to read the note but couldn't take the risk. Then suddenly the attendant walked out. Victoria expelled the breath she was holding. Then she discreetly took the note and flattened it on one of the pages. If the attendant came back in and approached her, she would turn the page and hide it. There were two sheets of paper. Her heart was beating so fast she was sure it would be heard by someone in the room. She took a deep breath and began to read the notes.

One was a map of the asylum, showing clearly how their plan tonight would work. She was to go to the bathroom of the dormitory at three in the morning. There was another door in the bathroom, but it was always locked. Mary would unlock it. This would lead Victoria into another room. The door would be left open and she could escape down the long corridor. This was where she could run into trouble if any of the night staff were around. But they normally took a break at five past three. Mary knew where the babies were, and she would grab the baby and meet Victoria at the bottom of one of the corridors. There was another door of entry that was used when they wanted to bring vegetables in from the garden. There was a wall almost surrounding the asylum but there were three gates and Mary had a key to one of them. Victoria would take the baby and go to the gate marked on the map. She would then open the gate and find herself on the river bank. Edward would be at the other side with a car. The river was fairly shallow at that point though a bit deeper at the middle. As she would be carrying the baby, she should not attempt to cross alone but should wait for Edward to wade into the river to guide her across.

She was so engrossed in the notes that she didn't realise there was a man standing over her. He was a new patient.

'*I want that book!*' he hollered.

She closed the book with the sheets in it. 'I will give it to you in a minute.'

'*Now!*' He started to cry louder and tried to grab the book.

The book opened, and the sheets flew out. As quick as

she could she grabbed the papers, dropped the book to the floor and ran from the room to the bathroom. She went into one of the toilets. There were no locks on the toilet doors of course. Her heart was frantic in her chest. She was terrified she would be caught. She held the papers in shaking hands and memorised everything on them, praying she was missing nothing, then shredded the papers. When she came back into the kitchen, she passed the fire and threw the shredded paper into it. It was burnt in a second.

Dinner was about to start. She normally sat beside Alice but she wasn't there. Perhaps she was delayed with the hens. In the afternoons, Alice looked after the vast number of hens that they had. She cleaned out the henhouses and made sure the eggs were collected and brought to the kitchen. Victoria hoped she was just delayed and prayed that was the reason she was absent. She was either late or gone for more treatment.

When Alice didn't arrive she realised it was the latter. Victoria could barely eat, thinking of her. Alice was such an innocent. The anger built up inside her, thinking of poor Alice in the heat tub or maybe some other experimental thing.

She saw Mrs Burns walking around, making sure everyone was where they should be, and the words were out before she could stop them.

'Why can't you just leave Alice alone? Did you ever think that maybe she's not mad and that she *can* see things – maybe God can see you all too and what you are doing to us!'

Mrs Burns glared at her. Nobody dared say anything.

'Watch your tongue and get out of this dinner hall! Apologise now or believe me you will be sorry.'

The anger was simmering deep down in Victoria's very soul. But she knew she had to calm down, or she could ruin everything. She had no choice, no choice at all but to apologise. She could be locked up and all chances of her escape gone.

'Sorry, Mrs Burns, I am very sorry. I have no idea what came over me.'

'*Go to the dormitory now!*' roared one of the attendants at Victoria.

She got up quickly and left the room. Please God, don't let them lock me up, she prayed. She was terrified of what she was doing. They would lock her up for ever if she got caught and she would never see her baby again. She had no idea how old she was. She had lost track of time.

But she had so wanted to see Alice, to make sure she was alright. She hated having to leave her. Alice would hardly survive in here on her own. If only she could take her too! But she would come back for her. When she was safe, and her baby was safe from this godforsaken place, she would come back for her.

She asked the attendant where Alice was. They had put her in a cell until she recovered from the treatment. God knows what they had done to her this time. Some of the patients were so unwell afterwards that they never recovered. She just wanted to hug her and tell her to stay strong and keep believing in the light.

One night, when for once the whole ward was asleep, Victoria had awoken and Alice was standing in the middle of the room, staring out of the window. There were no lights on, only an oil lamp. She was smiling and staring as if she could see something. She was singing what sounded like a hymn, in a whisper. Alice had a voice like an angel whispering. It was as if she was in a trance. Victoria was afraid to disturb her. She knew that this was the reason that Alice was locked up. Someone had thought she was mad because she seemed to be singing at something that was not there. She was holding out her hands and singing. Victoria had heard of apparitions. She knew that Alice believed that she was seeing something ethereal. She had told Victoria that it appeared like a light, the most beautiful light, and colours that you could not ever imagine. The light changed from dark to light to colours so tranquil that she couldn't explain them, or what colour, but when she looked at them it was as if they wrapped her up in an embrace.

Victoria had looked out and had seen only darkness but, looking at Alice, she believed that maybe she did see this light. It was as if Alice was too precious for this world.

She had gently walked her back and put her into her bed, before any of the attendants saw her and maybe locked up her again.

Every minute that night was like an hour. Eventually all the patients went to sleep and at ten to three she tiptoed to the bathroom. The door was unlocked. She could barely see where she was going but she saw the opening and again followed the instructions and escaped through another door and then up the corridors. She had only her nightdress and slippers on. She was afraid to bring anything else in case she was caught, and they would know immediately if she had anything with her. There was no one on the corridors. She pushed herself flat against a wall when she heard chatter, but then it died away. Eventually she came to the point where she was to meet Mary. There was no one there yet. She felt sick she was so nervous. Eventually she heard light footsteps and Mary appeared, looking petrified, carrying a sleeping baby. She put her finger to her lips in warning. She handed the baby to Victoria. Victoria could not believe she was again holding her baby. She knew instantly that it was her. She must be about two months old and she had a shock of red hair. She was wrapped tightly in a blue blanket.

'Oh God, she's beautiful!' Victoria whispered, her voice cracking.

'Go and for pity's sake be quiet. Never mention my name if you get caught. Here is the key. Hold it tight and for God's sake don't drop it. Run, your brother will be waiting for you. It has stopped raining but be careful when you come to the river – it's been raining so heavily all day that the water will be high. But your brother will be there to help you cross. Go!'

'Thank you,' Victoria whispered with tears running down her cheeks.

'Hush – run, for goodness' sake, run!'

'Alice – look after Alice for me. Please check on Alice for me – she works with the hens – please.'

'*Run, run!*' Mary said hurriedly.

Victoria held the sleeping baby close to her as she tiptoed down another corridor near to the kitchen. She found the door that Mary had left unlocked. Mercifully it did not creak as she went out and a minute later she was out of the building, the freezing air hitting her. She adjusted the blanket on the baby and made her way towards the wall. She walked for a quarter of a mile along the wall and then found the gate that Mary had drawn on the map. The key opened it and at last her heartbeat began to slow. She was well away now.

The moon was shining on the river, making it look like glass. She looked for any sign of Edward. There was no one there yet. She waited for a few minutes and the baby began to wake up and whimper. She could feel panic engulf her. What if Edward was delayed or even prevented from coming?

Minutes passed, the baby began to cry and Victoria sobbed with her.

No Edward. No help. Perhaps it was up to her alone to save her baby from this terrible life?

She could be pursued at any moment. She had to get across that river.

The water looked calm enough. Mary had said it was shallow but that it might be full after the rains. She looked down the river and saw that a tree had fallen across it, reaching more than halfway to the other side. That could provide something to hold on to.

She walked down to where the tree lay.

Holding her baby as tightly as she could and with one hand on the tree-trunk, she waded into the river. It felt like ice on her legs and the baby began to wail as water splashed up.

There was still no sign of Edward. She pushed on, fear threatening to overwhelm her. She tried to concentrate on the task. The baby was screaming now, her blanket and clothes well and truly sodden. The water was almost up to Victoria's shoulders now and holding the baby above water was becoming harder as the current became stronger against her legs. She lost her slippers to the current.

She was almost halfway when suddenly her feet were barely touching the bottom and she began to lose her balance. She grabbed the tree-trunk and found her footing again.

She gazed at the opposite bank and desperately began to wonder if she could swim the rest of the way. She couldn't, not without submerging her baby.

She must go on.

Heart pounding, she grasped the tree-trunk. She took one step forward and the current swept her feet off the bottom. Terrified, she hung on to the tree and grasped her baby desperately.

Then there was a flash of light and she heard a car engine.

Please God, let it be Edward! I beg you, Lord!

The baby screamed. The freezing water was now covering her little body. What if her head went under?

The light was gone and there was no further sound of a car.

Had she imagined it? Please, God, no!

Then a bobbing light appeared in the darkness. Bobbing closer. A torch.

Her heart lifted, tears flowing down her face. Had they really come, had they not forgotten her? Was she going to be rescued?

The current was strong. Her arms were so tired trying to hold on. She just had to hold on for another little while. She would not let her baby go. She would never let her go.

'*Victoria!*'

'*Victoria! We are here!*'

She could hear them now, clearly across the water. A man's voice and a woman's. Young voices. It was Edward and Edith. They were shining their torch on her. She tried to call back, but all her strength was needed to just hold on. The cold was barely allowing her to breathe. The water was like a hundred-thousand knives biting into her. Her baby had stopped screaming and that frightened her. Gazing down at her little face, it looked blue in the moonlight. Her eyes were closed. Even the cold itself could kill her.

But Edward and Edith were here. Her emotions were so high that if she called her brother's and sister's names, she would collapse with the depth of her emotion and gratitude that they had not forgotten her. Her breathing was getting very heavy with the cold, they were telling her to hold on, they were coming to get her. She was safe.

CHAPTER 24

Marlborough Asylum
2018

There was a narrow river that curved its way around the large high mottled limestone wall of the grounds like a moat. For some reason a shiver ran up her spine at the sight of it, but before she could analyse her reaction she had crossed the bridge over the river and saw a sign lying on the ground. It said **Saint Ita's Psychiatric Hospital**.

She drove through great iron gates and took a deep breath at her first sight of the immense redbrick building that once had been the Marlborough Asylum for the Insane. An austere redbrick building with several floors and many chimneys.

It was the windows, many of which were broken, that struck her the most. She imagined the ghosts of the people who had been incarcerated in this intimidating building looking out at her. A shiver went up her spine as she thought of her Aunt Victoria. What had it been like for her? She must have been only about sixteen or seventeen. Why had she been committed by her mother? Why such a mystery? Where was she now?

She drove up the avenue and parked near the building. She walked towards the entrance door which was, to her surprise, slightly ajar. There was a notice in black and red saying: **No Entry.** But she pushed the door open. It creaked as she tentatively walked in. The briars and ivy had begun to grow in and curl around the broken windows. Carefully she walked the large hallway where black and white tiles had once covered the floors. They were damaged and faded now and mould had taken over between the tiles. An old broken wheelchair lay abandoned in the hall with a faded gown left on the back. Carefully she made her way down the large expanse of hall, stepping over broken pieces of threadbare furniture, faded books and a collection of items from yesteryear.

She walked into a large room, the walls crumbling, drapes mottled with damp barely hanging on the windows. Broken pictures on the floor and a yellowed ceiling. A box lying in the corner caught her eye. There was a book or ledger sitting on top. She stepped over a broken window and tripped. The box and book were full of dust, but inside she could see a holy picture, some rosary beads, slippers and a lipstick. Carefully she lifted the book and opened it. It was a photo album. A photo of two boys and a young girl sitting on a fence. The picture barely visible, one of the faces so faded, she could barely make it out. The next page was a wedding photograph. Was it belonging to a patient? A life abandoned in a box. Pigeons nestling in the rooftops startled her and she let out a scream, thinking there was someone there, following her. But there was no one there, she was alone in this forgotten place. She put the album back and tried to imagine what it must have been like to be here all those years ago. Was there anyone who could tell her? The ghosts of those who had walked these corridors were silent. An eerie feeling flooded through her. She was grateful to step back outside and into the late afternoon sunshine.

Around the back were small sheds, where old buckets, shovels, spades and forks lay rusted. There had obviously once been gardens, but they were now taken over by weeds and the land had descended into a marsh.

She studied a large majestic clock sitting high on one of the wings of the building. Only one hand remained. Time! Yet the people that were locked up here had had their time taken from them.

She walked around the grounds. There was no sign telling anyone that they couldn't. She noticed some sheds up a hill a good distance from the hospital.

She met a couple, a man and a woman out walking dogs. The dogs were scampering around. It was the ideal place to let them loose, with no one around.

'Excuse me, can you tell what is up there where all those sheds are?'

The couple were friendly and were glad to stop and chat. The man was in his sixties and seemed quite knowledgeable about the place.

'There used to be a farm up there. In the old days. They grew almost everything they ate and sold produce too. There is also an old mill. There is very little else up there.'

'Did you live around here?' Lainey asked, delighted to have found someone who seemed to know the place.

'A few miles away. I have lived here all my life.'

'The hospital or "asylum" as it was called then – can you tell me anything about it?'

'There was little we knew, to be honest. The locals called it "The Mental". Growing up, we were all afraid we would end up in "The Mental". It was very private – the patients were never outside the grounds. In later years you would see some of them out for a walk. But in the forties and fifties, although it was packed, nobody was ever allowed beyond the wall.'

'How come it was so busy those years?' Lainey asked curiously.

'It was easy to put people away, I suppose. I don't think they were all sick, God love them. Unwanted was more like it. It was somewhere to almost get rid of people. It was very industrial too. They had pigs and sold the meat and there was a launderette. Oh, somebody's pockets were lined from the poor souls locked up here. I'm afraid it's part of Ireland's dark past. It did improve though in later years and conditions were good, I'm told.'

'Did you know anyone who was in it?'

'I knew some people who worked there, but not the patients.' He shook his head.

The woman spoke up. 'Are you on holiday from the States?'

'Yes, but I think my aunt was here, in 1954. I'm not sure for how long. I thought by coming here I might be able to find out something.'

'It would be hard to find anyone who worked here that long ago – most are dead now,' the man said.

'She was committed, she didn't work here.'

'Oh!' The man shook his head again.

The woman pointed up the hill. 'There is a cemetery of course,' she said.

'Who was buried there?' Lainey asked.

'Lots of the patients. A few were brought home and buried where they were from, but most were left here and buried here. Unfortunately, there are no markings.'

'What do you mean?' Lainey asked.

'There is a large cross, and a little plaque. But they were all buried together.'

A feeling of dread possessed her. God forbid her poor aunt had died within those walls. But surely, if she did, her family would have taken her home and buried her? But then there would be a grave in Kilbride. Yet the baby was there.

'But how does anyone know who was buried here then?' Lainey asked.

'I don't think they do,' said the man. 'I'm sure there were records of some sort kept. But as it's closed now I'm not sure where they would be. I know of someone who traced someone through the National Trust and then the HSE. It is very difficult though. She had to prove she was related. It took years to find out and receive the records. Nothing was very transparent then. They were different times.'

'She should talk to Paddy Boyle,' said his wife.

'So she should.' He nodded at his wife and turned back to Lainey. 'There's a pub in the village. It's there for many years. John Boyle runs it, but his father Paddy lives with him. If there's anyone can tell you anything, it might be him. He's a nice old fella, and very sharp in the mind but he must be near ninety.'

'Thank you so much! I might just call in. Do you think that would be okay?'

'I would say Paddy Boyle would love a visit from a lovely American lady,' he said with a laugh.

They bade each other goodbye and Lainey walked up the hill. She saw the old abandoned outhouses that had obviously once been a farm. She walked on. She could see the mill and tried to imagine it when so many were there working on it. It lay silent now, with only a few pigeons nesting in it.

Then in a small shelter a few hundred yards away from everything was a large cross. She walked up to it, the final resting place of so many. There was a small plaque beside it.

In memory of all who were buried at Marlborough Hospital from 1925-1979. R.I.P.

A mass grave. Lainey said a silent prayer that if Victoria died, she was not buried here in this heart-breaking place. Lainey was not religious but she said another prayer for all the people who had been abandoned here and ultimately left to die and be buried in such a bleak depressing place.

Back in the car, she put on some music to try and lift her mood and set out for the village.

It was only a short drive. The village was small with a shop and two pubs. She could see a sign for Boyle's pub. It was a very old pub. A dog sat outside the entrance and Lainey had almost to jump over it to get in. Inside there were two men having a drink at the bar. It was surprisingly bright inside, with a fire blazing and tea lights twinkling from the mantelpiece.

'May I have a mineral water, please? Sparkling?'

If the barman thought it was odd to see an American woman on her own in his little pub, he made no comment.

'Ice?'

'Please.'

'Right. Nice evening.'

'It's lovely.'

'Are you on your holidays?'

'Well, yes. But I'm also looking for some information on the asylum. I have just come from there.'

'Oh, it's going to be up for sale.'

'Really?'

'Yes, it was only decided last night at a County Council meeting.'

'My goodness. Who would buy it?'

'No idea. My father thinks Trump might come over and buy it, make it into one of his hotels.' He grinned as he handed her the bottle and glass.

Lainey spotted an old man sitting in an armchair by the fire. She had not seen him at first. He was very elderly. She knew he must be the man she was looking for.

'Is that your father? Paddy Boyle?'

The barman grinned. 'Go and ask him, why don't you? See what he says.'

Lainey looked at the barman questioningly.

'Go on!' he said. 'Ask him who he is!'

Realising there was some kind of joke afoot, Lainey approached the old man.

'Excuse me? Are you Paddy Boyle?'

'It depends on who is asking. If you are anything to do with the taxman I am not Paddy Boyle. But if you are here to give me money, I most certainly am Paddy Boyle.'

Lainey laughed. 'I have nothing to do with tax. I am trying to trace someone who was committed to the asylum here in the fifties. I met a man walking his dogs earlier. He thought you might be able to help.'

'Because I am the oldest person in the village, I suppose. Probably Jim Doherty with those two mutts of dogs that he has. Retired now with feck all else to do but take walks with the Missus.'

'I didn't actually get his name,' Lainey replied, smiling.

'Oh, he's an auld busybody, always walking those dogs and finding out information. So he told you I could help. Thinks he's thirty himself, you know. But sit down, girl, and I'll be telling you.' He gestured to an armchair opposite him.

Lainey sat.

'So, you are looking for information about the Mental?' said Paddy.

'I don't think it's called that anymore, Dad,' said John Boyle from the bar.

'Sure that's what it was called – the Mental – no point in pretending that it wasn't.' said Paddy. 'Sure, we were all half terrified of the place when we were nippers. I used to buy some vegetables off the Mental when I had the shop. I would have known a few that worked there but, God, I would not really remember much about them. Sure, there were thousands of poor people went through the door and it's a lifetime ago.'

'It is. It looks so forgotten. I walked up to the cemetery – it's really bleak. One large mass grave.'

'Sure, there were plenty of people ended up there and it made no sense. I do remember seeing them working out in the fields when I collected the vegetables. Mostly men worked outside. Some were old, but they all worked plenty of hours. Then there was little fuss when they died. No one rushed back to bring them home to bury them. Sure, they were trying to get rid of them when they were alive. They hardly wanted them dead.'

'But surely some were actually sick?' Lainey asked.

'Look, it's not for me to say, but they were definitely not all mad, if that's what you're asking.'

'I suppose I am, yes.'

'There were a few scandals up there too.'

'Really?'

'There was a doctor who did all sorts of strange stuff. Something to do with taking parts of their brains away. Experimenting, he was. Sure, they got away with all sorts. Different world today – they would get away with nothing now.'

'I'm sure the lady wants to hear about our local Frankenstein!' one of the men sitting at the bar quipped.

'She wants to know about the place, isn't that right, girl?' He leaned forward. 'What's your name anyway?'

'My name is Lainey and, yes, I really am interested in what happened up there. But, tell me – surely not all of them ended up in that graveyard? Some must have been there just for a time? Getting cured?'

'Yes, indeed – some only stayed a short time and some managed to escape and that was a hard job. You saw the big wall and of course the way the river curves around it. Sure, it was the perfect site to build somewhere to lock them up. Some managed to escape nevertheless. But it didn't always work out for them.'

'How do you mean?' Lainey asked, intrigued.

'Well, mostly they got caught and then they didn't see the light of day for months.' He got up to throw more turf on the fire.

'That must have been terrible.'

He studied Lainey as if making his mind up if he would continue talking.

'Then there was the story about the girl and her baby. It made all the papers. Very little wrong with her, but the mother had her put away.'

'What happened to her?' Lainey put her glass down, not taking her eyes off him.

'Drowned. They both drowned. They never found the poor baby. Oh, musha, unfortunately they were not the only ones that drowned. But there was an awful commotion because she was from the gentry.'

'Gentry?'

'Sure, I remember it well. She was a Protestant from one of the Big Houses. She was supposed to be a real beauty. Shocking it was.'

Lainey could feel the blood drain from her face.

'Can you remember her name?'

'No ... God, it's so long ago ...'

'Would you remember it if you heard it again?'

'Maybe. But I remember the place she was from – not its name though. I had to go there once with a horse, years later, but the man I was with told me that it was where the Drowned Girl had come from. That's what she became known as.'

Lainey could barely breathe. 'A horse?'

'Yes, they were big into horses. Beautiful horses. Only thoroughbreds. Wait a minute ... the name of the place ...' He closed his eyes. Then suddenly he opened them. 'I have it now. Kilbride. A Big House belonging to the gentry. She was from a place called Kilbride House.'

CHAPTER 25

There were two missed calls and a text on Lainey's phone from Ruby: '**Call me.**'

Lainey dialled the number and Ruby picked up straight away.

'Where are you? I'm back at Kilbride.'

'I'll be a couple of hours. I made a little trip. I'm about two hours away. Look, I'll fill you in when I get back. How's Edward?'

'Better, in bed resting. See you later.'

Lainey was glad of the drive to sort out her thoughts. She knew she had seen the river before. It was the river in her dreams. Had she had nightmares about Victoria drowning in it? It gave her the shivers to think about it. It sounded ludicrous, but was the ghost of her aunt haunting her? She put on some music to distract herself. It was no doubt a coincidence but the feeling that she had seen the river before in her dreams freaked her out.

She never failed to marvel at the grandeur of Kilbride House when she came upon it. The gardens had an autumn coat and it looked so beautiful.

After feeding the horses one of the mornings, Edward had shown her the orchard, the rose garden and all the little nooks and crannies of the gardens. It was magical. He showed her the pond with golden fish. He showed her where the beehives where, in a little shelter with some oak trees. Like his father before him, he collected honey. It was good to spend time with him. He reminded her of her grandmother. He loved showing her the beauty in things and of nature. He showed her where the birds nested in the stables and how he had hung old buckets years before into the rafters to make sure they had beds for the winter. He had a little flask of brandy with him and every now and then he had a little drop.

'Keeps the bones oiled.' He winked.

She was glad to get in to the warm stove. Ruby's timing was great – she had a fresh pot of coffee made.

'Wow, what's the gorgeous aroma?' Lainey asked.

'Cecilia was baking – it's nutty toffee cake. It does smell divine, lots of cinnamon in it. I can feel it on my hips already – she put about two pounds of pure butter in it. Go on, where have you been?'

Lainey took off her coat and pulled a chair closer to the stove. It was funny, but she felt so at home now at Kilbride. Ruby had done so much to help her feel at home. She loved the house.

'Well, not to shock you, but I took a visit out to that place – Marlborough Asylum.'

'What! But it's been closed for years.'

'I know, but it still exists though very much abandoned now, and according to this elderly man in a pub, it's up for sale.'

'What pub?' Ruby asked as she poured two cups of coffee.

'A village pub where I met this man who, get this, was around in the fifties.'

Ruby joined Lainey at the table. 'I leave for a few hours – you go off to an abandoned asylum and a pub. Go on – did you find out anything?'

'Ruby … I'm a bit shell-shocked to be honest … he was able to tell me what happened to Victoria.'

Ruby paled. Her hand flew to her mouth.

'Ruby, this is dreadful news. But it looks like Victoria had a baby and tried to escape. While doing so, she drowned. There's a narrow river that curves its way around the grounds. The asylum was possibly built there because of the river as it forms a bit of a natural barrier. They never found the baby.'

'Oh my God. Do you believe him?'

Lainey shrugged her shoulders. 'He had no reason to lie to me. He didn't know of the connection. He just started talking about her. He didn't even remember her name. He just said she was a beauty and this is the part that nearly made me fall off my chair – he said she lived in a place called Kilbride House – he'd been there for some business with the stables. He said the drowning was covered in the papers. I guess he meant the local newspapers.'

'Christ, the poor girl!' said Ruby. 'But why on earth were we never told about this? I wonder did my mother know? It's ludicrous to think we had an aunt and never knew. Why the secrecy?'

'I suppose it was considered a family disgrace – both the baby and the possible insanity – and the drowning itself. Maybe there was a suggestion of suicide? I have a feeling your grandfather knows the whole story but for some reason neither he nor my grandmother wanted to tell us about it. Sorry, I'm so shocked I haven't even asked you – how is he?'

'That's why I was ringing you. He's better but very agitated. I have a bit of a bombshell to report too. He has asked that you and your mum come to Kilbride House. He says he wants to talk to you, tell you why Edith left and never came back.'

'*What?*'

'I know. He says it's killing him keeping it secret all this time and now, with you both here and Edith dead, it's time you all knew the truth.'

'Oh God!'

'Can you get your mum to call over later with you?'

'I don't know. After the last visit, I'm not sure. She kind of knows that he knows something, and she was getting fed up to be honest – she said she wasn't coming over anymore. But look, I'll chat to her – we're having dinner at seven. What time will we come over?'

'Could you make it for half eight? Can't keep Grandfather up if he needs to sleep.'

'Okay.'

'Right – come on, our coffee is going cold. Have some cake.'

Back at the hotel, Catherine arrived down to the restaurant dressed in some orchid-white trousers and a pale-pink silk blouse, with black Prada shoes and a pink cashmere pashmina. Lainey was glad she had made a bit of effort and was wearing an emerald-green dress that suited her complexion. Her strawberry-blonde hair was loose over her shoulders. She hardly ever wore much make-up except a lick of lipstick and a bit of blush. Unlike Catherine, whose make-up always looked as if a make-up artist had just finished it. She could have easily had a career in make-up she was so good at it.

They ordered a green salad to start and then a risotto with basil and roasted vegetables. Lainey had asked Ruby to drop her down and later bring them back up to the house because she felt like having a glass of wine or two to calm her nerves. They ordered a chilled bottle of white burgundy that tasted delicious. She soon could feel herself relax a little and launched into telling her mother about her discovery.

Catherine was stunned. 'I can hardly believe it. Christ, what a lovely mother Gertrude Goulding was! It's a shocking story.'

'I just can't believe that Grandma never told us – surely she wasn't ashamed to tell us?'

'Mother was never that type. I can't imagine her shunning her sister like that. We may have had our differences, but your grandmother was a great supporter of anyone who needed help – she certainly would not have been ashamed.'

'Maybe Edward can shed some light on it all … Mom, he wants us to go up to the house later … he wants to talk with us about Edith.'

'So, he has decided to talk. That's big of him.'

'Look, I know you said that you wouldn't go back again. But please come with me.'

'Oh, very well. To be honest, I wouldn't miss hearing him finally spilling the beans.'

Edward was in the sitting room beside the fire. Lainey

216

thought he looked very shaken. She wondered if this was a good idea. He had been in hospital earlier that day. Ruby had said he had slept but he looked very weak.

'Hi, Uncle Edward.'

His eyes looked glassy, but he welcomed them and told them to sit near him. Catherine sat the farthest away.

'Thank you all for coming here. I have had time to think and for the life of me I am not sure why your mother, Edith, decided to ask you to come now and not when she was alive. Ruby, can you give everyone a drink, please? A brandy for me, make it a large one.'

When they all had a drink, Edward leaned forward and began.

'When your mother left Ireland we made a pact that we would lose contact. We knew it would be for a long time. I never imagined it would be for a lifetime. But the years passed and now she's gone.'

'There are boats and planes that go to New York,' Catherine quipped.

'Mom!' Laney pleaded.

'It's okay, Lainey, your mother has every right to feel upset. Allow me to tell you what I know.'

Ruby interrupted him. 'Sorry, but before you begin, Grandfather – I found some old documents in the basement. We found a document from your mother about your sister Victoria. There was a document about an asylum. I'm sorry, Grandfather, but we were going to tell you, and then I got the call to say that you were in hospital.'

Edward shook his head and looked at Catherine. 'I am sorry that you had to find out like that. I should have told you when you first arrived over here.'

'It's okay, Uncle Edward,' said Lainey, 'you can tell us now. But today, I drove over there. The asylum is closed now and very much forgotten. But I went into a pub where an old man lives with his son. The thing is, he ... well, he remembered Victoria.'

'Did he tell you that she drowned?'

There was silence for a few seconds.

'Yes, he told me that she tried to escape with a baby and they both drowned. He said that the baby was never found. Was it?'

Edward drained the rest of his brandy. 'It's a bit more complicated than that.'

'I don't understand, how can it be more complicated than that?' said Catherine aggressively. 'There is a grave marked Baby Goulding in your local cemetery. It's the same year as this aunt of mine died. Is that the baby? If it is the same baby, why was it not buried with Victoria?'

'Mom, give him time for goodness' sake!'

But Catherine drained her scotch and got up and walked to the fireplace.

'No, I think we have waited long enough. Edward, you may have made a pact with my mother to keep all this a secret. She literally banned me from ever coming here to Ireland. On many occasions I wanted to, but she would get so upset that I would have to back down. I grew up having no idea why we were so ostracised from our Irish family. I know I was born out of wedlock. I suppose that was it, was it? Shame. Was she run out of Ireland because of me? Run out by her own family? But, look, it doesn't matter any more. My mother is dead and it's all in the past. I live in the present. So, sorry, but it's all a bit late for cosy chats – can you just bloody tell us

218

what happened? All this secrecy, I am so tired of it! Now there is an aunt who must have had a baby out of wedlock too and was locked up. What a great family history! She drowned with her baby and you and my mother decided it was better to never mention it ever again. You both felt so ashamed that my mother left and made a new life in America and you both decided never to contact each other again. Oh, we heard how beautiful Kilbride House is, repeatedly, and all about Dingle and the Blasket Islands. But never in all those years and, let me tell you that is a long time, never have I heard about any family here. Then my mother dies and leaves it in her will that we must visit you here. How ludicrous is that? Why now, why after all these years? Why did she not bring me here when I was young and would have loved to run barefoot along the beaches of Ireland? Learn about its history and the people that lived here. I begged her to allow me to spend time in Dublin when I was young. I longed to act on the Abbey or the Gate stage, but I was forbidden. I wanted to come here, visit this mystical Kilbride House that I had heard so much about. But no. So, forgive me for feeling like an outsider.'

'Mom, please.' Lainey looked apologetically at Ruby who was almost in tears.

'Please, Catherine, my grandfather is not well enough to deal with this.' Ruby's voice shook with emotion.

But Edward put his hand up. 'Leave it, Ruby. She has waited long enough to hear the truth.'

He sat up in his chair and stared at Catherine, not taking his eyes off her.

'She lied to you to protect you.'

'What do you mean "protect me"? Protect me from what?'

'She never came back here because of the way she was treated.'

'What do you mean the way she was treated? Her sister was locked up and drowned trying to escape and it seems the baby too. What on earth happened to my mother?'

'The baby did not drown that night – I know because I was there,' Edward said in a clear voice.

'You were there?' said Catherine.

'Yes, I was there, and I know that baby did not drown.'

'What? Where is the baby then?' Lainey asked.

He looked at Catherine who had gone as white as a sheet.

'That baby that escaped in the arms of her mother was you, Catherine.'

CHAPTER 26

Marlborough Asylum
1955

Edward dropped his torch on the bank and waded into the river. Edith shone her torch to light the way.

'Hold on!' Edward shouted.

The tears were falling down Victoria's face. She was terrified she would lose her grip on her baby, her body felt so numb. The current kept sweeping her feet off the bottom. The water was so cold, like icicles on her body. Her baby was still silent, her eyes closed. She tried to check if she was breathing but it was impossible to say. She held her close.

'Stay until I reach you, Victoria!' Edward warned.

Edith threw the torch down and waded into the river.

'Edward! I'm coming in too!' she called. 'I can take the baby!'

'Be careful!' he called back. 'The current is quite strong!'

He had almost reached Victoria when Edith cried out.

Edward swung back towards her. She was up to her chin in water though still quite close to the bank and seemed to be floundering. She must have stepped into a pothole.

'Are you alright?' he yelled.

'I'm fine! Go on – get the baby – go!'

But as he watched she went under and then barely surfaced again gasping for breath, using breaststrokes to keep afloat.

'*Go! The baby! Go!*' she screamed at Edward.

Then she went under again.

He couldn't understand what was happening with her, so he lunged through the water towards her.

She surfaced and, spluttering, screamed, '*What are you doing? Get the baby! Get Victoria! Save them before they are swept away!*'

He turned back and half-waded, half-swam to the tree-trunk. Telling Victoria to hold on to the tree until he returned, he took the baby in one arm and used the other in a sidestroke that brought them to the bank in seconds. He laid the baby on the grass of the riverbank and plunged back into the river.

Victoria was screaming Edith's name. Edward couldn't see Edith but he went and grabbed Victoria and pulled her to the bank. He left her crawling to where the baby was and dived back into the river and began to search for Edith.

The baby was crying again and Victoria thanked God for that. She was alive. She held her close, her little body so cold and her baby clothes soaking. She huddled the baby closer. 'Hush, hush, we are safe now!'

The moon was under a cloud. She peered into the river, trying to see.

Then Edward surfaced and disappeared again.

A powerful dread hit Victoria.

Frantic seconds passed turning into minutes and eventually Edward was wading from the river, gasping for breath.

Edith was in his arms, her body limp with no sign of life.

He laid her on the ground.

'*Edith, Edith, come back to us! Wake up! Wake up!*' Victoria screamed.

Edward turned Edith over and water gushed out of her mouth. He turned her on her back again and began pressing her chest vigorously in a rhythm. Then he breathed into her mouth for a while before returning to pumping her chest again.

Victoria prayed as she watched.

He felt for her pulse, then went back to pumping again.

Time passed – how long Victoria didn't know – until he sat back on his heels exhausted.

Edith was completely unresponsive. He felt for her pulse in her wrist again, then shook his head and let the wrist drop.

'*No! No! No! No!*' Victoria screamed into the night.

'How could you, God?' Edward fell to the ground, sobbing as if his heart was broken.

Then there was quiet – even the baby in the sodden clothes had stopped crying. Victoria wondered was she in a nightmare. Was it real, how could it have all gone so horribly wrong? Her beautiful Edith!

She caressed Edith's forehead, singing a lullaby that their father used to sing to them. Stroking her hair.

Edward took the baby and cried for all they had lost, rocking his new niece to and fro.

Minutes passed and then Edward knelt beside Victoria, holding the baby.

'Victoria, we must leave – there is no time to lose.

223

Soon it will be light and they may notice you are gone. We must go ahead with the plan.'

Victoria looked at him. Plan? She hadn't thought any further than escaping from the asylum.

'What happened to Edith, Edward? She could swim. How could she drown?'

'There was a pothole there with a tangle of fishing line wound around a tree trunk in it – her foot got caught and she was pulled under.'

'Oh Edith!'

'Victoria, listen to me. You can't go home. Mother is not well – she will put you and the baby back there. Edith and I made plans for your future. We must go now before the alarm is raised and they come searching for you.'

'What? How can we go, Edward? Edith is dead, drowned. We must tell people!'

But even as she spoke she realised that Edward was right.

'Come – we must get the baby into dry clothes – look, it's blue with the cold. Come, Victoria, quickly!'

He raised her to her feet and hurried her to the car. She sat in and he turned the heater on.

Then he took some baby clothes, blankets and a bottle of milk from the back seat and helped Victoria get the baby into dry clothes and wrap it in a blanket.

Victoria began to feed the baby who sucked hungrily at the bottle.

'We can't leave Edith here, Edward. She told you to save us, she died for me and my baby.'

'Then the last thing she would want is for it to be for nothing. Victoria, hear me out – I have a plan and I think it is a good one. You and Edith look alike. It would not be too difficult to believe that one of you was the other – other than that your hair is shorter now. Victoria, we must convince everyone that Edith is you. That you tried to escape and drowned with the baby. We can put your nightdress on Edith. You see, her clothes are in the car because she was running away with you. And she must have something like a nail scissors we can use to cut her hair. When her body is found, they will let Mother know but I will come and identify Edith as you.'

Victoria was appalled at the idea.

'We have to, Victoria, it's your only chance.'

Victoria shook her head. 'I can't do that to Edith! And what about the baby – there will be no baby with her!'

'They'll search the river, but when they can't find the baby, they will just presume that it has been swept away. And they won't want to prolong the search – they'll want any fuss to die down for fear of scandal. This will give you your freedom.'

'But, but … if they think Edith is me, what happens to me then? There can't be two Victoria Gouldings.'

'You will become Edith. We booked a passage for both of you and the baby to New York. I have passports for both of you. I have all Edith's papers and her money – the money she inherited when she turned eighteen – a substantial sum. It will set you up in America in a new life.'

Victoria was so overwhelmed it was hard to think straight. 'New York? What about Canice?'

'I will try and get Canice released. When I know it is safe, I can tell him where you are.'

'How can I manage all on my own in a new world, just me and the baby?'

'You must. You know you must.'

'But won't Mother search for Edith?'

'I have a letter for Mother from Edith,' Edward said. 'Saying she has taken her money and is beginning a new life and she never wants any contact again. She and Mother have hardly been speaking since you were taken away. But, come on, Victoria – we're wasting precious time. They could soon be looking for you.'

He was right. The day was dawning, casting shards of silver light across the river.

Warm and fed, the baby was now asleep. They left her in a nest of blankets on the passenger seat.

Victoria changed into some clothes belonging to Edith. With Edward's help she took her sister's clothes off and dressed her in her own wet asylum nightdress. Edward found a nail scissors in Edith's handbag and managed to cut Edith's beautiful hair. Edith's hair was slighty darker and not as curly as Victoria's but not so different that anyone would notice. Victoria noticed a gold slide with ruby-red roses in Edith's hair. Their father had brought it for Edith when she was sixteen. Edith adored it. It was so beautiful. Gently, with the tears streaming down her face, she pulled the slide away and put it in her pocket. The hair Edward put in the car, to be disposed of later. They said a prayer and wept again, their arms wrapped around each other. They had lost Edith forever.

Victoria kissed her on the cheek. It took all her strength to walk away.

As they looked at the river for the last time, the dawn was about to break, and a mist was beginning to form. They knew that the mist and that dawn would stay and haunt them until their dying day, making them remember all that was lost.

They went back to the car.

Edward lifted the baby out as Victoria slid into the back seat.

'What are you going to call her?' he asked as she took the baby from him.

'Catherine. I am going to call her Catherine.'

CHAPTER 27

Kilbride House
2018

Ruby sat down on the floor beside her grandfather.

'What are you saying, Grandfather? How can the baby be Catherine?'

Catherine had literally collapsed on the sofa. She was staring into the fire with Lainey beside her holding her hand.

'Mom, Mom, are you okay?' Lainey asked gently.

Catherine said nothing for a few minutes then it was as if she found her voice and it was very clear. She stood back up and looked at Edward who looked like he had physically shrunk.

'I am not listening to these lies. How dare you drag me over here for – for some stupid fabrication about my mother's past.'

Edward looked up and spoke, his voice gentle. 'I know you are angry but, please, just hear me out.'

'Mom, please just hear him out,' Lainey pleaded.

She stood and grabbed Catherine's hand, then led her back to the sofa.

Edward took a deep breath and continued.

'It was my sister Edith and I that had made Victoria's

228

escape possible. We knew a girl who worked in the kitchen of the asylum and we had it all arranged. But the river, normally quite shallow, was higher after the rain and both Edith and Victoria got into trouble in the water. Victoria was clinging to a tree that had fallen across the river and trying to hold you, Catherine, above the water.' His voice almost became a whisper, as if he were back there, watching the scene.

'Grandfather, this is too much for you,' Ruby said, clutching his hand.

'No! She must know. She must know the truth.'

He looked at Catherine and there were tears spilling from his eyes.

'Edith screamed at me to save you and your mother first. I knew Edith was going under. I had seconds only.' His voice broke. 'I grabbed you, brought you across and laid you on the river bank. Victoria had swum to the side and was crawling out of the water. I couldn't see Edith and now in the darkness was uncertain where exactly she had gone under. I dived and searched again and again. She had caught her foot in a tangle of fishing line and by the time I found her and freed her, she was lifeless. I tried to revive her but it was too late.'

Edward's body slumped, and Ruby put her arms around him.

Tears were streaming down Lainey's face, but Catherine was dry-eyed, her face frozen.

With effort, Edward continued, his eyes fixed on Catherine. 'When your grandmother Gertrude discovered your mother was pregnant out of wedlock she acted very badly. My mother and father were good parents when we were young, and my father was the kindest soul you could imagine. But when he died our mother changed so much that we could hardly believe it. She was terrified of her two beautiful daughters going astray. Then Victoria and Canice, the love of her life, decided to run away. Canice was an islander, a Catholic and from a humble background. Mother would never have accepted it. With the advice of the local doctor she had Victoria committed to an asylum, thinking she had been brainwashed. We were not allowed to visit her. We were told that the baby would be adopted and that your mother would have treatment to make her forget what had happened. There was no talking to my mother. In some terrible way, she thought she was doing the right thing. She was assured by the hospital that it was the best decision for her daughter. We knew differently and so we formed a plan. We knew that if we failed, my mother would have her committed again and the baby would be given away. So, we bought three passages for America. Your Aunt Edith was to go with you and your mother to America.'

Catherine still didn't react.

'When the accident happened, we had to make a terrible decision. We pretended that Edith was Victoria.' He spoke now as if to himself, staring into the distance. 'We left our poor sister's body beside the river in Victoria's hospital nightdress. We cut her hair as Victoria's had been cut at the asylum. They looked alike which allowed us to fool everyone. We drove away leaving her there, and it has haunted my nights since. We knew that people would think it was Victoria. It worked. They brought her body back and searched the river for the baby. They assumed the baby had drowned too.'

'But the 'Baby Goulding' in the graveyard. Who is that?' Lainey asked.

'I was lucky to call the local vicar a good friend. He was the only person aware of what had gone on. I trusted him with my life and yours and Victoria's and he never let me down. Those were different times. There were no questions by the gardaí. We said we had found the body of the baby and we would bury it. This was to halt any suspicion about the baby's survival. But we buried only a small empty coffin. Mother never asked to see the bodies of either Edith – Victoria as she thought – or the baby. We knew she would not.'

'So my grandmother used her sister's passport and documents,' said Lainey. 'Even her birth certificate.'

'Yes. Edith had all her documentation with her. So Victoria became Edith.'

'Why should we believe you?' Catherine asked.

'I can only tell you the truth. Whether you believe me is up to you, Catherine.'

'My father? She said she had barely known him. He was passing through. She had a photograph of him.'

'You knew about that photograph!' said Lainey. 'I saw it in her drawer when it was too late to ask her about it.'

'Yes, I saw it once.'

Lainey had the other photo in her bag. She pulled it out and gave it to Catherine.

'Somebody else knew – they pushed this under the cottage door the first night that I stayed here. Winnie told us that he was from the island. Is this him?'

Catherine took the photograph and looked at it. 'Yes, it's him.' She handed it to Edward.

'Yes, that's your father,' Edward said. 'Canice

Meagher. A poet, singer and a grand fellow – but my mother would never accept him. He died, shortly after you both left. He was originally from the Blasket Islands. I am ashamed to tell you that our mother had him arrested for abduction and rape. Which was of course untrue. He deeply loved your mother and she loved him too.'

'Yes, Winnie told us he died,' Lainey said. 'She thought it might have been a work accident in England. Do you know if it was?'

Edward sighed. 'I had planned to help him to get out of prison, but somehow he escaped before I could get word to him that you were safe and on the way to America. I promised Victoria I would give him the passage to go when he was released. He heard that you both had drowned. He took the boat for England and word came back that he had died. There were different stories about how. Yes, some said he had fallen from some scaffolding. Some say he fell off the boat on the way over. Inevitably, there were suggestions of suicide.'

The others were silenced, horrified by this possibility.

'He was the finest singer you ever heard,' Edward said then, his voice full of regret.

'Where is he buried?' Lainey asked.

'I don't know – somewhere in England if it was not a drowning and the body not recovered. I did try to find out. Possibly a pauper's grave.'

'Can I have a drink?' Catherine asked.

'Ruby, I think we all need another drink,' said Edward. 'A large brandy for me, please?'

Ruby got up to get the drinks. 'Catherine?

'Scotch on the rocks.'

'So, my aunt died that night so that you could save us first? Is that what you're telling me, Edward?' Catherine said as Ruby handed her a large glass of scotch and ice in a crystal glass.

'Edith loved your mother and was broken-hearted about her being locked up. She blamed herself, because she was worried about her and had told my mother that she thought she was running away. Victoria had not told us about her courtship with Canice. So, Edith was the older sister and worried about her. Victoria and Canice had planned to run to England and get married. But Mother wasn't long in finding out what your mother was up to. They stopped them at the boat. I am afraid that Canice had asked his friend Freddy to drive them to the boat in Cork. His friend unfortunately confided in a girl he was courting at the time. The girl was a sweet girl and meant no harm but she told her aunt who happened to be a patient of Doctor Ford and the woman reported it to him immediately. Freddy had only left her when he went to pick up Canice. Mary confessed all to Doctor Ford who wasn't long getting the gardai involved and of course my mother.'

'And all these years, why did she never come back? I was a grown woman. Nobody could have taken me from her.'

'My mother lived until she was ninety-eight. Victoria would never come back when she was alive. I think it was too painful. We lost so much. We thought it better to try to forget. Then too much time had gone by. We didn't know how to begin again. She had given up so much. Your mother adored Kilbride. She adored the peninsula – she was part of it. Even though she and Canice came

233

from different backgrounds, they were the same – unique and wild as the wind. She used to ride the beaches for hours, always wanting to be near the water. She had to leave it all behind, including her beautiful mare Silver. Silver missed her as much as I know Victoria missed her. The pain of Edith was crucifying. I think she may have felt that she would not have been able to bear it if she came back. I lost both sisters that night.' Then he broke down and cried. All the years of secrecy were tumbling down. 'We were wrong – we could never forget. We could never forget what we had lost that night.'

Lainey had gone quiet. She looked at Edward as if afraid to ask something.

'Lainey, are you okay?' Ruby asked.

'If Edith was brought back to the asylum, where was she buried?' The image of that mass grave came back to her. She prayed he would not say the asylum graveyard. 'Please tell me you brought the body back to Kilbride and she is not buried at the asylum.'

Edward shook his head. 'No, thank God, she is not buried there. The vicar helped me again. Mother was allowing her to be buried there. She refused to allow her back to Kilbride. The vicar got a plot for me in a quiet churchyard a few miles away from the asylum. I know this is an awful lot to take in. But when I saw you, Lainey, your eyes were so like Victoria's that I was shaken. Catherine, you look like her too, yet it is Edith that you remind me of.'

Catherine drained her drink and stood up.

'I need to leave.'

'Okay, Mom, I'll go with you. I'll ring the hotel and ask them to send a cab.'

'I need to leave.'

'Yes – I said I'll take you back now.'

'Thank you, Edward, for clearing all this up,' said Catherine. 'I have only waited over sixty years to know the truth and to know who my father is. But for what it's worth, it doesn't matter now, it's too late. It no longer interests me.'

CHAPTER 28

Catherine had begun to pack when her phone rang. It was Lucille her assistant.

'I can get you on a flight at twelve-forty tomorrow Irish time. You need to be there two hours before.'

'Okay but check if you can get two seats. Also, can you book me a hotel close to the airport for tonight?'

Lainey came out of the bathroom.

'Mother, what is going on?'

Catherine was ferociously throwing her clothes into her case. 'This was a mistake. She has got her bloody wish for us to come to Kilbride. Now I am leaving, and I want you to come too. I am staying in Shannon tonight.'

Lainey looked at her in amazement.

'What are you talking about? Why now, with everything that Uncle Edward has told us? We can't go now!' She was gobsmacked.

'That is exactly why we need to leave. Call him what you like. But I have no uncles. I never have had, and I have managed quite well. I certainly don't need one now. That ghastly story about asylums and graves. I have the shivers even thinking about it all.'

'So, you are running!' Lainey replied.

'I am not running! I am going back to my life. The life I have spent all these years creating. If my mother had wanted me to know any secrets, she should have told me when she was alive. Not now when I can't ask her anything. How convenient! Send them over when I am dead and let them figure out what happened. How dare she? How dare she land all this on us now. She should never have asked us to come to this godforsaken place. I want to go back to my life and never hear of Kilbride House ever again. Do you hear me?'

'I hear you, Mom, but I don't understand you. What are you afraid of?'

'I have no interest in hearing about how someone died to save me and my mother. I simply don't want to know.'

'Why?'

'Because I don't. That's why. I don't even know if any of this is true. It could be all some crazy story and I have no intention of finding out any more about it.'

Lainey sat down on the bed, grabbed a pillow and hugged it to her.

Catherine looked at her daughter. Everything would be so easy if Lainey were not involved. If her mother had only requested her to travel over. She would never have told Lainey any of it. They would be better off. What good did knowing all this do? But her mother was more clever than that – she knew Lainey would have to get to the bottom of it.

'Mom, please don't go. I need you here.'

'For what? Just put all this rubbish out of your mind and come home. Lucille is looking for two flights as we speak.'

'I am not going anywhere,' Lainey replied adamantly.

'Lainey, please. I am not staying here a moment longer than I have to and I don't want you to either.'

Lainey shook her head. 'You are running because it makes you uncomfortable to think that someone cared so much for you and your mother that they chose to die for you. You can't tolerate even thinking about it. Because you keep everyone away, everyone away that loves you. You build this big wall that protects you from everyone. Well, I have news for you, Mom. It's just me! That's all! I am the only one constantly trying to break down that wall. But go ahead and build it up. You have done it all your life, why be any different now?'

Catherine took a deep breath. She was just about holding it together. Lainey was right, she had built a wall around herself and it did protect her. The truth was, she was terrified. There was so much untold about her past, but she had no intention of dragging it up. She wanted it left there in the past, where it couldn't hurt anyone. Maybe when she was younger there was a time for all that. But Edith had made sure that she never knew. Now it was too late. Her life was in New York, not in this ghostly place that seemed to be at the edge of the world.

'You know I care about you,' she said. 'I know I don't often show it. I am not like you or my mother.'

'Why? Because you don't need anyone. Guess what? I do. I needed you when I was little, but you were never there, and Grandma had to step in.'

'That's not fair, Lainey. I had a career.'

'You had a daughter, but the theatre always came first. Just go – run away!'

Catherine threw her hands up in the air in frustration.

'What do you want me to do?'

'I want you to stay here. At least for a few days. Stay with me while we try to digest everything we have been told.'

Catherine shook her head. 'Why? What good will it do?'

'I don't know, but if it's true and that young woman died that night, surely we should visit her grave and pay our respects. It's the least we can do.'

'I'm sorry, Lainey, but I have had enough. I am certainly not going on some wild goose chase looking for a grave that means nothing to me. I am leaving tonight.'

Lainey grabbed her hand. 'Please, Mom, don't go! Stay at least for a few days like you had planned.'

But Catherine was not to be persuaded. 'No, I have made my mind up. Come with me.'

Lainey threw the pillow on the ground and got up and went to the door. Tears were flowing down her face.

'Please, Mom, don't go, please.'

Catherine wanted to hug her and tell her that of course she would stay. But something inside just would not allow her to.

'I'm sorry, Lainey, but no. Please come home with me.'

But Lainey left, banging the door behind her. Catherine could feel herself crumple. Her daughter needed her. Had pleaded with her to stay. But she wanted to run faster than she ever had in her life. She found a cigarette in her bag, opened the window and lit it.

Lainey's words had stung. Had she been a bad parent? But it had suited everyone. Edith had needed someone, and Catherine had felt so suffocated by her. When Lainey came along, Edith had poured out love to her. She stopped watching every move that Catherine made. She was consumed with love for her new granddaughter. It had given Catherine her freedom – she could pursue her own love, the theatre. Her marriage was just as restricting. It was not that she didn't love him. She just didn't need him. But he needed her, and it sucked the life out of her – she had to break free. There were other relationships, but again she needed none of them. She was happier on her own. But what Lainey said made it sound like she had abandoned her. Her career meant everything to her, she knew that, but she had loved her daughter. Just because she was not always the one to put her to bed or collect her from school hardly made her a bad mother. With the nanny and Edith, Lainey was fine – she had a great childhood. But seeds of doubt were hard to get rid of. Edith had begged her to spend more time with Lainey. But she just felt it was Edith's way of controlling her again.

She felt ill after the cigarette. She sprayed some mist in the air to get rid of any smell. She felt suffocated. For her own sanity she had to leave Kilbride now.

Everything was packed. At least she had a flight. Lucille had emailed her to say that she had a room booked at a hotel called The Park Inn. Catherine mailed her back to tell her she needed only one ticket.

She didn't want to admit it to Lainey, but she did believe Edward. Somehow it all added up. She always knew there was more to the story her mother had told her about her father. She said he was passing through but she had no forwarding address, so he never knew. Years later, when she tried to find out more, her mother refused to talk about it, saying that she would never be able to find him. But Catherine had found the photo that she had hidden. Outside the thatched house. She knew he was her father. She suspected that he was possibly married. But now she knew. Why had Edith not told her the truth? Why create some other story? None of it made sense. What was Edith afraid of? So, her father was a man of no means. So what?

'Buried in a pauper's grave.' That was what Edward had said. His name was omitted from her birth certificate. *Bastard*: that's what was written. Her mother was marked as a spinster. That's how she had been treated here in Ireland. Well, it was all too late for the truth. She wanted nothing to do with any of them or Kilbride House. The ghosts of the past could stay there. She wanted to jump on that plane and get as far away as she could. What good would seeking it all out now do? None. She would go to New York and hopefully Lainey would follow shortly.

She needed to go through Security and then she would be out of here. She normally liked the airport. It was anonymous. It suited her. She grabbed a coffee and sat down.

A woman sat down beside her. She had a baby asleep in her arms. It could only be a few months old. Her mother looked professional, possibly in her early thirties.

She tried to push the thought of her own mother away – crossing to America with her as a baby on a ship. She was so young and alone. How terrible to leave her sister's body beside the river! How heart-breaking that would have been. Leaving her brother that she cared about and Canice Meagher the father to her baby, locked up for something he didn't commit. How did she have the strength to go? But Catherine knew why. She did it to keep her daughter from being taken from her. She could not bear that. Is that why she was always so terrified of anything happening to her? Why she tried to wrap her in cotton wool? Why she never wanted her to come to Ireland? Where they had tried to take her from her mother. No wonder she never wanted her to come back. It was all too painful. She never recovered from having to leave Edith and the only way she could cope was to never talk about her, because possibly if she did she could not carry on. The precious hair slide. With the ruby-red roses. She saw her mother hold it to her and cry like her heart would break, thinking no one was looking. But Catherine was, hiding behind the doorway in her velvet dress, waiting to go to her dance class, wondering how on earth a hair slide could cause her mother to cry like she had lost everything. Because other than her baby she had lost everything. Her sister died to save her. And then there was the terrible pact she made with Edward to pretend it was she who had died. But this meant she would never see her beloved Kilbride again.

Kilbride House. It was beautiful. Everything her mother had described.

They were about to go through Customs. But she knew where she had to go. It would be a nightmare. Her baggage had gone through and would have to be retrieved later. She got up and walked out of the airport towards the cabs.

'I need a cab to Dingle, County Kerry?'

'Dingle, County Kerry? Sure that's a couple of hours away.'

'I know. Can you take me?'

'Hop in, love.'

242

CHAPTER 29

Lainey had the dream again, but this time it was even more frightening and vivid. In a slumber where she wasn't sure if she was dreaming or awake, there was an awareness about it now, perhaps. She could see a girl in the river like a shimmer of light in the dark glassiness, an illusion disappearing into the water. Lainey could feel her own body being pulled in. It was cold and the light from the moon was disappearing. The woman's form was merging with the greyness of the water. Lainey was trying to reach her. The splashing and screaming seemed distant. Then the glimmer of light in the river was gone. It was dark.

She awoke, her breathing panicked. A dream. Another nightmare. The same river. The river she had seen at the asylum. But that day it had looked peaceful, without a ripple. She remembered the pungent air, so full of musty earth. But in the dream, she imagined it smelt of nothing.

It was as if she was being haunted by what had happened. She now knew that the woman drowning must be Edith Goulding, who had screamed for her sister and her niece to be rescued, knowing that she herself was drowning.

243

Beads of sweat on her body made her light pyjamas stick to her. She turned on the light and opened the window slightly to let in some air. The past was being unearthed and it was frightening her. Now at least she knew what had happened. She also knew that Edward was telling the truth.

Her mother was halfway across the Atlantic now, back in New York. She wanted to tell her about the dreams. Catherine would call it hocus-pocus but she still wanted her to know. It seemed important to her that she did, for some reason.

She waited for the light to come and, as soon as it did, she was up and dressed. She needed to get out in the air, things would be clearer then. She threw on jeans, a jumper and a jacket. She headed down towards the stables. The yard was quiet. John would be up shortly, and the work would begin.

Murphy, a graceful dark chestnut, was in a stable at the bottom of the yard. She had ridden him in the ring and on the pathways with John Hogan or Seán the stable boy. John was a man of few words. Ruby had told her he was a widow and his son lived in London as a lawyer. Lainey admired how this gruffness disappeared when he handled the horses. His voice became almost a whisper as he softly patted them and nudged them. They whinnied in delight when they saw him. She marvelled at their intelligence. They know how kind and patient John Hogan was with them. His patience did not transfer to people. Lainey reckoned he was about sixty, a rugged man with twinkling blue eyes. Ruby had remarked that he preferred spending time with horses than people.

She fetched a saddle and bridle and left a note in the

tack room for John, to say she had taken Murphy out and would be back in an hour or so. She was heading towards the beach. She had ridden on the beach with John on a different horse, but it was lame. She knew that Murphy was not as quiet as the other horse and that John might not approve, but she could deal with that when she came back. He had also told her not to go to the beach alone, but she needed time to think and clear her mind.

Murphy was delighted to be on an early-morning ride out and he almost danced in excitement. She grabbed a riding helmet, put on riding boots, mounted and headed down the avenue. It had rained heavily, and the clouds looked like it would soon again. There was a break in the fence across the field that led to the woods. She had taken it with John. She could ride through that and it would take her towards the beach.

It had rained, and the smell of the damp earth and leaves met her senses. Crows cackled in the trees, watching for early worms in the soft earth. The worn path was smudgy with puddles as Murphy clip-clopped down the path.

Then Murphy began to pick up a little speed.

'I think you can smell the sea.' Lainey laughed aloud.

Another few minutes and she crossed a small road to get to a narrow sandy path. Within minutes the path got wider, and she could hear the waves and the early-morning gulls swishing towards the cliffs.

She could feel Murphy gather speed.

'Steady now.'

Murphy slowed as she tightened the reins.

It felt good to be free, the wind chopping at her as if slicing her face. Her mind was tired from thinking about everything. She had been so angry with her mother for leaving. She knew she could leave too. But not yet anyway. She wasn't ready. Her uncle had told her about her grandmother in Kilbride when she was young. She tried to imagine her here, wild and free on her beloved horse. How different to the woman that she knew! She had never even known she could ride. According to Uncle Edward she was a very talented rider. Another secret from her past. Surely she must have longed to ride again? It seemed to have been a huge part of her life here in Kilbride. But that was possibly why she didn't ride. It reminded her too much of what she had left behind.

The beach was deserted. There was a fishing boat moored there and the remains of a small fire. Murphy's thunderous hooves skimmed the water. She loosened the reins and he began cantering, the wind behind them. She smiled in delight at the speed. She held the reins and kept her legs close to his sides to steady herself. The rhythm of Murphy mixing with the sound of the waves crashing was magic.

'Go on, Murphy!' she urged.

She could feel the horse shifting rhythm and soon it was as if she was gliding, the canter getting faster until, as if changing perfectly into gear, his hooves moved to a gallop. The sea spray washed her face. The pure strength of Murphy made her feel safe. He was so solid. Then she noticed the gulls gathering in the distance, just at the edge of the sea where it ebbed and flowed. The frothy foam like white bubble bath covering the beach.

'Whoa, Murphy, slow down, good boy!'

He began to slow but he didn't see the flock of gulls. Alarmed, they took off like a white fluttering cloud.

Murphy slowed abruptly and bucked and Lainey could feel her body being thrown with a thud and a splash into the water. Her leg was caught momentarily in the stirrup but luckily it released itself as she crashed to the ground.

She was shivering and wet. Her foot was in dreadful pain when she moved it. Murphy was standing close to her, looking sorry for himself, his legs slightly shaky in the water.

'Oh no!' she exclaimed as she touched her face. '*Ow!*' She must have torn it when she fell. Her back was painful. She knew she had been stupid to ride so fast and to ride Murphy into the gulls.

She looked over at him.

'I'm sorry, Murphy, it was my fault. I should have been more careful.' She tried to get up and walk but it was so painful she had to sit down on the sand.

Then she could hear a car engine. She looked up and gave a sigh of relief as a Jeep came into view. It was John Hogan. She was sure she would get an earful from him and she wasn't looking forward to it. There was someone else in the Jeep. She squinted against the light to see who it was. At first, she thought it was another man, wearing a big coat and boots. Then, to her utter surprise, she saw it was Catherine – dressed like she had never seen her before. She wasn't sure if she was more shocked to see her at all or more shocked to see her dressed like somebody going to do farm work.

Then Catherine was running towards her.

'*Lainey, Lainey, are you okay?*'

'I'm fine. I've hurt my foot but I don't think it's broken. And Murphy is okay, I think.'

John Hogan was with Murphy, checking out his legs.

Now he approached Lainey and he was angry. 'What were you thinking of? I warned you not to go to the beach alone. Anything could have happened. The horses are accustomed to go at full gallop here and you are not experienced enough to control them.'

'I know. I'm sorry.'

'Can you walk?'

'Well, I can limp.'

'Okay, grab hold of me and let's get you to the jeep.'

She leaned on Catherine's shoulder on the other side and limped to the Jeep.

They helped her to clamber in.

Then John turned to Catherine.

'Right, you drive the Jeep back to Kilbride. I'll bring Murphy back.'

'What! Me? Drive a Jeep?'

'You can drive?'

'Of course.'

'Well, then, what are you wasting time for?'

Catherine looked at him, aghast. 'But I can't …'

But he had already walked off to get Murphy.

Catherine stared after him.

Lainey burst out laughing. 'Sorry, Mom, but it was worth falling to see you dressed like that and gaping at John Hogan bossing you about!'

'Well, I am delighted you are so highly entertained. I nearly lost my life when I saw you fall.'

Lainey was shocked to see that Catherine had two big fat tears rolling down her face.

'Mom, are you okay?'

'I would die if something happened to you, Lainey,' Catherine whispered. 'I would simply die.'

'Oh Mom, I'm fine.'

'Fine but next time go for a walk on foot,' Catherine said, wiping her tears away.

'Why did you come back? I rang the hotel and they said that you had left for the airport.'

'I know. I couldn't leave. I wanted to. But I knew I needed to come back.'

'Was it just for me?'

'Partly. But it was also partly for your grandma. I finally got it. All these years, I held the fact she kept us away from here against her. But now I know how much she lost in keeping me. And what she was protecting me from. How traumatic it was for her – and Edward – it scarred them for life. My aunt saved my life – as did Edward. You're right. We should visit the grave. It still all gives me the creeps, talking about graves and cemeteries. But we need to do it. I need to do it and I will be glad to have you there. But there is another reason why I wanted to come back. My father was from here, from those islands. I know nothing about him. I know what he looked like from that photograph. He went to England. I have pretended all my life that I never needed a father. But I want to know what happened to him and maybe see where he was from.'

'I know it was hard for you, Mom, to come back.'

'I wanted to leave all this behind me. But I suppose no matter what you do you can't leave the past unearthed. One thing that still puzzles me is why she wanted us to come *now*.'

'Maybe she simply could not face telling us.'

'That's what makes me sad now. If only she had, things might have been different. Right, we must get you to a doctor. Let's hope I can drive this thing.'

CHAPTER 30

'The roses that you ordered have arrived. They are stunning, Catherine!'

Ruby was showing Lainey and Catherine a beautiful wreath created from scented red roses.

They were having a coffee while they waited for the vicar to arrive. Catherine was dressed in a two-piece suit in a rich emerald green and a burgundy camel coat. Her auburn hair was in a perfect chignon. Lainey wore a raspberry-coloured wool dress and Ruby a long gypsy-style dress and coat with brown boots. Edward was taking them today to where Edith was buried. They planned to say a few prayers and then go for lunch.

'Red roses – how apt, Mom.'

'How do you mean "apt"?' Ruby asked.

'Grandma had a hair slide that was precious to her. It was one of her most prized possessions. I lost it once and she nearly lost her life. It had ruby-red roses set on a gold slide. She always seemed to have it. She used to say that it belonged to someone very dear to her. I asked Edward about it yesterday. He told us that when Grandma was leaving Edith at the river, she took the slide from her hair and put it in her own. It was the last connection she had to her sister. Her slide of ruby-red roses. Their father had bought it for Edith when she was sixteen.'

'Oh God, how poignant!' said Ruby.

'I always knew it was precious to her, but I had no idea how precious. I now know why she was so upset when I lost it.'

'How is Edward?' Catherine asked as she lifted her cup.

'He's better really – it's as if a terrible weight has been lifted from him, now that we all know.' Ruby lowered her voice. 'I have noticed him being quite forgetful though – he went to boil two eggs yesterday, then forgot he put them on and the saucepan burnt to bits. Then last night he rang me to remind me to bring home his newspapers. He had rung me half an hour earlier to ask me the same thing, but he didn't seem to remember. Maybe it's just everything taking so much out of him, but I certainly won't be going back to London any time soon. I spoke to Mum. She will hopefully be home for Christmas and then she is heading to Syria. It will be great to see her, but it will be a flying visit. So, it's up to me really to make sure Grandfather is okay. I could never put him in a home. Winnie adjusted fine and is happy, but Grandfather would slowly die there. His life for better or worse is in this house. I will never change that.'

'It must have been so difficult all these years,' Lainey said.

'Yes, but it's a pity they left it so late. I would love to have met your grandmother, my great-aunt. She sounds wonderful. To think I have been in New York and we have never met. I just regret that I never met her.'

'Well, at least we have met now,' Lainey replied, smiling.

'I know. I always wanted a sister, so I'm thrilled to have you. We have so few relatives. We have to stick together.'

Edward arrived down dressed in a suit, shirt and tie and a smart overcoat. They had all agreed to dress up.

'You all look lovely – thank you,' Edward said. 'Catherine, as I said before, if your hair was darker, you'd look very like Edith. You are like her too in personality. She never left the house without being turned out perfectly.'

Catherine looked at him, not sure if it was a compliment or not. Lainey and Ruby laughed.

'Victoria, on the other hand, wasn't that bothered,' said Edward. 'A real tomboy, always climbing trees and riding horses bareback. Oh, we had such fun! Of course, we were forever in trouble, but our father had a way of getting our mother not to scold us too much. There were plenty of good times when we were young. We played for hours in this house when the weather was too bad to go out. Our own personal playground.' He smiled, remembering.

'How was your mother after everything happened?' Lainey asked.

'Mother lived her remaining years mostly in the confines of her bedroom. She rarely went outside. She could never talk of her two daughters. My wife was kind to her and she never really recovered when my wife died of cancer so young. From the moment her daughters were gone, it was as if she gave herself her own life sentence. I could not forgive her, but she was still my mother, and the memories of when my father was alive stopped me from hating her. We had a happy upbringing, but the effect of his death on my mother was devastating for everyone. I often remarked that it was as if I lost both parents as I barely recognised my mother after. She seemed to withdraw from everyone and most of all her children.' He looked around at the assembled company. 'Well, let's move on. I hope Pierce is not bringing that wife of his – she would wear the ears off you. I think I will get a little drink, for medicinal purposes of course.'

Ruby threw her eyes to heaven. 'I don't argue anymore,' she said.

Edward went to the cabinet, took out the bottle of brandy, poured a good measure and then threw it back as if it were medicine.

'Now, are we ready?'

The previous vicar had found a burial plot for Edith in a pretty church cemetery which was surrounded by chestnut trees. The plot was in a secluded spot and there was a simple headstone on it. *Edith Goulding, Kilbride House. 1936–1955.* It was very well maintained.

What could have been a very sad morning turned out not to be. They laid the wreath on the grave and huddled together.

Pierce, who had not brought his wife, said a few prayers.

Then Edward said a few words.

'Edith, we are here today to remember you. Remember how your beautiful life was cut short. But know that not a day has gone by that I have not thought about you. I do believe that if Victoria were here she would say the same. You adored your sister, even though she was a rascal. How I have missed you all these years! I know that you are in heaven and you are looking down on us. The beautiful baby is now this famous actress in New York, can you believe it? She reminds me of you in so many ways. This is your granddaughter Lainey and let me tell you she has many traits like our sister Victoria, including a mad passion for the horses – only the other day she had the heart across us when she took out a fresh horse and got thrown off down on the beach. It reminded me of what Victoria would do. This is my granddaughter Ruby who is a mixture of both of you. She is bossy and has a heart of gold like you, Edith, but there is a wildness like Victoria mixed in there too. Our little sister is in heaven now too, Edith, so I know you are now together again, looking down on us. I miss you both, my dear sisters. But today is not for sadness – God knows we have had too much of that. Today is a day to remember how happy we were once. Sweet dreams, dear Edith, until we meet again.'

There was silence as they all bowed their heads in prayer.

'That was so beautiful, Grandfather,' Ruby then said, with tears in her eyes.

He nodded. 'This is a good day.'

Catherine could not speak. She wiped the tears from her face and composed herself.

'The hotel I booked for lunch is only a few miles from here,' Ruby said. 'Is everyone ready?'

They were a silent little group walking away from the old cemetery.

The hotel had given them a private little alcove which was very quaint with a marble fireplace and a fire ablaze in it. After lunch they ordered hot whiskeys and a coffee for Ruby as driver, and lingered for a while by the fire.

Then they went for a little walk around the hotel gardens.

'Are you okay, Lainey?' asked Piece, drawing level with her. 'It's quite an emotional day for you all.'

Lainey was not sure how she felt. Then for some reason she felt the urge to tell him about the dreams.

'Can I ask you something, Pierce? It may sound a bit strange.'

'I'm intrigued,' he replied.

'Well, ever since I arrived here, I have been having nightmares. It started in a hotel in Tralee on my first night. I had a dream that a woman was drowning in a river. It was very vivid. I saw myself at the river too. I have had the dream several times since I arrived in Kilbride. After visiting Marlborough Asylum, I know that the river in my dream is the river there. I can never really see the person in the river but now, of course, I think it must be Edith.'

'My goodness, quite frightening for you really, considering you had never heard anything about this until you arrived at Kilbride.'

'I haven't told anyone in case they think I'm bonkers. But it's beginning to freak me out.'

'I can imagine.'

'Do you think it could be my aunt in the dream?'

He looked perplexed. 'How do you mean?'

'Do you think I'm being haunted by my dead aunt?'

'Look, there are so many theories out there ... but at the end of the day I am a vicar ... and as such I believe in spirits and, indeed, spirit possession ... but the Church is less clear on haunting!'

'Do you believe it's possible?'

'Honestly, I don't know. It does sound plausible. Yet in the land of psychiatry there is possibly a reasonable explanation for it. But let's say it is your aunt – why would she be trying to haunt you? Perhaps she may have wanted to be acknowledged and now you have acknowledged her.'

'I hope so. I was going to tell Mom, but she is still a bit freaked out herself about everything.'

'Still, keeping it all to yourself is not good. Being here today may help. Let's hope you don't have any more dreams but, if you do, tell your mother and perhaps Ruby. Something like that is very frightening.'

'I hope it helps, I hope it stops. Thank you for listening, Pierce.'

'You can talk to me any time you need to.'

Later that evening, when Edward was having a lie-down, the landline rang and Ruby went to pick it up. She spoke for a few minutes and then put the phone down. Lainey and Catherine were just about to head off.

'That was Winnie on the phone.'

'Is she okay?' Lainey asked, noticing the worried expression on Ruby's face.

'She said that she wants to see you two immediately.'

'That's Winnie who used to housekeep, you said?' Catherine asked.

'Yes.'

'Why would she wish to see me?'

'I can't imagine.'

'Well, I am going back to the hotel to have a lie-down. My flight is tomorrow evening, but I will see you and Edward before I go.'

'Catherine, it sounded like it was really important. She said "immediately". Could you both not swing by the nursing home for a few minutes?'

'God, not more news from the past! I don't think I can take any more revelations.'

'Please, Mom,' Lainey said worriedly.

'Oh, go on, but I am staying only a few minutes. I don't like places like that with all those old people.'

Winnie was sitting with her friends, chatting, when they arrived.

'Help me up, Lainey, and we can talk in my room.'

They settled down in her small bedroom.

Winnie stared at Catherine, not taking her eyes off her.

'My goodness, you look so like your mother Edith Goulding!'

Catherine moved uncomfortably in the chair.

'I called you because I have some news, but I don't want Edward Goulding or anyone else getting hold of it. Dragging up the past, as I said before, is bad for people. But I couldn't help thinking it was a coincidence to hear this now and I thought I'd better share it with you.'

'What is it, Winnie?' Lainey asked.

'There was a new patient arrived yesterday. Her name is Anna Morrisey. Her mother was a Boylan from the islands and a sister to that Canice Meagher's mother.'

Catherine started and leant forward in her chair.

'The poor woman got a stroke, but her mind is very clear. I asked her how many years ago Canice Meagher died, because it must have been in the early fifties. Sure, I thought she was mixed up when she answered me, but as I said she was very clear – you can talk to her yourself.'

'What did she say?' Catherine asked.

'That's the strange thing. Didn't she tell me they found out years ago that he didn't die at all.'

257

'*What?*' Catherine exclaimed.

'He was afraid he would be thrown back in jail, so they only made it up that he had died.'

Lainey could feel the hairs standing on the back of her neck.

'When did he die?' Catherine asked.

'That's the thing. Anna said that they had heard something from him a few years ago. He was in London. He possibly is dead by now – he is in his late eighties. But maybe he's not. Isn't that a coincidence for you? He was alive, she said, a few years ago and they've heard nothing to say he died in the meantime.'

Lainey looked at Catherine. The colour had completely left her face.

CHAPTER 31

'A gin and tonic and a scotch on the rocks – actually make the scotch a double,' Catherine said as she drummed her fingers on the counter.

'Take a seat and I will drop them to your table,' the barman said in a soft polish accent.

They were back in the hotel and Catherine had barely spoken since Winnie's revelation. There were a few couples in the candlelit bar. They found a table close to the turf fire.

Catherine sipped her scotch, hoping it would calm her mind. Right now, she really needed to be on her own, to try to digest this latest news. But she didn't have the heart to say that to Lainey who was all chat about going to London to try to trace Canice Meagher.

So, she had a father after all these years. Living in London. The father she had often wondered about – though, over the years, time had stopped her wondering. He believed his child had drowned that night. That was the great lie that Edward and her mother had decided on. But, unfortunately, the lie had also fooled Canice before Edward could reach him. He had absconded to London, never knowing that they had escaped. Living all these years never knowing he had a living daughter, she wondered if he had ever thought of her or if he had just moved on and begun a new life.

She had studied in London. She may have passed him on the street or sat in a coffee shop not knowing her father was at the next table. He could be a cab driver. Did he do well for himself? Did he marry? Had her mother ever known anything about him? It seemed unlikely. According to Edward they were very much in love and she thought he had died. Had her mother mourned him all these years, believing he was dead? Then a thought crossed her mind. He might have children. She could have half-brothers or sisters.

She felt sick. She ordered another scotch.

'Are you okay, Mom?'

'Not really, to be honest.'

'How do you feel about it?'

'I don't know. It's all too much right now. It's hard to take in. It was bad enough to deal with everything else, but now this. What other secrets are going to fall out of the closets? I have had quite enough.'

'We must try to find out about him. With the internet it couldn't be too difficult. Canice would be an unusual name in London, I imagine. She said he lived in Kilburn. I think lots of Irish lived there. Somebody may have heard of him.'

Catherine put down her drink and looked at Lainey.

'*No!* I don't want you digging anything else up. Not yet anyway. I'm not ready for that, Lainey. I'm tired. It has been such a long day.' She put her hand to her head. 'I can't deal with this right now.'

'Okay. When we finish our drinks, I will get the hotel to order me a cab and we can talk in the morning,' Lainey said reluctantly.

They sat for a little while in the small alcove of the hotel, gentle piano music playing. Lainey's cab arrived.

'Don't forget my flight is tomorrow night,' Catherine said.

'I wish you could stay longer – it's been so good having you here. Would you think about staying longer?'

Catherine shook her head. 'I need to go back, Lainey. Not just for work – I need some time to adjust to this.'

Lainey shrugged her shoulders. It reminded Catherine of so many times when she was a child and had asked her to play or read with her, but there were always lines to learn or a new play to read. The guilt came out of nowhere and almost smothered her.

'The thing is, he may be alive,' Lainey tried again. 'We can't really let the opportunity of finding him pass us by.'

'Please try to understand. I need time to think. I never expected to find my father when I was past sixty. It's a joke. When I found out that Claude was not my biological father, there were times I thought about finding him, but not now. He is more than likely dead and the last thing I want is to find some family in England who are now my half-brothers and sisters. It's too much.'

'But … he could be alive.'

'I'm not ready to go there in my head … I'm sorry.'

'Okay, go back to New York if you have to – I can drive you to the airport.' Lainey grabbed her coat and gave her mother a hug. 'See you in the morning.'

Catherine hugged her tightly, inhaling the jasmine smell from her reddish-gold hair. She pushed back a few strands from her face. It suddenly struck her – the red hair, they had always wondered where it had come from. He had red hair, she just knew it. The photo was black and white, but somehow she just knew.

Her mind was racing. What good would it do, to meet some old man and tell him that his long-lost daughter was alive and well. 'How do you do, Dad? Fancy catching up on the last sixty or so years – oh yeah, sorry we were actually alive and well all the time, pity about the mix-up.'

She had another drink. Eventually she decided to get to bed and just put it out of her mind.

But she couldn't sleep. She had a bath and then some camomile tea. Eventually she pulled some sleeping pills out of her bag and took one. She hated taking them and knew that she shouldn't with the scotch, but tonight she was glad of the chemical oblivion for a few hours.

She awoke groggy and with a dreadful headache. Hopefully a coffee and a shower would do the trick. She needed to check her flight and pack. New York had never seemed more appealing. She couldn't wait to get back to her apartment and away from Kilbride House with all its secrets. Lainey had offered to drive her to the airport, but she might just book a cab. It was a long drive back for Lainey on her own. She was just finished packing when her mobile rang. It was Lainey.

'Mom, I know you told me to leave it, but I just can't. This man is my grandfather and your father.'

'Yes, I told you to leave it and I'm telling you again now! Lainey, just leave it for now. When all this sinks in, we can talk about it.' The pills from the night before had left her feeling wretched and the last thing she needed was more chat about her long-lost father.

'I'm sorry, Mom, I know how you feel, I really do, But I just couldn't help myself. I've been up all night.'

Catherine could now hear the excitement in her voice and a feeling of dread made her close her eyes.

'Up all night doing what?' she asked.

'I couldn't sleep, so I began tracing him on the internet.'

'Lainey! I asked you not to!'

'I know, calm down … wait until you hear this. At first, I could find nothing, but I slightly changed the spelling of Canice and then I found it.'

Catherine held her breath. 'What did you find?'

'I think I found an article on him in a London paper.'

'An article?'

'I know, I was shocked, but I think it's him – it doesn't show a picture or anything, but it says he lives in Kilburn town, in London. I found a piece in the paper that spoke of an Irishman who had accidently joined the choir and was a wonderful singer. Apparently, he spent a lot of time in the church and one day, while the choir was practising the "Ave Maria", he began to sing. They said he began to sing from the back of the church, and the choir stopped in awe of his voice and when he had finished they all broke out in applause. It says his name is "Cannice" Meagher, originally from Kerry. And this is the part that made me catch my breath.'

'Go on!' Catherine could feel her heart beginning to race.

'It says that he comes every day to sit at the statue of Mary with the Child Jesus and that he left Kerry in 1955. The year of the drowning. It adds up. The newspaper article is dated only four years ago. It goes on to say that the choir were due to do a charity recording and now they have Canice on it singing the "Ave Maria". How unreal is that? It has to be the same Canice Meagher.'

There was no getting away from it now. Catherine tried to answer her, but she couldn't. She was glad there was no one there to see her – she could feel herself crumbling.

She took a deep breath and said as breezily as she could, 'Lainey, a porter is at the door with my breakfast, I'll have to call you back.'

'Okay, but we need to reach out and see if he's alive. My goodness, there's a chance that he is! Can you believe it?'

'Chat in a little while – sorry, he's at the door.'

'Okay, but my goodness, I am so excited! Talk to you after your breakfast.'

There was no porter at the door. Catherine could barely breathe. She took a few deep breaths to try to calm herself. Damn her mother for bringing all this on her. Her mother who had devoted her life to her and to Lainey. Never to know that the man she had loved and was father to her child was alive and mourning her in London. All these stupid wasted years. It made no sense. It would have been better if they had never come to Kilbride. What good would it all do now?

But she knew by Lainey's voice that she would not be able to stop her looking this man up. Going to London possibly to try to find him. She couldn't stop her. That's what her mother had done to her, stopped her from coming until now. All the years her mother had dissuaded her from coming to Ireland. Now it all made sense. It was best to leave it all here, buried. This place was enchanting if you could ignore the secrets and the heartache. Kilbride House with all its secrets lay buried for over sixty years. She had seen a portrait of her grandmother Gertrude Goulding. She looked very beautiful but austere. How could she do what she had done? Locking her own granddaughter and daughter up. Oh, she had read about it, she had done her own research since Edward had told her about her past. Some of the children from the asylum never left there, some went to industrial schools and worked for years in appalling conditions. That's what might have happened to her, if her grandmother had got her way. She had locked up her father and got him charged with rape. What kind of person was she? Her parents were torn apart by this woman. Catherine had never felt such hatred for a human being. She was glad she was dead, she hoped she was not at peace for what she had done. She was a baby and she could have drowned in that river, only for Edith and Edward. Her heritage was so complex. She had Edith who gave her life so that they could live and her grandmother who may have locked them up for ever. She felt a shiver going up her back. It was so much easier not knowing.

She ordered a pot of coffee. She couldn't eat.

Now she would have to ring Lainey back. She could try to dissuade her from digging any further, but that was what her own mother had done – dissuaded her in every way possible from trying to follow her roots. Lainey had the right to trace her grandfather. She just hoped they wouldn't regret it.

CHAPTER 32

Lainey's body ached. She had barely slept. She didn't want to worry her mother any more, she knew Catherine was finding all this business stressful enough.

The dream had woken her again last night. This time it was even more vivid. She could clearly see the river. It was the one at the asylum. Then she could hear cries for help. She knew there was someone in the water. She sounded young. But she could never really see her face – but she looked so white, almost like an angel, and then she became a shimmer of light disappearing in the river.

Lainey had awoken with tears flowing down her face. It had frightened her. So much for the dreams stopping. This one was worse than ever, she felt she was going mad.

She had hoped that after the prayers at the graveside it would all surely stop. She didn't really think she believed in anything like that, but perhaps it would help. It all sounded a bit bonkers, but she felt she was being haunted by whoever was in the dream. Perhaps it was her mind playing tricks on her.

She was exhausted, but sleep evaded her. That's when she had begun to search the web for information about

266

Canice Meagher. It just had to be him. Imagine, living all these years never knowing that Victoria and their baby had not drowned. Well, she had every intention of finding him. Maybe he was dead, but there was a good chance that he was alive. He would be almost ninety.

She checked her email and there was a mail from her grandmother's lawyer in New York asking her to contact him as soon as possible. It was too early to ring, so she mailed him and told him she would call around lunchtime Irish time.

Ruby had asked them all to come for lunch at the house. She would pick Catherine up first and then they would head back. She needed to have one more chat with her to see if she could convince her to stay. If she did find her grandfather, she wanted Catherine to be with her.

Catherine wasn't in the foyer. Lainey rang her, and she told her to come up to the room. Lainey was expecting to see her dressed and her make-up as immaculate as ever. But when a pale Catherine opened the door in a dressing gown, Lainey was taken aback.

'Mom, are you okay?'

'I'm fine, just a little shaken to be honest.'

Lainey went in and threw her keys on the table. The bed was unmade, and Catherine's clothes and things were still not packed.

'Mom, I thought you would be packed by now. I know how organised you like to be. Ruby has that lunch organised. I'll tell her you're not up to it if you like, but you might want to say goodbye to them before your flight. Are you sure you're okay? I've never seen you look so pale.'

'You rarely see me without make-up, that's all. You had better make my excuse though to Ruby.'

'But you need to say goodbye to them later, Mom – you can't just leave like that. Ruby has done everything to make us welcome. She is caught up in this too.'

'I'm not going.'

'Suit yourself,' said Lainey. 'But you're being insensitive – if not rude.'

'I'm not going home.'

'*What!*'

'I rang Juniper. I can't act with all this hanging over me. I wish that I could just fly back and never think of all this again, but I know that I can't. As much as I hate it, I need to find out what happened to my father.'

Catherine sat on the bed and looked at Lainey.

'As a little girl, I had everything. Mother loved me enough for two parents. Too much. I can't honestly say that I often thought about my father. I believed her story. They had fallen passionately in love for a few weeks and then he had to go. She had not kept in contact and when she found out she was pregnant there was no way that she could contact him. There was no ill feeling from her – she told me he was kind, handsome and funny.'

'I still can't believe I never knew about it. I really did believe that Claude was my grandfather, even though I had never met him.'

'Well, Claude was that in every way that he could. I have no doubt he loved my mother and did everything he could for her. We agreed when you were little that you did not need to know much about her past. Well, like many secrets, this was another. It worked. We were all happy. But now I want to know. I am dreading it, to be honest.'

'Mom! What are you saying? Are you agreeing to search for him?'

'Yes, I am. God knows what we'll find out. Imagine if he had children?'

'That woman in the nursing home didn't mention any children.'

'That's true.'

'So what's our next step?'

'Lainey, I am going to London to see if we can find my father or at least find out what exactly happened to him.'

Lainey hugged her and suddenly tears came down her face. 'Mom, I am so glad. I really need you now.'

Catherine hugged her, taken aback at her tears.

'You look exhausted, Lainey – are you okay?' she asked worriedly. 'Well, of course you didn't sleep last night, you said, searching for Canice.'

'Well, it wasn't just that ...'

'What was it then?'

'Mom, I keep having dreams, more like nightmares. From the first night in Ireland. There's a river in the dream and a girl drowning, I think. And after seeing the river at the asylum, I know it's the one in my dream. It really frightens me.'

'Why did you not tell me?'

'In case you thought it was bonkers. I think it is. I'm being haunted by the ghost of a girl in the river of an asylum – not exactly after-dinner chat. If it was the fifties, Gertrude Goulding would possibly have me locked up.' She smiled ruefully.

'Lainey, why did you keep all this to yourself?'

'You have enough going on – anyway, I thought it would stop to be honest, especially after yesterday. You see, at first I thought it was Edith in the dream but last night I saw a girl, a fair-haired girl, white like an angel. I was almost afraid to go back to sleep.'

'You poor thing! I'm sure there is some sort of reasonable explanation for it though.'

'I told the vicar yesterday. He suggested that maybe the dreams might stop after we prayed over the grave yesterday – after we accepted Edith. It didn't work. But of course the girl isn't Edith. But, anyway, I know you think all that praying is hocus-pocus.'

'I don't think that. I respect religious beliefs. Believe me, Mother was not very happy when I brought you up without any religion. I used to relent when she wanted to take you to church for Christmas and Thanksgiving.'

Lainey grinned. 'We went a lot more than that. We had a track worn to the church. I loved it, and we always went for hot chocolate afterwards. We never mentioned it to you as we were afraid you would not approve.'

Catherine smiled. 'Mother knew I wouldn't, but I am grateful to her – she was wonderful to you.'

'She was more than wonderful. I miss her so much and seeing all this without her tears me apart, not being able to share it with her. I can hear her all the time telling me about stuff. Like the garden and the roses that her mother grew, the village and how it looked on market day when the farmers would gather to sell their wares. I so loved listening to her tell me how the old roses and brambles would burst into bloom in spring and it would seem the walls of the stables were painted in pink and white. I miss her.'

Catherine hugged her again. 'I know, you miss her more than me, I know that.'

'She was so protective of you – is that what caused you to drift apart from her?'

'I think so now. I could not be everything to her,

nobody can be that to anyone. But it felt like that was what she wanted. I had no idea she had lost so much. She was possibly afraid that she would lose me and, by tying me so tightly to her, in a way she did.'

'I could never understand why you were so cold to her. At least now I understand a little more.'

Catherine walked around the room as if trying to find the right words.

'Lainey, I know I have not always been there for you either.'

Lainey shrugged.

'I should have been.'

'I was happy with Grandma, but I did miss you.' Lainey could feel herself getting choked up. She was not ready for this conversation.

Catherine sensed it. She brightened up and grabbed Lainey's hands.

'Look, let's go to London together. Even if we don't find anything to do with this Canice Meagher, we will at least get to spend some time together.'

'Brilliant. Thanks, Mom.'

'We will have to get to the root of these dreams too though.'

'Thanks, Mom. Look, I'd better head over to Kilbride.' Lainey checked her phone. 'Oh, I'd forgotten – Grandma's lawyer mailed me this morning to get in touch. I don't know why. I tried to contact him and left a message saying I would ring back. I will try it now.'

'What could that be about?'

'I don't know.'

Lainey dialled and got through to him. She talked for a little while.

'Well?' Catherine demanded when the call finished.

'There's a letter. A letter that Grandma wrote and asked him to send me while we were here. I asked him to scan it in and send it to me by email.

'What on earth is this about?' Catherine threw her eyes to heaven.'

'I have no idea. I'll just grab my laptop.' Another piece of the puzzle!

'Give me strength!' Catherine exclaimed and made for the bathroom.

Lainey made a cup of tea while she waited.

Catherine emerged and put on an elegant pair of Dior jeans, a red cashmere polo and a soft pair of white loafers. She left her hair loose and her classic make-up was pared down. She looked like a glossy ad for how to mature gracefully.

'You always look amazing, Mom.

'Appearances count.'

Lainey laughed. 'Come on. I'll take the laptop with me in case that mysterious letter arrives.'

When they arrived at Kilbride John Hogan was walking across the gravel forecourt. He stopped to talk to them.

'I have to go over to the Blaskets later this afternoon. All you Americans love it. You can sit in if you want.'

Lainey noticed that he was speaking to Catherine and to her shock she agreed.

'Fine, I would love that.'

'Right, I'll pick you up at about three o'clock and for Christ's sake put a proper pair of boots on you.'

Lainey was waiting for her mother to give him a sharp retort but to her amazement Catherine nodded and smiled.

'What on earth was all that about?' Lainey asked as they walked on

'I am not quite sure,' Catherine said, looking slightly shocked herself at what she had just agreed to.

When Lainey opened up her laptop in the drawing room, she was surprised to find that the letter had already arrived.

'My goodness, it's here!'

'What is?' Ruby asked.

'It's a letter sent by Grandma's lawyer. It was written by her shortly before she died. She wanted us to have it when we were in Ireland.'

'Read it aloud, Lainey,' said Catherine.

'Okay, here goes: "*My dearest girls, I trust you are both in Kilbride now. I do hope you are in Kilbride House, the home that has stayed with me all these years. I do hope you have fallen in love with the beauty of it and indeed of the whole area. I am so sorry I am not with you. How I have dreamed of it! The cliffs, the dunes, the gulls and the salty scent of the sea. Have you met Edward, my dearest brother, forever young in my heart? Somehow, I believe you have figured out the rest. How our beautiful sister died the night that I escaped. How I stole her name to escape. Believe me, there was never a day passed that I did not think of her. How wonderful she was! You remind me so much of her, Catherine. She was beautiful and talented too. You have given me so much. I know I held you too close. I could not bear to lose you, but my knot was too tight. I know that now and I am sorry, truly I am. Lainey, my gorgeous Lainey, forgive me for not telling you the truth. We have shared such a special time. You have so much love in your soul. Please fly high, Lainey, and don't be afraid, I will always watch over you."'* Lainey's voice broke on these words and she paused. 'Sorry, give me a moment. Okay. *"Canice Meagher was the love of my life. I loved Claude too, but the love I had for Canice can never leave me. My heart breaks to think he died believing we were dead. We missed out on so much. I am just glad you can see where he was from because seeing the islands is like seeing a piece of him. His soul was enshrouded in the Blasket Islands. There is one more thing I need help with."'* Lainey glanced at Catherine who rolled her eyes. *'"When I was sectioned and locked up in that terrible place, I befriended a young girl. Her name was Alice. She was fifteen. She was like a fairy, all blonde and pale. Alice had visions. Unfortunately, this was why she was in Marlborough. Her family had most probably been advised to put her there. She spoke of her family and they seemed gentle people. Unfortunately, they had heeded the wrong advice. In her visions she saw a beautiful light. Once in the middle of the night I awoke in the dormitory and she was in a trance. She was softly singing like an angel. I never got the chance to say goodbye the night I left, but I always told her that if I did escape I would come back for her. She was so fragile and so gentle. I can't imagine how she survived in there. So many times I have thought of her. But I was fearful to contact anyone in case I was found out and, as ridiculous as it seems, I was still terrified that Catherine could be taken from me. I tried to find out about her by ringing the asylum. I was absolutely terrified I would be recognised. They just told me that she was gone and refused to give me information about her family. It is on my conscience now. I know it may be a difficult task but if you can find out what happened to her, it would mean so much to me. If by any chance she is alive, tell her that I never forgot her.*" Lainey paused. "'*I love you both, forgive me for keeping the truth from you. Quite simply I was afraid. Love always,*'" she looked up, "'*Victoria Goulding Lee.*'"

Lainey needed some time to digest her grandmother's latest revelation. Seriously, Sherlock Holmes could not get a family with as many secrets. It beggared belief. Now this. Her grandmother had been the most wonderful person in the world to her, but she was beginning to wonder did she know her at all. She had not even known her real name.

'My goodness, Grandma signed it *Victoria* – it makes it all so real now,' she whispered.

'It sure does,' Catherine sighed.

Edward was quiet.

'You okay, Grandfather?' Ruby asked.

'I am, but it's as if she is here with us.'

'I agree,' Catherine replied dryly. 'My mother had a strong presence to say the least.'

'This request. How are we going to meet that? 'Lainey asked.

'We will contact every office until we find out what happened to this girl,' Edward stated.

'Look, I know someone who might help – leave it with me.' Ruby said.

'Really?'

'Yes, he's into that type of thing, a kind of historian-researcher. To be honest, we kind of have a thing going. I just don't know how I feel now. When I was in London that seemed to be my life but then, Grandfather, you were ill and Winnie was ill and I came home. At first, I thought

I would be back in London shortly, but since I came back to Kilbride, I have this weird connection to it. To be honest, it's not just you, Grandfather, that's keeping me here. I feel I don't want to leave. I spent so many years in London, it seemed more home to me, but now it's as if the peninsula is drawing me back. I can't bear to think of leaving it now. Anyway, this guy that I was seeing – Harry – we are still very much in touch. I will ring him later and see what can be done. He will know where to start at least. I know these things can be difficult to find out, especially if we are not family.'

'I think she drowned,' Lainey said.

Ruby looked at Lainey. 'Why would you think she drowned?'

'Look, I've been having nightmares since I arrived in Ireland, about a woman drowning in a river – before I ever heard anything about the asylum. When I visited the asylum and saw the river there – it was the river in my dreams. I'd been thinking the woman was Edith but the girl I saw last night was just like this Alice. A pale angel.'

Ruby hugged her. 'Lainey, you should have told us. But dreams are only a way of sorting stuff in our head. There is something somewhere back in your memory resurfacing. Probably something Edith mentioned to you.'

'It's okay, Lainey – we will sort it out. Ruby, will you work on this and ring this friend as soon as possible?'

'I will, Grandfather.'

'Thanks, Uncle Edward,' Lainey said. 'I was afraid I was cracking up.'

Edward laughed. 'Sure everyone is cracking up.'

'Edward, we have other news,' Catherine said. 'We are heading to London.'

'Oh? Why London?' Edward asked.

Lainey had told Ruby Winnie's news about Canice. But they had yet to tell Edward. It took him a while to digest the news.

'I can't believe it – imagine Canice Meagher was alive all these years! All these years not to have known. Why would he not have got in touch?'

'Well, he believed that they had both drowned,' Ruby said gently.

'I should have looked for him longer. When I heard he had escaped from the prison, I tried to find him, but I couldn't, then I heard the news that he had died. I never thought that it might not be true.'

'You couldn't have known, you thought he was dead, there was nothing you could have done about it,' Lainey assured him. 'Imagine trying to find him in London in the fifties. It wasn't like today with the internet.'

'Mother had a good life, Uncle Edward,' said Catherine. 'It was tragic that they did not know, but no one was to blame, especially not you. You did everything you could. We'd better let go of what might have been, but we are going to try to see if we can find him. We have no idea if he is still alive or not though.'

'A lifetime has passed since Victoria left. A lifetime!' Edward lamented.

'It has, and there is no more time for secrets,' Catherine responded.

'Right, let's eat some lunch,' Ruby said. 'Myself and Grandfather have been busy in the last couple of hours. No, not making lunch, Cecilia did that. We went down to the basement – well, John Hogan and myself did. Grandfather had told me about two trunks of clothes that were never thrown out. They belong to Victoria and Edith.'

'Oh, my goodness!' Lainey exclaimed.

'I had a quick peep – they look very much intact – they were packed up well.'

'Mother would have had that done,' Edward replied. 'I think she always believed Edith would come back. She made sure the room was never touched – though she never allowed anyone to use Victoria's either.'

'I thought that was you, Grandfather, that you had kept them as a shrine?'

'No, Mother may have been cruel, and I know it's hard to understand, but I do believe she did think that she was doing the right thing. She really believed Doctor Ford knew best. She told people that Victoria was gone to a finishing school and she even planned to take her on a shopping trip when she came home.'

'What did she think was going to happen to me?' Catherine asked.

'I really don't know,' he said. 'She would never discuss it and to the day she died she never did. But when she heard of the drowning, she locked herself away as if in Purgatory. She would not allow anyone to touch either bedroom. I remember we had a maid as well as Bessie – they gathered all the clothes and Mother told them to arrange them in these trunks, and under no circumstances were they to give them to anyone. You, Catherine, in all your lovely clothes, have obviously inherited your Aunt Edith's great love of style and it was that thought that made me remember the clothes and I am so pleased that they are still here.'

'Like a treasure trove! Oh, I can't wait to see them!' Lainey said in excitement.

'I'm really glad you're not going back yet, Catherine. It really means so much to me,' Edward said. 'I know it's difficult, but I can't begin to tell you how happy your visit has made me. I was worried first about dragging up the past, but we should never be ruled by fear.'

'That's for sure,' Catherine said with a warm smile.

After lunch they went into the large sitting room where the fire was lighting. They opened Victoria's first. On the top was an elegant tweed riding jacket and brown jodhpurs. Lainey took them out as delicately as she could. Then she pulled out a princess ball gown in a delicate oyster silk with a draped skirt embellished with sequins. She left it carefully on the back of a chair. Wrapped in a piece of linen was a gorgeous red chiffon cocktail dress. A mink stole was wrapped in another length of linen. And a Chantilly lace veil.

'My goodness, they are beautiful!' Ruby exclaimed.

Next was a black suit nipped in at the waist with daisies embroidered on the collar. Then an evening dress in an aqua taffeta with pearls and sequins adorning the waist.'

'They are so tiny,' Catherine said as she gently touched the fabrics.

'She was only a slip of a thing,' Edward remarked.

'Such beautiful clothes. Where did they go in them?' Ruby asked.

'Mother always liked the girls to have the best in clothes and she bought them in Dublin and sometimes had them made. There were plenty of dances to go to. Always run by the Protestant community. We rarely went to anything else. Mother also loved to have dinner in the

Shelbourne when we were in Dublin and then we would all get very dressed up.'

'My mother always bought me the best too in New York,' Catherine said. 'She went as far as Paris to get the latest fashions.'

Then they opened Edith's trunk. This was a treasure trove of silks, taffetas, sequins, organza.

'I told you she was very fashionable,' said Edward. 'She loved all the glamour of Hollywood and adored going to see the latest big film. Believe me, when Edith was dressed up, she was very striking.'

'Oh my, I would have loved to have known her!' said Catherine, holding up a beautiful jacquard suit. 'You say she was like me. I must have reminded my mother of her so much.'

'When you walked in that door for the first time, I almost believed it was Edith with reddish hair. Of course, you had a shock of bright-red hair when you were born. Your father had the most striking red hair you could ever have imagined. I went to visit him in prison. He was dying in there and I promised to get him out. It was so tragic that he never knew that you lived. I am so sorry, Catherine.'

'What's done is done, Edward. We cannot rewrite what happened.'

'Uncle Edward,' said Lainey, deciding to try to lift the mood, 'we have another bit of news.'

'Oh?' he said.

Ruby and Catherine looked enquiringly at Lainey.

'Mom is going off with John Hogan to the Blaskets.'

'What!' said Ruby while Edward looked bemused. 'He never allows anyone to go with him.'

'I am to wear boots, more suitable,' said Catherine, straight-faced.

'Knowing John, it better be hiking boots. I'll see if I have anything,' said Ruby.

Watching Catherine jump into the jeep in hiking boots and a wax jacket was a sight to be seen.

Lainey was giggling. 'Opposites attract, obviously.'

It would be difficult to get two people so different as John Hogan and her mother. Yet if she thought about it there were some similarities. They had no time for small talk and almost preferred their own company. They were completely passionate about what they did for a living. As if nothing else mattered. It would be interesting to see how the afternoon went though.

CHAPTER 33

London
2018

They were flying to Heathrow.

'I have a feeling Canice Meagher did not stay in a hotel when he first arrived here,' Catherine said.

Lainey had managed to get in touch with the choirmaster, a George Williams, who had agreed to meet them for a coffee, but had given her no information at all so far. He couldn't or wouldn't even confirm that Canice was alive.

'I had forgotten how much I adore London,' Catherine remarked.

'Have you agreed with Juniper to come to London for the play yet?'

'Well, she will come either way, but I need to tell her if I am on board or not shortly.'

'It's not like you to hesitate.'

'I know. I was hesitant before all this, now I am not at all sure how I feel. Part of me wants to get back to New York and never leave again. Maybe it's my age.'

'It will be hard to turn down Juniper.'

'Another part of me now wants to linger.'

'Is that anything to do with your date with John Hogan?' Lainey said with a giggle.

'I keep telling you it was not a date! But I did love the outing. Oh Lainey, you must go out to the islands as soon as you can! You will love them – they are so beautiful and wild. The birds are mesmerising – everything from sea gulls to puffins and fulmars. John is so knowledgeable about the land. It's so remote and unspoilt. I can imagine it may have been a difficult life, but to think of being born there and then having to leave it!'

Lainey hid a smile. It was so strange and endearing to hear her mother romancing about the islands. 'Yes, it's mad to think that our relatives were island people, that they lived that life – it's not like it's that long ago. It's like a glimpse of a vanishing Ireland. I am going there with my camera as soon as I get back. The views from Ventry are amazing and I have already got some great shots. I am thinking of doing an exhibition back in New York at some stage. I would like to base it on my trip here. So, I need to build up my portfolio.'

'I would like to explore it more myself, to be honest. I can see where the poets and playwrights got their inspiration. John was a really great guide. He only talks when necessary which suited me. He points out the most unusual things, like a stream flowing with the sun shining on it, looking like melted crystal. He has an unusual turn of phrase. He talks a bit of Irish too. I love listening to it even though of course I have no clue what it means. But it suits him somehow. He is the quintessential quiet Irish man.'

'He wasn't very quiet when I took Murphy for a ride. The next time I went down to the stable he tore strips off me again, some in Irish too!' Lainey grinned at her mother.

'He is very passionate about his horses and he thought you were irresponsible. I think you were too. You gave me the fright of my life.'

'Are you going on any more private little tours with him?'

'Well, I told Juniper that I would let her know after today when I am due back in New York for definite. So, depending on that.'

'Hmm, so you might go on another with him?'

'As I said, he is the perfect guide. You can come with us.'

'I wouldn't dream of it,' Lainey said with a grin.

Catherine gave her a nudge.

Heathrow was a buzz of activity. As they had only hand luggage they went through Customs quickly and went outside to grab a cab.

'The Stafford, please,' Lainey instructed. She knew how Catherine enjoyed her luxury and she had stayed at the Stafford herself only a year before on a trip for work.

Catherine looked as elegant as ever, in a closefitting grey jersey dress, a white cashmere coat and soft grey leather gloves. Her hair was in an elegant chignon and dark glasses were on her head.

'Let's get this meeting over,' said Lainey in some trepidation. 'He was giving nothing away on email or on the phone. He seemed quite wary of me to be honest.'

'It may turn into a wild goose chase, but we can always go shopping,' said Catherine but she looked nervous too. 'Where are we meeting him?'

'Starbucks in Kilburn.'

After they settled in their beautiful rooms, they freshened up and met in the foyer.

They grabbed a cab to Kilburn.

George was waiting for them in the coffee shop, a coffee half-drunk in front of him. Lainey introduced herself and Catherine. She had told him that Canice was a relative, but she had not said that they now knew he was much more than that.

He went and brought them two coffees from the counter.

'But I recognise you?' he said to Catherine after he sat down again.

Lainey could feel her mother bristle. One thing that her mother did not look for was any celebrity status. Truth was, even though she was a famous theatrical actress most people did not know her. Obviously, theatre lovers recognised her and the cream of high society in New York who made a point of knowing lots about the theatre. Catherine had of course no time for anyone who talked about theatre just to impress. She simply ignored them. They tainted the name of theatre, but as Juniper pointed out 'They buy tickets and put bums on seats and that is all we can ask for.' But Catherine knew that, like her, Juniper would do theatre even if she was penniless. She could not do anything else. Luckily, they were able to make a living out of it. It did help that her mother had left her a wealthy woman. If she decided not to work, she was very much financially secure. Lainey reckoned that was another reason she always turned down any TV or film work. To be recognised on the street would be something her mother would hate. Catherine could not understand why people craved fame. Celebrity lifestyle was vulgar to her. 'If you have an art, use it properly, not to get noticed for anything other than your talent.' This was what she constantly said to young actors who had got bitten by the celebrity culture.

The man was staring at Catherine, trying to figure out how he knew her.

'I spent some time here when I was young, perhaps we met at some stage?' Catherine said sweetly.

'My goodness, you are Catherine Lee Miller! The actress! I saw you at the old Vic, playing Blanche in *Streetcar*. My dear woman, you were fantastic! I know you got a Tony and an Olivier for it.'

Catherine softened a little. Obviously, this man knew his theatre.

'Mom prefers to live very quietly offstage,' Lainey said.

'Of course, but I am honoured to be in such a theatrical presence.'

'Thank you,' Catherine replied.

Lainey gave Catherine a warning signal to be nice. This was the only lead she had to Canice Meagher.

'So, Canice Meagher?' Lainey asked. 'We're trying to trace him. We have no idea if he is alive or not.'

'When I received your mail, I just wanted to see who you were before giving any information about Canice. I can see now it is very genuine and of course having Mrs Lee Miller here gives great credibility to your enquiry.'

'Call me Catherine, please.'

George beamed. He was a stout man, possibly in his late sixties. He had a very open face and big blue eyes that crinkled up when he smiled, which was practically all the time.

'I have no hesitation in telling you about Canice. Yes, Canice is alive. He is in his late eighties, but he is remarkably well. A gentleman, I might add.'

Lainey looked at Catherine, who looked like she just might faint.

'Are you okay, Mrs Lee Miller – *ahem* – Catherine?'

'Our flight was very early, and Mom hasn't been feeling well. I'll get you some camomile tea, Mom, okay? Leave the coffee.' She was trying to cover up their shock.

'I'll do that,' said George, getting to his feet.

'Thank you, that would be lovely, George,' she replied sweetly.

He went to the counter.

'Mom, Mom, are you okay?'

'Alive! Just like that. I was sure he was dead. We would lay a flower like at Edith's grave. But he is alive. My father is alive. I don't know how to react. I am shocked – my God, he is alive!'

George arrived back with the camomile tea.

'Thank you, George,' said Catherine. 'I find it very soothing. It really was a very early flight – it seems to have hit me just now.'

'Flights are ghastly these days, I dread flying. I was on a flight recently to Paris and we were delayed at least three hours, then I was on a flight to Berlin and that was worse.'

George chatted for a few minutes, giving Catherine time to recover.

Lainey felt he had picked up on the atmosphere. At length she asked, 'You were telling us about Canice?'

'Yes, well, Canice arrived over here in the fifties. Like many men from Ireland, he worked on the buildings. But I think he was a bit lost in life. He had no family left as far as I am aware. So, I am sure he will be delighted to meet you.'

'Thank you – we are doing a family tree, so it would

be great to get all the links,' Lainey said. 'But better still to meet him.'

'Ah, yes, indeed! He's a wonderful man. And what a singer! He still sings with us at times. Beautiful. I think with the right training he could have been really something. Anyway, you probably know the story, but we were rehearsing and there was an elderly man at the bottom of the church. I had seen him there often when we were rehearsing. There is a statue there of Mary and the Child Jesus. Apparently, Canice had a wife and a baby in Ireland and as far as I know they drowned. Poor man never got over it. Had you heard about it, seeing as you are relatives?'

Lainey and Catherine caught their breath. This man would fall off his chair if he knew that the drowned child was sitting in front of him in Starbucks having camomile tea.

'No, we hadn't – what a dreadful thing to happen!' Catherine replied, the actress in her coming into play.

'Anyway, we were just about to do the "Ave Maria". We have a few soloists and we were trying to figure out who would be best to sing the first verse on their own. The music began to play and suddenly the man at the bottom of the church began to sing. His voice was startling and very Irish. Believe me the choir hardly breathed while he sang, it was that beautiful. It took a lot of persuading to get him to agree to recording it with us but, as it was for charity and a homeless shelter, which was close to his heart, he agreed. I have the CD with me.'

'When you say it was close to his heart, what do you mean?' Lainey asked tentatively.

'Canice has lived in a shelter for the past sixty years.

I'm sorry, I thought that you knew that?'

'No, we had no idea,' Lainey almost whispered.

'Yes, I think he slept rough at the start. But he has been at Saint Aidan's since it opened, their longest resident, even though they don't house residents. It's not a long-term set-up. You must pack your bag in the morning and leave and then reclaim your bed at night. There were many organisations that were aware of Canice's living circumstances, so he was offered alternative accommodation on many occasions.'

'Well, why on earth is he still there then?' Lainey asked.

George looked at her and at Catherine. 'Quite simply, it is his home, call it what you like.'

He spoke so softy that Lainey wondered if the penny had dropped – was he beginning to have a suspicion to who they really were?

'Perhaps he is institutionalised,' he went on. 'But I think it is more than that. Saint Aidan's is where he learned to find peace again after whatever trauma happened to him. I do believe it was a trauma. It wasn't alcohol. He would take a drink but only one to two bottles of ale. He loves his tea and a big treat for him is going into the coffee shops. He loves a cup of tea in the Coal Café. He likes to write – he will sit there for hours watching the people go by. He is very well known and loved too. As I said he may be poor, but he is very much a gentleman. But things are changing now of course, and it can be so dangerous for him. He has been mugged and even got a terrible battering one night. But he will not move to anywhere else.'

Catherine looked pensive. She put down her cup.

'You have been very honest with us, George. I think we

289

must give you the same curtesy. We would ask for your confidentiality. I am an actress, but I value my private life very much.'

'Of course, be assured, I am very discreet.' George looked like he would do anything for such a talent.

Lainey gave her a nudge of encouragement.

Catherine took a deep breath. 'We believe that this man is my father.'

CHAPTER 34

London
1955

Canice Meagher knew from experience that the streets of London were far from being paved with gold. It had been tough when he was here before, but everything had changed since then. He had arrived before to find work and there was plenty of it. He had worked laying gas pipes from early light until dark. He had even dared to dream. He could sing and write and in London there were theatres and concert halls. He never told anyone except Victoria. Things happened in London, good things, there was a chance, there was none on the islands. Victoria had believed in him, she had listened for hours to him singing, he had shown her poetry that he wrote and songs.

Yet he had missed the peninsula and the Island when he was here before. The very air was different. The air on the Great Blasket was the purest, it fed his soul. But it was not work he had arrived for this time, it was to disappear from Ireland, a man on the run. But more than that, he could not tolerate living in a country that had stolen so much from him. There was a black hole where his heart should be, and it was close to destroying him. He was afraid hate and bitterness would become so powerful that he could be consumed by it. He had to stay away for good this time. He would never set foot on Irish soil or the Island again.

If only he had stayed in London and never went home that first time, made a life in Kilburn and accepted his fate! It was a little over two years since he had returned to Ireland. But now there was no return. All bridges were burned. Ireland might be only across the Irish Sea, but it might as well have been in another galaxy. Indeed, it felt like a dream now. Had it all really happened? Sometimes he wondered was he going mad.

That day in the bog field had changed everything. When he slept he dreamt of her. Her gentle voice that teased him about his island ways. When he awoke it took him a few minutes to realise that she was gone and then a cloud of darkness wrapped him up so tightly he thought he would die. Her wild carefree beauty had stolen his soul like a Celtic goddess. She had loved him – he was sure of it. He was as sure of that as he was of the moon reappearing in the sky. He remembered the passionate bond they had shared. He knew now the memory would have to last him a lifetime. He could not think of the child that was lost. He had put that out of his mind, for if he was to dwell on it he would have been better off throwing himself off the boat that bore him back to London.

When he was locked away and knew what they had done to Victoria, he thought he would lose his mind, caged like an animal. Then he heard from Edward that the baby was born. He vowed that he would get out and get her out too. Edward was trying to talk them into dropping the charges. It made him sick to think of what they had charged him with. Rape and abduction. Her mother had to know that it was a lie. He was an innocent man who loved her daughter with every breath that he took. He was poor and a Catholic and of course they had committed the worst sin in holy Ireland: created a baby out of wedlock. He tried to stop imagining what the baby must have looked like. Was she like Victoria? All silky skin and dark hair? What was her name? If only he could stop the thoughts. Stop them tearing him apart.

He had been spotted on the boat. Seán O'Connor had recognised him. Seán was from a village just outside Kilbride. All ready for his big chance in London, with his make-do case and his few shillings. Seán could have shopped him as soon as he stepped off the boat in Swansea. But luckily there was another man, Joe Dwyer, a man Canice had worked with on the roads of London and shared a house with off the Kilburn Road. Joe believed him, he knew he was no rapist or abductor. He agreed to help him. He would help him to disappear.

Canice hid on the boat until the passengers were all off. It was easy to get a rumour started and Joe made sure that happened when Seán O'Connor said that he thought he had seen Canice Meagher on the boat.

'Canice must have fallen over the edge of the ship – he had the drink on him!' Joe shouted. The rumour would reach Ireland as soon as the ship returned if not sooner.

Ironically, he had struggled with wanting to throw himself in that night and many times after that. Sometimes he could feel a pull from the dark waters of the Thames. But then he would simply be another Irishman who lost his way.

They would have had a life in London. He knew she would have missed the wildness of the peninsula. He could still smell the saltiness in the air himself, hear the gulls and early evening curlew. He could see the cliffs as the silver waves crashed and when on a wild night the wind howled so loud down the chimney that the roof felt like it would fly off. His childhood of stories, fisherman, fairies and hardship stayed with him. He was haunted by his mother's cries as she left the Island, the only home she ever knew. How on earth would she cope? He could almost smell the flowers that only grew on the islands. The songs that had filled his soul, the land that had stolen everything from him.

Victoria would surely have missed Kilbride. Her heart would weep for her beautiful Silver, Kilbride House would forever remain in her memory. She had longed to tell Edward and Edith, but he was afraid of how they would react. He had asked her not to. If she had, maybe none of this would have happened. But it did. Her mother had her locked up. Was she a witch or was she just brainwashed into thinking she was doing the right thing? Protecting her daughter. That's what the great doctor had probably told her.

He remembered his vicious words when he came to see him in his prison cell.

'You are not fit to shine Victoria Goulding's shoes, you rogue! You are lucky I am not a violent man, or the gardaí would have had to pull me away from you that night. What are you? I'll tell you, you're a nothing! That's what you are – home from England where you drank everything you earned like all the other labourers. Well, you can head back, that is if they don't lock you up for good. Your poor mother will rue the day you were born. You are caught now like the rat you are. You came from squalor and you are not dragging her into it. You could have had a decent life. You had a few acres from the land commission and a few hours on the estate. But you wanted what wasn't yours, and you will pay.'

So, Gertrude Goulding had locked her away in that gaol of a hospital. Well, Mrs Gertrude Goulding of Kilbride House had her own sentence to live out now, one of her own making. Her daughter would not shame her anymore. She could never apologise for what she had done and try to make amends. She could never tell her daughter that she loved her, and she was sorry. She could never hold her granddaughter and feel the warmth of her soft skin. She had destroyed it all. Canice was fighting with himself not to hate her with all his might, but if he did she would win. Victoria had no hate – it was what he had loved her for. She was free of bitterness, judgement and prejudice. He would not hate Gertrude Goulding because if he did he might as well have jumped that night off the boat and be done with it. He knew the dark nights that would now surely be his path and he prayed that he would survive them.

Instead he tried to see it as Victoria would have. How she would have loved London! The energy of Fleet Street where every respectable newspaper had an office, knowing everything about the world a day before everyone else. She would have marvelled at Bond Street where the ladies shopped, dressed in colourful clothes and fancy shoes. He would have shown her the Tower of London where history was embedded in the walls, Windsor Castle to watch the guard change. He would have shown her the West End where theatre and musicals were on nightly.

He would have taken her to Kilburn Road. Sure, it was practically Ireland. Full of men from every corner of the country who had left with a dream of returning. He had watched them in Ireland making their way to the boat. With their cardboard cases and their peaked caps. Not an inkling of what London was going to be like.

In Kilburn the Ganger arrived every morning to collect men to work that day. There was plenty of work. Hard, backbreaking work by Irishmen who helped build Britain after the war. Women too, working in shops and factories. Big families waiting for the money in the envelope to be sent home to the rest of them. The men worked fourteen-hour days. Shirts and vests would come off and like savages they would work with sweat on their brows. Hard, difficult and sometimes hazardous work, where you needed nerves of steel to carry a bucket of cement up scaffolding so high you'd think it should touch the clouds. Don't look down or you were a goner.

He must stay away now from the usual haunts. He was officially a man on the run. He would not visit the Crown bar where he used to cash his cheque on a Friday. He would drink and buy the Ganger a few too, making sure he got some work the following week. At least the Irish hired the Irish. There were plenty of signs saying NO IRISH NEED APPLY scattered around London. So, they looked after their own. Most of the time.

He had told Victoria all that was good about London. The money that she had would help get them started and he would work hard. He would have hated to bring her to some crummy bedsit.

He had no place to sleep when he arrived in London. He wandered into a church and at the feet of a statue of

Our Lady he fell and cried until he thought he would die. He slept and had a fitful dream, watching a grey mare race over the beach, crashing across the waves, galloping as her mane danced in the morning light. She was searching, searching for her mistress.

He slept rough, often wondering if he would live until morning. He slept in doorways and anywhere that he could feel safe. He made friends on the street, other men who had found the streets of London had become their home. The human spirit amazed him. They talked of Ireland and they sang her songs. They looked out for one another. Then he found Saint Aidan's, a shelter for men that housed mostly Irish. You got a bed and hot porridge in the morning with bread and a mug of tea. Then you packed your bag which wasn't very hard – it consisted of a sleeping bag, a rug as a pillow and a few clothes items – and you waited until later when you could come back in and get a bed. There was a soup kitchen that he was welcome to visit at around noon. He made friends with the people and accepted their kindness with gratitude. They asked no questions of his past, he supplied none. He became known simply as Canice.

He still prayed every day. Catholicism was in his blood – even if he wanted to walk away from it he couldn't. Every day he walked to the same chapel and knelt and prayed at the statue of Mary and Jesus. He prayed for Victoria and his baby. Often, he stayed there for hours. There was something there that he was searching for. He had found a peace of sorts. Something in his heart kept him living and wanting to live. While he had life, he would try to see the good. He had a pen and an old copybook, and in the darkest hours he wrote it down –

everything, the passion, the pain and the love he knew he was lucky to have had. She was gone but he knew it would endure. A love like that would endure forever.

CHAPTER 35

London
2018

George looked as shocked about their news as they were about his.

'My goodness, are you quite sure?'

'Quite sure,' Catherine replied.

'How can you be so sure it's Canice? He told me that his baby and the love of his life died. He never elaborated. But he was very sure that they were dead.'

'My mother Victoria Goulding had a relationship with Canice Meagher who was originally from the Blasket Islands. But her mother Gertrude disapproved. She was only sixteen, a Protestant from a village called Kilbride. The Gouldings were very much the gentry, living in Kilbride House, and she was brought up in an elitist circle. I am afraid Gertrude acted very unwisely. Victoria became pregnant by Canice and they tried to elope to England but were stopped at the boat under the instruction of Gertrude. She had Canice arrested and my mother was sectioned to an asylum. Apparently, it was relatively easy to have someone committed. I was born there. But we escaped in 1955, while Canice was still in prison, held for the abduction and rape of Victoria, which we of course know were lies. My Aunt Edith died trying to help with our escape – she drowned in a river which ran around the asylum. My mother assumed the identity of my aunt. This way we could escape. You can understand why I would like to keep this story quiet. But, George, I somehow trust you, that is why I am telling you this.'

George blushed and promised that she was assured of the utmost discretion.

Lainey admired her mother's skills. She had poor George ready to jump into the Thames if that was what she wished. He was smitten and in the palm of her hand.

'Anyway, we began a new life in New York. Canice escaped, and my mother believed that he died shortly afterwards, never knowing we had lived. Victoria had a substantial amount of money and she also married a man called Claude. He died when I was very young so my memory of him is dim. But he was very kind – I do remember that he indulged us both. He left us very secure financially. We lived in New York high society. Finally – my mother stipulated in her will that we should visit Kilbride and there we stumbled over some information about my father.'

George sat with his mouth opened. Lainey had to stifle a grin at his appearance. He could hardly believe what he was hearing.

'I know it is a lot to take in,' said Catherine. 'But I assure you, it is the truth.'

George eventually closed his mouth. His face had become quite red. Lainey wasn't sure if it was the heat or the proximity to Catherine that was affecting him. Then he found his voice.

'To be honest, I do not doubt it,' he said. 'I am just not sure how Canice will take it.'

'Do you think it will be too much for him?' Lainey asked.

He considered it and moved his cup around on the table.

'What choice do you have but to tell him? He has been denied the truth all these years. It is quite a heart-breaking story.'

They all sat in silence for a few minutes, trying to absorb what they had heard.

'I think if I call to see him first and maybe arrange a meeting for you in the Coal Café. Perhaps it would be best if I tell him this news and see how he takes it all? He is very healthy, but I would be worried about the shock and the effect it might have on his heart. I think we need to tread carefully.'

Lainey looked at Catherine. It seemed a good option. They both nodded in agreement.

'Okay, you have my cell number,' Lainey said. 'Thanks, George, for your help.'

They got a cab back to the hotel and headed for their respective rooms. Catherine decided to lie down, and Lainey turned on her laptop.

So, she had a grandfather, living all these years in a hostel in London. She looked around at the luxury in her bedroom. She was used to it. She had grown up with it, never knowing anything different. He had possibly never stayed in such a hotel. Never knew what luxury was. His treat, the local coffee house. Lamenting for a lost lifetime, his lost daughter and the love of his life. It was heart-breaking. He had never met anyone else.

She was exhausted but almost dreaded going to sleep,

although the night before had been undisturbed. She didn't have the nightmare. Was it to do with the letter about Alice?

She looked up the hostel that George had mentioned. It had been opened in 1965. It was for homeless men and during the sixties and seventies it was ninety per cent Irish. The forgotten Irish. The men who had helped to rebuild a war-torn London. The men who had sent money home to educate the children of Ireland, in some cases to put bread on the table for their Irish families. It seemed as if they were forgotten. They had left their homeland, many never being much further than their own towns before. Now they had no one back there, all being dead or moved on, and they lived on the outskirts of society. Not really belonging to either place.

It was almost three when her cell rang.

It was George. He had gone to visit Canice and found him at the church on his daily visit. They had gone for a cup of tea and he had told him what he knew. He said that Canice was overwhelmed with grief and they had to call the doctor. He was fine now though and resting at the shelter. The staff had great fondness for him. But he had some good news. Canice wanted to meet with Catherine and Lainey.

'Oh, my goodness, that is wonderful news!' said Lainey. 'Where shall we meet?'

'I think his own surroundings would help. I'll bring him to the Coal Café tomorrow at eleven if he's up to it. I will let you know for certain when I call for him in the morning.'

'Perfect.'

'Did you listen to the CD?' George enquired.

'Not yet. My mother has been resting. We'll listen to it now.'

'Regards to your mother. I'll be in touch tomorrow morning.'

Lainey dialled her mother's room and filled her in on the news.

'Can you play it on your laptop?'

'You bet.'

'Okay, see you in a minute in your room.'

Lainey popped the CD in.

'There is only one song on it, I think,' she said.

'It feels odd to think that this is the first time I will hear my father's voice,' Catherine said, her own voice choking.

Lainey pressed play.

It began with a very professional orchestra. The intro to Shubert's 'Ave Maria' filled the air and then a male voice began to sing. It filled every fibre of the room with a remarkably beautiful tenor, his accent accentuating his Irishness. It was not until towards the end that the choir joined in, like a background of angels swelling to a wonderful finale.

Lainey and Catherine were in floods of tears by the end of it. Whatever they expected when they found Canice Meagher, it was not to be so moved by the sheer beauty of his voice that they could not speak.

'Oh my God, what a voice!' said Lainey. 'He is like the finest secret tenor of Ireland. Magical.'

'You know, this is why my mother constantly listened to John McCormack when I was little. On her own, always on her own. He reminded her of him, it was how she felt close to him. Christ, it all makes sense now.'

'I feel she is close to us today. I know she is gone, but somehow she is guiding us.'

Catherine opened the mini bar. 'I need a drink. Have one?'

'Love one, gin please.'

They sat with their drinks and listened to it again, his beautiful voice bringing powerful emotions to the surface.

'I really hope he is okay and can meet us tomorrow.'

'Yes – yet I am half dreading it. I hope it's not all awkward.'

Catherine was dressed in her usual style, which meant very elegant with a hint of glamour. Lainey had a simple outfit of tailored trouser and shirt under a warm dark woollen coat. The cab driver dropped them off at the Coal Café. They had agreed with George to allow him to get Canice settled first – they would arrive a little after eleven.

It was busy with the usual chit-chat of a local coffee shop. The smell of melted chocolate hit their senses. It was quite an old-fashioned coffee shop with a very homely essence to it.

A woman of about fifty came out to meet them.

'Hi, I'm Cheryl. George told me to expect you. We normally give Canice a window seat, but he is down in the little alcove there today.

'Thank you,' Catherine said.

They made their way down to the alcove.

'How did she know it was us?' Catherine whispered.

Lainey didn't state the obvious. It would not be too difficult to describe Catherine Lee Miller to anyone.

They spotted George raising a hand in greeting.

There was an elderly man seated beside him, dressed in

a suit. tie and overcoat. He stood up when they arrived and then put his hand to his mouth in disbelief.

Lainey knew he needed no proof, with their strong family resemblance.

He opened his arms then embraced Catherine as only a father could a child he had lost for sixty years.

Catherine was overcome with emotion. George, being the perfect gentleman, guided her to her seat.

Canice took both Lainey's hands in his. Looking deep into her eyes.

'Thank you for finding me.'

He embraced her as she broke into floods of tears.

The emotion was tangible as they sat down.

'We heard you sing the "Ave Maria" from the CD that George gave us,' said Catherine. 'It is so beautiful.'

'Ave Maria – I have great belief in Holy Mary and indeed she did not let me down. All these years I have prayed to be with you again. I just never thought it would be in this lifetime.'

'I am so sorry we have only found you now,' said Catherine. 'I cannot bear to think of all the years that my mother silently mourned for you. While you have been here, never knowing. It's almost unbearable.'

'I think I had better leave you,' George said, obviously feeling he was intruding.

'Please, there is no need,' said Canice. 'That article in the paper would never have been written if it wasn't for you, George, and Lainey here might never have found me.'

George beamed at him. 'I think some pastries or fudge cake then to celebrate!' he announced.

CHAPTER 36

'It feels odd to be going back to the hotel and all this luxury while he must go back to the shelter. It seems so wrong. I just wanted to grab him and bring him with us,' Lainey said to Catherine.

It was almost lunchtime and they had just left the Coal Café.

'I know, but George is right – we need to tread carefully. He has his pride – we can't offer to put him up in the Stafford, just because we can. I'm not sure what we should do, but I think we did enough today. We must allow him to come to terms with everything.'

'Seeing him with his sleeping bag, waiting to go back in to claim his bed. It all feels so wrong. We could make his life so much more comfortable. Can you imagine if Grandma knew? Surely she would want us to?'

'Yes, but she would know he has his pride too, Lainey.'

In all her time Catherine had never imagined her father to be living in a shelter. To think that he was here all these years, claiming his bed every night! She thought of her beautiful apartment in New York and her childhood one with Edith, all the hotels she had stayed in. She had never

306

seen a glimpse of a life like his.

However, he might be living in a shelter but that did not take anything away from him. He had a quiet dignity about him and he spoke with an Irish elegance. He was an Irishman through and through. She could imagine him living in Kerry.

She knew she needed to give him time. She didn't want to go and flash her credit card around and tell him she was from the elite of New York Society and they had done quite nicely without him.

'George told me that he has a little room in Saint Aidan's that they keep for him always. But he would never impose on them, so he prefers to leave each day and not have any special arrangements made for him. But the same room is always kept regardless. Imagine living there all those years! I can't quite get my head around it.'

Catherine was trying to keep her emotions in check. She had always managed to have a steely exterior, except for the theatre, where every emotion known to humankind seemed to embrace her. But she had kept her emotions in control in her personal life – it had suited her. But that day that Lainey had been thrown by Murphy, something had changed for her. Theatre had always been everything, but now she was not so sure. She didn't want to wake up one day and find it was too late to repair the relationship with her daughter. She knew she was lucky – Lainey was forgiving. She could be bitter about all the time she had devoted to her career rather than family, but she wasn't. How many times had she taken her shopping, or taken her on holiday? She could scarcely remember any.

Now this big thunderbolt was thrown into their lives.

Canice Meagher. He certainly was a gentleman, a man of his time. Lainey wanted to go buy him new clothes and perhaps have him live with them – she knew how her daughter worked. But she was wiser and knew that life was not that simple.

She had no idea what the future of the relationship with Canice would bring. She needed some time to absorb it all herself. So much had happened since she left New York. And now, for the first time in her life, the allure of the theatre was not as strong.

She found herself thinking of John Hogan, he was so different to any man she ever knew. He had no idea who she was for a start – he was certainly not interested in her as a theatrical star. She was in her sixties now, he was possibly the same. Since she hit sixty, she had decided enough was enough. She had never needed a man really. She had loved Lainey's father, but of course never really needed him. As she let go of youth and middle age, she certainly did not need a man in her life. Men simply bored her. But John was different. She loved his passion for horses. How he saw the landscape as if from an artist's eye. His appreciation of a flight of starlings and how they floated together across the sky. He spoke only when he needed to. But they did have a connection. He was very assertive and, although he could be curt, he was still quite chivalrous in an old-fashioned way. He was a very conscientious man – she had met plenty of the other kind. She had seen plenty of it, directors thinking they were gods and ordering actresses around. Well, she had made sure that they never ordered her, and they would get the viciousness of her tongue and her actions if they dared.

'You will never work in New York again – go back to

the hovel that you came out of!' she had said to a pretentious young director she had found in an indecent situation with a very young, very cowed wardrobe assistant. 'Get out, you animal, or I will call the police and have you locked up and on the front page of the newspaper in the morning. She is under age, you imbecile!'

He had scampered with his trousers in his hands, shouting insults at her. She had warned the girl to develop some gumption if she planned on staying in the theatre. If not, she strongly advised her, she'd better go home, find a nice husband and stay there.

'Let's do the galleries – we are in London,' Catherine suggested.

'Okay, we could have some lunch there,' Lainey replied.

They spent the next couple of hours blissfully going through the National Art Gallery and then chilling having lunch.

'It's lovely to just sit and not rush, isn't it?' Lainey said.

Catherine watched her and knew she needed to say the words that were in her head.

'Lainey, I'm sorry – we should have spent many afternoons in galleries and shopping. I know I was always consumed by the theatre. Can you forgive me?'

Lainey smiled back. 'I would never have had the relationship that I did have with Grandma if you were around. I did miss you but, being so close to Grandma, I see the world a little like she did. She is with me all the time and I miss her so much.'

'I know you do, Lainey, but know that I am here now.' Catherine grabbed her daughter's hand and held it.

Coming to Ireland had changed Catherine's perspective on a lot of things. Perhaps that was another reason why Edith wanted them to visit Kilbride – the place of their ancestors, the place where their past decided their future. New York seemed far away now. She would have to ring Juniper to let her know when she would be back. She needed to make some decisions.

Catherine picked up her wineglass.

'What shall we toast?' Lainey asked, holding up her own glass.

'Let's toast Victoria Goulding Lee, my mother and your grandmother.'

'To Victoria!'

'To Victoria!'

The next morning George rang to say that Canice was in very good spirits and had asked if he could meet with them in the morning. Lainey agreed to meet again in the Coal Café.

Cheryl greeted them as they arrived.

'What can I get you? Canice is not here yet.'

'Some tea, please,' said Lainey.

They sat near the window and as they looked out, they could see George and Canice crossing the street.

'He has his sleeping bag again,' Lainey remarked.

'Say nothing, Lainey. I know you want to look after him, but take it gently, we just can't rush things.'

After they greeted each other and they had all settled down with drinks, Canice spoke up.

'I have been thinking about things and there is something I want to ask you. I am so glad you did find me. My spirit is lifted more than you will ever know. For the first time in all these years, I went to bed last night knowing that you did not drown, but lived a full life. Yes, it was tragic that we all never knew, but there is no point holding any more regret or heartache. It only has the power to build a dark hole in your heart. Believe me, I know. We must take what we have now. So I have a request. When I dream, I see Victoria in Kilbride, wild and free. I believe her spirit is still there. Perhaps she has guided us to each other since her death. I would like to be close to her again. This is what I want to ask you. Will you take me to Kilbride for one last visit? I know it may seem a big thing for a man of my years, but I would like to see the Island that I grew up on, where I was wild and free too, with the wind behind me. I loved Victoria so much. In the darkest nights the love we had made me survive until morning. If I could just touch the earth there, I know I would be close to her again.'

Catherine looked at this stranger who could arouse such emotion in her. If this was what he wanted, she would not deny it.

'Of course we will,' she whispered.

'You can stay in Kilbride,' Lainey said eagerly. 'You don't have to go back.'

'Thank you, Lainey, but this is my home. I have good friends like George and I want to die here amongst them. They have been my family all these years. George here has been very good to me.'

George blushed and smiled. 'It has been a pleasure, Canice. There are many people who care about you here in our little community.'

'I will make the arrangements – but he will need a passport, George,' said Catherine.

'We can probably get an emergency one,' he replied.

Canice looked at Catherine, his eyes glassy. 'I have travelled in my dreams so many times – even in my writing.'

'Your writing?' Catherine asked.

'Well, yes, it is what has kept me going all these years.'

'I am no expert,' said George, 'but I do believe it's rather good. More than that. Canice has written a memoir of sorts and a play. He has beautiful poetry too, though he is quite hesitant about showing it to anyone. I assure you it's wonderful.'

'May I see some of it?' Catherine asked.

'I often questioned why I wrote it, now I know why. I think I wrote it to have for you, Catherine, never knowing you would actually read it. I would be delighted to show it to you.'

CHAPTER 37

Lainey put the phone down. It was Ruby. She had been right when she had said that her friend Harry was used to this. He had managed to trace Alice. He had obtained some files in relation to the asylum. There was a patient called Alice O'Sullivan in 1955. She was in the asylum the same time as Victoria was. The records said that she was released back to her family.

Somehow, he had managed to contact a member of the family, a niece who was married in Dublin. She was very cooperative and told him what had happened.

Apparently, Alice had tried to escape and had almost drowned. She couldn't swim. Luckily a man had seen her struggling in the river when he was out hunting. He rescued her, contacted the gardaí and they had insisted her family was contacted as well as the asylum. It was discovered that they were doing experimental treatment on her. There was an investigation and her family had her taken out of the asylum. She had soon after entered a convent, an enclosed order in County Clare, and apparently she was still there.

'Oh, Ruby I am so relieved she didn't drown! Tell

Harry that I am so grateful.'

'He's pretty highly connected, so that helped.'

Alice was alive. A nun. And her grandma need not have felt so guilty all these years.

It wasn't too hard to find the convent on the internet. They had a website! They hosted retreats for people looking for solace and time out. Mindfulness and prayer. She wasn't sure what she expected an enclosed order to be, but she had assumed it was a silent order. She hoped Alice had been happy.

She knew she needed to see her, find some closure for her grandmother. She had to be quite elderly now. She contacted the order.

'Please just tell her that I am the granddaughter of Victoria Goulding, and I would so much like to see her.'

The nightmares had almost stopped but somehow she knew she needed to see Alice.

It was so good to be able to talk to her mother about the nightmares. Normally she would have talked to her grandma about stuff like that, but she was glad that now she could talk to her mother. She knew that she thought it was just a coincidence about the nightmares. But she never judged her or said that. She had grown closer to her over the last few weeks. Her grandmother, in her wisdom, had known what she was doing. There was something about Kilbride and Kilbride House. It was as if their ancestors were with them there, guiding them.

Lainey had plans. She was going to stay in Kilbride, at least for a while. She wanted to learn more about the horses – it was in her blood. She also wanted to photograph Ireland and especially Dingle. She could never get tired of looking at it. Whenever the light changed it almost changed the landscape. What a landscape it was! She had also noticed a vanishing Ireland, an old Ireland in Dingle that contrasted with many other parts of the country. This was the Ireland that she had heard her grandmother talk of, with its stone walls, thatched cottages, the small pubs with their threadbare couches and turf fires that had a welcome like no five-star hotel could ever have. It was a precious piece of Ireland but a vanishing one. She wanted to try to capture the beauty of it.

She planned to move into Kilbride House. There was a lovely guest room and Edward and Ruby had told her that it was hers. It looked out over the garden. It was decorated in a delicate flower wallpaper with a white wooden bed and a white wooden floor. It had a big bay window that allowed so much light in. She loved it. She had spoken to Ruby about her plans.

Ruby had decided not to return to London. She would look for something part-time in Dublin, she had lots of contacts. But she needed to know that Edward would have someone when she was working. Lainey was glad of the opportunity to get to know him better and Ruby was glad to have some family to help her look after him.

But Kilbride House needed vast repair. Lainey had told them of her idea. It would need investment, but she had some money left to her from her grandmother. Kilbride could provide the perfect equestrian holiday. The old stables could be converted into self-catering cottages. The rides out on the beach would be ideal. She had the money to invest. She would rent out the apartment in New York for now and see what the future held. Ruby was delighted with the idea and Edward approved too. John Hogan would of course still be head of the stables. The profits could eventually help in the maintenance of the house.

Lainey knew her grandmother would approve. There had been a lot of pain but there were also great memories in the house from when Edward, Edith and Victoria were small. She wanted to breathe life into it again. Kilbride House would be beautiful. It deserved to be. It was her heritage.

Her phone rang. It was the convent. She could come up the following afternoon and see Sister Francis. Alice was now Sister Francis.

Catherine had gone off touring with John Hogan and they were going for dinner in the Old Schoolhouse Café afterwards which was opened for dinner at the weekends. They were spending a lot of time together and she had never seen her mother so happy and relaxed. Lainey was free to make the journey to Clare.

With Google maps she easily found the convent.

The gardens were pretty with lots of roses and overlooked the sea. She could see how people might like to come here to get away. It was the perfect retreat from the modern world.

She rang the bell and a lady of about thirty in plain dress opened the door.

'Good afternoon, I'm Sister Joan. You must be Lainey. Sister Francis is just chatting to some of our guests before they leave. She will be with you in a jiffy.'

Whatever Lainey was expecting it wasn't this – she had vaguely expected them all to be walking around making sign language.

She must have looked a bit taken aback as Sister Joan

went on to explain. 'An enclosed order is a little different today, Lainey. We have to survive in a modern world, so we open it up to guests who are seeking a contemplative few days away. A kind of meditation. Would you like some tea?'

'Thank you, that would be lovely,' Lainey replied.

She followed the nun into an office.

'I look after all the office stuff for the convent. We have a bit of a following on social media, Facebook and Twitter. I do a blog too – you know, about different things that we do here. We are also known for our singing. A few times a year we perform for charity, so we are constantly singing. We have a farm too and live off the land mostly. But in between all that we do live a contemplative life.'

'It sounds wonderful.'

Sister Joan seemed to hesitate as if she was trying to phrase what she wanted to say.

'How much do you know about Sister Francis?' she asked then.

'Well, my grandmother was sectioned many years ago when she became pregnant out of wedlock. She was in an institution and it was there she met Alice, now Sister Francis. My grandmother died recently but it was her wish that I find out what happened to her friend.'

Sister Joan smiled. 'Sister Francis has been in the convent a long time. When she was young, she said she saw an apparition of light, like an angel. We know that she still does. Her family originally locked her away for it. All we can say is that Sister Francis has brought so much light and love into our lives – she is the darling of the convent and loved so much. When she was younger she would sing, and it was like an angel had arrived from the heaven to sing for us. I believe she has been very happy here. People believe what they need to. I believe Sister Francis believes she sees a light and it is something that has sustained her in her earlier life. Now I just must answer a few emails but please make yourself at home and have a walk around. I will see where Sister Bartholomew is and ask her to bring some refreshments. Sister Margaret has been baking so you can have some nice scones too.'

With a big smile, she left.

Within a few minutes a little nun dressed in a grey habit came in, followed by a larger nun carrying a laden tray.

'Lainey? I'm Sister Francis.' She smiled and her eyes twinkled. 'And this is Sister Bartholomew with our tea.'

When Lainey stood up, the little nun took her in her arms and embraced her.

'Come, let's have tea and you can tell me everything.'

The other nun unloaded the tray and left with a smile.

'My goodness, when I heard that Victoria lived, I did a dance! I think the guests thought that I was a little crazy, but it wasn't exactly the first time anyone thought that.' Sister Francis smiled a mischievous smile.

Over tea and the lightest scones Lainey had ever tasted, they discussed the last sixty years. Lainey told her all about Victoria, even showing her the letter. Alice told her how she had escaped, almost died and been rescued. Shortly afterwards she had entered the convent.

Then Lainey told Alice about the nightmares.

'There is so much we don't understand in this life,' Sister Francis said. 'I will pray that the nightmares leave you now.'

Lainey admired her faith. It was a gentle one, not a

318

faith she wanted to push at anyone – it was simply her belief.

By the time she left the convent Lainey's heart felt lighter than it had in weeks.

There was a four by four parked at Kilbride that Lainey didn't recognise. She went into the kitchen. She could hear a man's voice with a strong Kerry accent.

Edward and Ruby were sitting chatting to a man in his thirties. He was dressed in jeans, a wax jacket and brown boots. He smiled and stood up when Lainey walked in.

Ruby introduced them. 'Lainey, this is Robbie O'Shea – he's from just outside the village. Robbie, this is my cousin Lainey.'

They shook hands and Lainey noticed how his eyes crinkled up when he smiled. He was handsome in a very outdoorsy kind of way. He looked like he would be more comfortable on the land than anywhere else.

He grinned. 'So you're the wild one that took out that fresh thoroughbred? John Hogan was telling me about you.'

'John was not too pleased, I'm afraid – he has banned me from riding out on the beach.'

'Oh well, I ride out most mornings. I know the horses here. I'm sure Prince is not too fresh and he is good for following another horse. I can take you out any morning.'

Lainey wasn't sure what to say but found herself agreeing to meet him the following morning. What was it about these Kerrymen?

'Anyway, Robbie has a bit of news for us, Lainey,' Edward said as they both sat down.

'Oh?' Lainey said curiously.

319

'Yes, more like something to explain,' said Robbie. 'My grandmother was Sarah Quinn – she was great friends with Victoria Goulding. We were reared on stories from her childhood. She tried to go to see her when she was incarcerated, but of course she was not allowed. She said she was almost put in herself, she caused such a row trying to see her. Sure, she was broken-hearted when she heard she had died. Anyway, years later, she received a letter from Victoria telling her that she was alive. My grandmother died when I was very young, and she never told anyone about the letter as Victoria had begged her not to. About a year ago, we were going through some stuff and we came across the letter Victoria had written and a photograph of the man she had wanted to run away with.'

Lainey was taken aback. Was it he who had put the photograph under her door that first night?

'Well, my sister Lily has special needs – she's fourteen years old and her mind is quite childlike. Kilbride is small and news spreads like wildfire. So Lily overheard talk about the fact you were coming to visit. And she knew from family discussions that the photograph was something to do with your aunt. She normally walks her little dog in the morning, but the morning after you arrived she got up very early and we were looking for her for ages. My mother was on the verge of calling the gardaí. Luckily, she turned up and said she had just gone for a longer walk than usual. Anyway, she told me last night that the morning she went missing she brought the photograph with her. She walked down the avenue here. She saw your car parked outside of the cottage and slipped the photo under the door. I just wanted you to know who it was and how we came to have it. I've given the letter to your grandfather here.'

Lainey noticed then that Edward was holding an envelope in his hands.

'Goodness, I had almost forgotten about that little mystery,' she said. 'But, now that you remind me of it, I am very glad to know.'

'Grand, I'll be off so. Thanks for the tea, Ruby, and the cake. Lainey, if you want to have Prince saddled up in the morning, I normally hit the beach around six.'

'*Six!*' Ruby and Lainey exclaimed.

'Yes, six – sure it's nearly tea break at that stage. See you in the morning, Lainey. Don't worry, Edward, I'll take good care of her.'

'I am sure you will. Thanks, Robbie, for the letter. Sarah and Victoria were some pair. Always up to mischief. It's a lovely reminder.'

Lainey's phone rang. It was Catherine, so she excused herself to chat to her. She sounded excited.

'Lainey, I read a play that Canice wrote. It's a beautiful touching story about the Irish in London in the fifties. How they emigrated and some never made their way back. It centres around a boy who grew up there, almost on the streets. I thought it was so good that I sent it to Juniper. I just wanted to get a second opinion. I didn't tell her who wrote it. I have tears running down my face here, Lainey. You know I trust Juniper's judgment. She just mailed me wanting to know who the playwright is – she reckons it's a masterpiece. She adores it and has asked me if she can obtain the rights to stage it.'

'Christ are you serious? What does Canice think?'

'I didn't tell him that I sent it to Juniper. I'm not sure if

he'll be pleased or not. I have read some of his poetry too
– Lainey, he is so talented! We nearly never met him, we
almost missed out on all this.'

Lainey had rarely heard her mother cry. She was taken
aback.

'Are you okay, Mom?'

'I'm more than okay, Lainey, much more than okay.'

CHAPTER 38

The Great Blasket
2018

Canice Meagher with his granddaughter and his daughter by his side, stepped on the Great Blasket Island after leaving it over sixty-five years before. When he had left on that last boat to England, a lifetime had passed. In all his years in London, he had never thought he would feel the Blasket salty air on his lips again.

'Are you okay, Canice?' Lainey asked.

'Never better,' he said.

She was worried it was all too much for him. The water had been choppy getting into the boat. The crew knew what an emotional journey they were taking and had been very kind to them. They had gently helped Canice put on his lifejacket and offered him the best seat in the boat.

Canice looked across the island, his large body now slightly bent over and feeble, his once fiery red hair now silver, but his eyes were still a piercing blue.

'I can't help thinking of all the people who never went home,' he said. 'The ghosts of Kilburn and Cricklewood, the Irish people who worked so hard, never dreaming they would never see their land again.

They got lost, you see, lost between the two. I met so many men on the streets of London. With their holy pictures, their old photos, not accepted by their own or those in London. They were in a kind of no man's land. Yes, very often the only comfort was in the darkness of alcohol. Used to numb the loneliness. They too dreamed of their home, the bog and the gulls. It may only have been across the Irish Sea, but it was a lifetime away. Life had moved on and left them behind, forgotten, the forgotten Irish. I think of my fellow men and women now, hardworking decent people. God rest them. I too dreamed of the Island and it has remained in my heart. I never thought I would see it again in this lifetime. The people of the past are with me on my journey. I can hear them speak in the purest form of Gaeilge. If I listen hard I can hear them sing, the fiddle playing and the dancing. Their spirits free. We did not know as children that we were poor. We were so rich with time and the splendour of the islands. Look over there, 'tis the cottage that we grew up in. My brother and my mother and father. The sea was all around us. It was our life. Our island life. I remember stepping into a skin currach and taking the trip to the smaller Islands, my father and his two brothers rowing us across. Big strong men. How I remember it! Only a mile as the crow flies, but with weather and tides it was normally three. Their weather-beaten faces laughing at our excitement. They were excellent rowers. They had to be, their lives depended on it. There was great trust between them. Good people that looked after each other. So many memories in my heart, but I am grateful to see the Island once more, the Island of dreamers, poets and writers. Thank you for bringing me home. In a way I never left. The weariness of my age has left me for now, I am young again with dreams of what might be.'

'We brought some tea with us, Canice, would you like some?' Catherine asked gently.

It was such an emotional day. Lainey had her camera out and was in heaven taking pictures. How happy she looked now! How free and at ease! They were closer than they ever were. Her mother knew what she was doing when she requested both of them to go to Kilbride. It had changed their relationship.

For the first time in Catherine's adult life, the pull of the theatre had lessened. She had told Juniper that she would go to London. She could be close to her family here and get to know her father a little more. He had eventually agreed to move into an apartment very close to the shelter. His routine every day had not changed. Catherine had employed someone to call and see him twice a day. He still went to the Coal Café every day but now he went for his breakfast, before his visit to the church. He visited the shelter every day and had coffee with his friends. Getting to know him was something she knew she would always cherish.

They shared so much. Although he was never formally educated, he was well read and especially loved the Irish writers. They discussed Becket and Joyce. He read poetry and when she could they both visited the theatre. He was overjoyed that his play would see the stage.

Edward had insisted that Canice visit Kilbride House. He had invited Winnie and some good friends from the village. He had met Canice at the door. The two men wept as they met. Their lives had been entwined for a lifetime.

'Canice, I am so sorry you were not welcomed to Kilbride House all those years ago. I can only apologise for my mother's unforgiveable behaviour.'

Canice shook his head.

'No regrets, Edward, we did the best we could with the hands we were dealt. My Victoria loved this house, it broke her heart to leave it. She had good memories of her childhood and I am sure they withstood the test of time.'

Cecilia had gone into overdrive with the cooking and the table was laden for a buffet. Lainey, Catherine and Ruby had dressed up in their finest and the champagne was flowing. There had been enough sadness and loss.

Canice sang a beautiful rendition of *My Lagan Love* that brought the whole room to tears and wild applause. He really was a beautiful singer. John Hogan surprised everyone by singing, especially Catherine who seemed to be by his side for the night.

She had become close to John. She knew it surprised everyone. But there was something about John – the land deep in his blood, his love for the horses. She knew he felt the same about her. They had their separate lives and they respected that, but they acknowledged the bond there was between them.

Lainey had settled into Kilbride. The beauty of her career was that she could work anywhere. She was riding out on Prince with Robbie almost every morning and, once the horses were fed they often went into the village for a late breakfast in the Old Schoolhouse. He had brought her out to a party in the local pub which finished up at three in the morning, with lots of singing and laughing. There was something special about Robbie. It was as if she finally had met someone who really got her. But it was early days. She had met his sister Lily and had fallen in love with her. Lily loved taking photos too and Lainey had bought her a good camera.

She was working on getting the cottages converted for the first booking for the equestrian holiday. Luckily John was happy with the idea. He could still breed his thoroughbreds, but this would add a new dimension to it. He would be in total charge of all the horses and Lainey would help. They had hired a riding instructor. The beautiful beaches and land around Kilbride were the perfect escape for lovers of riding. The profit would sustain Kilbride House for years to come. They were all merely the caretakers of such places.

Now Catherine looked at the remains of what was her father's home. It was difficult not to compare it to the grandeur of Kilbride House. Her family had lived there for generations. Edward had walked with her around the gardens. She saw the glittering golden pond that she had heard her mother talk of so much. He had explained that over two centuries earlier their ancestors had brought trees from all over Europe and changed the landscape of Kilbride Estate. Originally over a hundred acres were vast gardens. There were ornamental lakes, secret hollows, statues and treelined walks. An exotic number of flowers and shrubs. But in later years the gardens were turned back into land and paddocks for the horses. There was still a substantial garden, all walled in by a tall austere wall.

The difference between all that privilege and her father's upbringing was immense. She was a mixture of gentry and the island people. It was in her blood. But she was also very much a New Yorker. She adored New York, but it would wait for her. She needed to spend time here now and in London.

She watched Canice slowly walk around the island of his youth. Then he came to her.

'The people who lived here were your people, Catherine. We thought we were at the edge of the world. My mother said it was the last piece of earth that God created. It was perfect, so he rested and blessed it. There is a wildness and a beauty here not known in any other part of the world and it is your heritage.' He slid an arm around her shoulders and looked at her, tears in his eyes. 'My beautiful daughter, how grateful I am to God for allowing me to meet you. My heart is lighter, knowing you lived. Your mother was always with me, in my heart.'

There was a fog over the island, but it was shifting now and Canice could almost see the ghosts of the past shimmering on the mystical land.

'If I close my eyes I can see Victoria,' he said. 'I can see her in the bog field with her hair wild and free, her horse as majestic as Niamh's in Tír na nÓg. She adored this place and I believe it adored her. It cried out for her to go dance in the woods, the streams and the wilds of Kilbride. It mourned her when she was gone, I am sure of it. The peninsula lost its brightest jewel which brought so much love and light. They say that people never really leave this land – part of them remains forever on the ancient bogs and beaches. I like to think she is free now and, like an angel on a white horse, she can ride across the bog and the cliffs with the wind behind her, forever free, my beautiful Victoria.'

THE END

ALSO FROM POOLBEG

THE INHERITANCE

ALLY BUNBURY

When Anna Rose arrived in London to start a career in PR with the fabulous Gilda Winterbottom, she hadn't banked on falling for the city's most eligible bachelor, art dealer and heir to a fortune, George Wyndham.

But as love strikes, fate plays a brutal card in the form of Sofia Tamper, a ravishing Hollywood actress, who serves up a dish of ice-cold revenge.

With the inheritance of his ancestral Scottish estate under threat, George is forced to make the most drastic choice of his life – one with devastating consequences.

Set in a world of opulence and privilege, where sex and money go to battle with tradition and romance, *The Inheritance* is a fast-moving, plot-twisting story packed with characters you won't want to leave behind!

'Pitched as *The Devil Wears Prada*
meets *Bridget Jones* this sparkling debut
novel embodies the best of both'
The Sunday Independent

ISBN 978-178199-840-3

TYRINGHAM PARK

ROSEMARY MCLOUGHLIN

Shortlisted for the *Bord Gáis Energy*
Irish Book Awards 2012

Tyringham Park is the Blackshaws' magnificent country house in the south of Ireland. It is a haven of wealth and privilege until its peace is shattered by a devastating event which reveals the chaos of jealousy and deceit beneath its surface.

Charlotte Blackshaw is only eight years old when her little sister Victoria goes missing from the estate. Charlotte is left to struggle with her loss without any support from her hostile mother and menacing nanny. It is obvious to Charlotte that both of them wish she had been the one to go missing rather than pretty little Victoria.

Charlotte finds comfort in the kindness of servants. With their help she seeks an escape from the burden of being the unattractive one left behind.

Despite her mother's opposition, she later reaches out for happiness and believes the past can no longer hurt her.

But the mystery of Victoria's disappearance continues to cast a long shadow over Tyringham Park – a mystery that may still have the power to destroy its world and the world of all those connected to it.

'Dark and densely plotted, this is *The Thorn Birds* with a dash of Du Maurier's *Rebecca*' *Irish Daily Mail*

ISBN 978-184223-520-1

RETURN TO TYRINGHAM PARK

ROSEMARY MCLOUGHLIN

An admirable doctor in charge of a small, isolated hospital in outback Australia swaps his wife's second stillborn baby for an identical twin born to an impoverished farmer's wife who already has seven other children. Both mothers are unaware of the deception. Only one person, apart from the doctor, knows what happened, but no one believes him. The doctor leaves for Ireland immediately afterwards so that his crime, committed on impulse, will remain undetected.

The stolen twin is destined for a future of privilege as the heir to her aristocratic mother's wealth and status, while her sister in Australia faces a life of hardship and loneliness.

The differing fortunes of the twins, the doctor's guilty conscience, the burden of the man who knows, the jealousy of an older sister, the fate of the mothers and the ambitions of the older generation, all combine to create a dramatic and explosive climax.

'Fans of *Tyringham Park* won't be
disappointed'
Irish Independent

ISBN 978-178199-909-7

ALSO FROM POOLBEG

RESCUED

MARIA MURPHY

In 1889, on the beautiful Mizen peninsula lives a young woman called Ellen. Although the daughter of a simple fisherman, she is no ordinary woman. Ellen is a healer, with a heart and spirit as wild and free as the Atlantic Ocean she lives beside. She devotes her life to helping others, often in secret. But when a stranger, in the fine clothes of the landed gentry, is washed up on the sand in front of her remote cottage, she is fearful of helping him because of the trouble he could bring to her and those she loves.

Trying to stay faithful to a warning her grandmother passed on to her, Ellen has to do all she can to protect herself and her home from this stranger.

But perhaps it's the stranger and his heart that needs protection from her?

'Absorbing from the dramatic first page
and very hard to put down' *Irish Independent*

ISBN 978-178199-862-5

THE SECRETS OF ARMSTRONG HOUSE

A. O'CONNOR

Present day – Kate and Nico Collins are filming a docudrama about life in their home Armstrong House in Ireland, during its golden age at the turn of the century. When they discover a cover-up of a terrible crime involving Nico's great-grandfather Lord Charles Armstrong, they set out to solve a mystery over a century old.

1888 – Arabella Tattinger arrives to attend a glittering ball at Armstrong House as the family's younger son Harrison's fiancée. Her head is turned by the glamorous aristocratic family, and most of all by the eldest son and heir, the exciting but dangerous Charles. A chain of events unfolds from that night which casts the family into years of a bitter feud.

1899 – When American heiress Victoria Van Hoeven marries into the family, she is determined to bring peace at last to the Armstrongs. But everywhere dangers are circling and secrets are ready to emerge from the shadows. Not just from outside the house but from within their golden circle. Victoria is stepping into the firestorm.

Kate and Nico press on in their efforts to uncover the truth – but are some secrets best kept hidden?

ISBN 978-184223-626-0

ALSO FROM POOLBEG

THE LEGACY OF ARMSTRONG HOUSE

A. O'CONNOR

2017 – At Armstrong House, Kate and Nico Collins are looking forward to a bright future with their young son Cian.

When archaeologist Daniel Byrne arrives in the area to investigate life there during the Great Famine, he soon crosses paths with Kate. Through Daniel's work, Kate is horrified to discover that a vicious sexual assault occurred in their home in the 1860s when the occupants were Nico's ancestors Lord Edward and his wife Lady Anna. Kate sets out to use all her investigative skills to discover the circumstances of the crime, the identity of the victim and the guilty party.

1860s – After Lawrence, the long-awaited heir to the Armstrong Estate, is born Lord Edward and Lady Anna take great joy in watching him grow up. But somebody else is watching

– Edward's cousin Sinclair who has always felt cheated of the Armstrong legacy by the unexpected birth of Lawrence. As Anna's past comes back to haunt her, life at the house is a tangled web of deceit, blackmail and betrayal that shatters in the summer of 1865.

2017 – As Kate's detective work edges closer to discovering the truth behind the assault, she and Daniel uncover a mystery that goes much deeper. Kate realises that if the truth is ever revealed it will not only destroy the legacy of the Armstrong family but also her marriage to Nico.

Secrets, Love, Lies, Murder – the legacy passes
through the generations

ISBN 978-178199-821-2

BY ROYAL APPOINTMENT

A. O'CONNOR

*The love affair that almost
destroyed the monarchy*

**In 1861 nineteen-year-old Bertie, Prince of Wales, began
an affair with the Irish actress Nellie Cliffden.** By Royal
Appointment *is a fictionalised account of their story, based
on true events.*

In the years following the Great Famine of the 1840's,
Queen Victoria has become deeply unpopular in Ireland. In
1861, as an official visit from the monarch is planned to
win over her Irish subjects, her son Bertie is dispatched to
County Kildare for military training as part of the charm
offensive.

Bertie has undergone a life of duty, protocol and a harsh
educational regime. As a frantic search is under way to find
him a suitable princess to marry, he relishes the prospect of
freedom from court life in Ireland. There, he is quickly
introduced to a life of decadence and soon presented to the
notorious actress Nellie Cliffden.

Nellie is as famous for her shocking behaviour as her
beauty. A famine orphan who has climbed the ladder of
society by any means she could, even she is shocked to find
herself in the company of the Prince of Wales.

When Bertie and Nellie fall in love, the royal family is
engulfed in a scandal threatening the future of the monarchy
and Nellie becomes a pawn in a dangerous world of power,
politics and blackmail.

ISBN 978-178199-807-6

FOR THE LOVE OF MARTHA

MARIA MURPHY

Though separated by one hundred and twenty years, two strangers need each other. Their worlds collide in Carissima, a beautiful old house in County Monaghan, Ireland, when mysterious events begin to unfold.

All Martha wanted was to be with Edward. As governess to the Pershaw family in England, in 1888, she never thought she would know a man like Dr. Edward Adams or experience such passionate love. And she would do all in her power to be with him.

When photographer Juliet flies off for a holiday in Florence, she doesn't realise she will be sharing an apartment with a distractingly gorgeous stranger. Happily indulging in a little holiday romance with Logan Pershaw, before returning to her life in London, is just what she needs. She certainly has no intention of uprooting and following him back to an old house in Ireland where she has to fight for their love.

There, Juliet comes to realise that the mysteries within Carissima can lead her to the fulfilment she craves – if she can just manage to bridge time and unlock them . . .

ISBN 978-178199-911-0

HOME TO CAVENDISH

ANTOINETTE TYRRELL

They have never met ... but their lives are bound
together by the love of one house

The Irish Civil War is raging across County Cork, and sixteen-year-old Edith Cavendish, bored within the confines of her privileged life, embarks on a forbidden love affair with local rebel Tadgh Carey. But Edith is unaware of the dark secrets surrounding her, both outside Cavendish and within its walls, in the very rooms through which she walks.

Eighty years have passed, and Elenore Stack has inherited her beloved childhood home, Cavendish Hall, from her recently deceased parents. Charming and magical, if in need of much loving and expensive care, Cavendish is woven into the tapestry of Elenore's life. She must somehow find a way to ensure its survival while preserving its dignity.

Then she meets and falls in love with Donnacha O'Callaghan, a property developer, and together they begin to work on changing Cavendish into the family guest house of her dreams. He, however, unbeknownst to her, has plans that will change the house beyond recognition and wipe away her precious childhood memories.

As Donnacha's past shady dealings surface and the prospect of losing Cavendish looms once more, Elenore's life begins to unravel. Then a fateful discovery in a forgotten corner of the house links her to a young woman from Cavendish's past – Edith Cavendish – and becomes her lifeline.

ISBN 978-178199-7727